MUSKOKA HEARTS

PRAISE FOR CAROLYN MILLER

Praise for the Original Six series

"I LOVE THIS BOOK!! I love the uniqueness of the characters - we don't see too many hockey player heroes which is a true shame because THOSE KISSES!!"~ *CARRIE BOOTH SCHMIDT, Reading is my Superpower blog*

"I loved the dialogue and the hero and heroine, the very authentic and real challenges they faced and the unique setting and hockey slant." ~ *RACHEL MCMILLAN, bestselling author*

"A touching romance set on the breathtaking shores of Canada's Lake Muskoka. Sarah and Dan are so vividly drawn they practically leap off the page! Their sweet, slowly evolving friendship deepens into the kind of lasting love Christians long for. A must read!" ~ *MEGHANN WHISTLER, award-winning author of The Billionaire's Secret*

"I have been waiting for TJ's story and am so glad it's here! It's perfect...This is truly a story about loving the unlovable and the blessings that come as a result." ~ *GOODREADS review*

"There is nothing like a wonderful redemption story where someone changes their life and becomes a better version of themselves. It is a good reminder to me that God offers incredible grace to all of us." ~ *GOODREADS review*

"Carolyn Miller keeps on turning out these beautifully written, tender hearted books!... There was humor and brilliant bantering conversations, heart stopping romance, as well as exciting descriptions (and sometimes dangerous passages of play) of hockey games. Well worth the late night/early morning read!" ~ *KAYE'S REVIEWS & NEWS*

"A sweet love story that continues the Original Six Hockey series by Carolyn Miller. The setting of Montreal with the Gardens and all the French woven throughout was delightful!" ~ *GOODREADS review*

"I am emerging out of my book hangover after reading *Checked Impressions* by Carolyn Miller....The romance, humor and themes of identity are so enjoyable and make for a great read!" ~ *BECKY'S BOOKSHELVES*

"Adrenaline, chemistry romance, and lots of wooing!...You do not have to be a fan of sports or even knowledgeable in hockey and short track to appreciate *Love on Ice*." ~ *GOODREADS review*

"Carolyn Miller scores another win with *Love on Ice*, the second book in her Original Six Hockey series. I absolutely loved the faith thread in this story. It's message that success does not lie on what we do, but who we are is powerful." ~ *GOODREADS review*

"*The Breakup Project* is a fun, charming, and faith-filled contemporary romance with adorable characters set in the competitive North American ice hockey world. Highly recommended." ~ *NARELLE ATKINS, Author of Solo Tu & Her Tycoon Hero*

MUSKOKA HEARTS

CAROLYN MILLER

Visit Carolyn Miller at www.carolynmillerauthor.com

Cover design by KT Design

Edited by Elizabeth Lance

ALSO BY CAROLYN MILLER

The Original Six hockey series

The Breakup Project

Love on Ice

Checked Impressions

Hearts and Goals

Big Apple Atonement

Muskoka Blue

Muskoka Romance series

Muskoka Shores

Muskoka Christmas

Muskoka Hearts

Muskoka Spotlight

Northwest Ice hockey series

Fire and Ice

Trinity Lakes collection

Love Somebody Like You

The Independence Islands series

Restoring Fairhaven

Regaining Mercy

Reclaiming Hope

Rebuilding Hearts

Refining Josie

Historical:

Regency Wallflowers
Dusk's Darkest Shores
Midnight's Budding Morrow
Dawn's Untrodden Green

Regency Brides: Legacy of Grace
The Elusive Miss Ellison
The Captivating Lady Charlotte
The Dishonorable Miss DeLancey

Regency Brides: Promise of Hope
Winning Miss Winthrop
Miss Serena's Secret
The Making of Mrs Hale

Regency Brides: Daughters of Aynsley
A Hero for Miss Hatherleigh
Underestimating Miss Cecilia
Misleading Miss Verity

'Heaven and Nature Sing' from the Joy to the World Christmas
novella collection

CHAPTER 1

"... I can't begin to tell you how much I love you, and hope to share the rest of my life with you. Please, say you'll marry me."

Toni Wakefield froze, the heartfelt words uttered in deep tones rushing through her. Oh, how romantic. How special. How she'd *longed* to hear him say these words. Even if she'd never have picked a New Year's Eve party at her home as the place to pop the question. Still, with the sound of soft music, and the gold and silver decorations from Christmas still brightening their home, she supposed some might consider it a romantic-enough location.

"Please, Serena," Joel continued. "Say you'll make me the happiest man in the world."

Toni's heart kicked. When she'd moved to search the spare room closet to find the painting she'd done long ago, never in a million years would she have expected her brother was about to propose to his girlfriend in this room. And never would she have expected him to sound quite so... anxious. Or impassioned. Or romantic. Ugh. The awkwardness of it all.

And now she was trapped here, crouched behind the open

closet door as her brother proposed to Serena Williamson, trying to make it look like she hadn't overheard, while the rest of their friends continued their karaoke countdown to New Year's. She could only pray that Ethan wouldn't wake and demand attention...

"Of course I will," Serena's soft voice came, followed by a noise that sounded suspiciously like a kiss. A long, passionate kiss that drew new meaning to the word awkward.

Toni eased back on her heels in her hidey-hole between the wall and the door, wincing as her leg began to cramp. Okay, so this was *really* starting to get uncomfortable, as the kissing and whispered words of devotion continued.

Her nose wrinkled as dust from the long-untouched canvases wafted through the room. A sneeze threatened, the irritation building, building, building—

"Ah-*choo*!"

Toni slapped a hand over her mouth, as a wince shivered through her entire soul.

The door slowly opened wider and she peeked up to see her brother's face loom overhead. "Surprise."

"Toni? What on earth are you doing there?"

She pushed to her full height, summoning a contrite smile. "Hi." She peeked behind his shoulder. "Um, hi Serena."

"Hi, Toni," Serena said, a big smile on her face unable to disguise the fact that her mussed hair and swollen lips made her look thoroughly kissed.

Toni glanced back at her brother. "So, um, congratulations."

His mouth tweaked. "You heard that?"

"Yep." She glanced apologetically at Serena. "Sorry to intrude. But hey, if my brother isn't going to check the room is clear before getting his proposal on, well, what's a girl gonna do?"

"You could've mentioned you were here," Joel grumbled, even as he slipped an arm around Serena.

2

"I was deep in the closet looking for—ah, this!" Toni held up the painting with triumph—and relief. "Looks like that is my cue to leave." She mouthed a "sorry" at Serena, who simply grinned and drew her into a hug. "I am really happy for you though."

"Me too," Serena said, glancing up at Joel like she thought he hung the moon.

"And you too," Toni said, giving her big brother a squeeze. "You might be a doofus, but you couldn't have chosen better."

"I know, right?" He kissed Serena again, and they were soon lost in each other again.

Judging this moment as being as good as any, she stole back into the hall where the sounds of merriment drifted from the living room.

"There you are!" Anna Morely, one of Toni's—and Serena's —close friends waved her over to where she stood with Rachel and Damian Taylor, both here enjoying a child-free night. Judging from the beverages Rachel was knocking back —which had led to some very spirited renditions of *You're the One that I Want* and *Love Somebody Like You*—Rachel might be enjoying the party a little *too* much. "I was beginning to think you must've got sucked into a time warp or something," Anna said.

"Nope." Admitting what she'd just witnessed wasn't her news to share. "It just took a while to find this." She held up the artwork.

"That's so good." Anna gestured for their friend Jackie O'Halloran to join them from where she'd been talking with their pastors, John and Angela McPherson, and Dr. James Wells and Staci Everton. Staci was one of Toni's favorite authors, and had shocked them all earlier this evening by declaring that she was moving from Chicago to Muskoka Shores to help care for her grandmother, Rose.

Anna shot the new couple a look and grumbled, "I still can't believe my luck. Hot doctor was only here a month and already he's been snapped up."

Damian murmured something about more punch and wandered away, as if the talk of hot doctors wasn't fit for his ears.

Toni nudged Anna. "I think you embarrassed Damian."

"Damian?" Rachel said. "Aw, bless. He's never been great with girl talk. Which is why I need you gals in my life."

Gladness stole through Toni, treacly thick and warm. How glad she was to have been adopted into this group of women, a group that seemed to be expanding with Staci's arrival in—or was it return to?—Muskoka Shores a month or so ago. A group where it was safe to be real, to relax, to enjoy Serena's delectable cooking at her girl-gathering soirees, and talk that ranged from favorite books to Bible verses, times of praying together, movies, and more. A place where Toni was accepted, mistakes and all.

"It's like I'm never going to find a man," Anna complained. "First Dan, then Joel, then James."

"Dan?" Jackie asked. "You mean Dan Walton?"

Dan Walton. Toronto's hockey defenseman extraordinaire. He had a summer cottage nearby and attended their church on occasion.

At Anna's nod, Jackie's brow cleared. "Girl, you've got to let that one go. He was never going to be yours."

He'd married an Aussie singer last year, Sarah somebody, and now they spent most of their time in the city. Toni knew that much at least.

"And surely you can't begrudge Serena and Joel?"

"No, of course I don't. You know I'm super happy for them."

Toni sensed that was true too.

Rachel snatched a corn chip from a nearby tray and dragged it through a bowl of salsa dip. "As for you and James, well, obviously you two weren't meant to be."

"Obviously." Anna sighed.

"You need to stop looking at him," Jackie said. "You don't want to make Staci feel like she's not welcome here by gazing at her boyfriend for too long."

"I can't help it. Every time I see his smile and those eyes, part of me melts."

"So how are you managing to get through your workday?" Toni asked.

Anna worked as a receptionist at the medical clinic where James worked when he wasn't rostered on at the hospital.

"With difficulty."

Toni exchanged smiles with Jackie, as Rachel downed her second margarita.

"Mmm. I needed that," Rachel said, smacking her lips. "I'm pretty sure that's gonna make my new year's happy."

Toni chuckled, happy for a virgin version.

Anna swallowed the last of her pink drink, a non-enhanced punch. "Hey, have you seen Serena anywhere? Or are she and Joel off kissing again?"

Well, judging from what Toni had witnessed before, "They're probably kissing."

"Everyone's pairing up," she grouched.

"Not everyone." Toni held up a hand, paint-flecked but ring-free.

Anna snorted. "You could if you wanted to. I noticed your friend Matt has barely stopped staring at you all night."

Toni tensed, refusing to glance in the direction of the kitchen. There was a reason she hadn't exactly hurried back to join the party. And a big, tall part of that was the man standing there in the kitchen, whose gaze felt heavy on her. Joel's best friend, Matt Vandenburg. "We're not together."

"Sure." Rachel smirked. "Not yet anyway."

"No," Toni corrected her. "He's not my type."

"Yeah, well, he seems convinced that you're his type," Anna

said. "I did my best to flirt earlier, but all he wanted to talk about was you and Ethan."

He had?

"It's not fun always being left out," Anna grouched. "And now Serena's so happy, I bet she won't want to do the Galentine's Day dinner again this year."

"The what?"

"Galentine's. It's when the single ladies get together on February fourteenth and commiserate over cheese and wine about the sorry state of available single men for Christian women."

"Huh. I thought it was for the empowerment of women to remember their inner awesomeness and that they didn't need a man to complete them," Jackie demurred.

"Yeah, well, that too." Anna shrugged. "I'm just getting tired of feeling this empowered all the time, you know what I mean? I'd be really happy to switch it up for a Mix and Mingle event instead, and find a man who could appreciate my awesomeness instead."

"Here, have a chocolate." Rachel shoved a Lindt chocolate ball at Anna, before sending Jackie and Toni an eye-roll that suggested she was as tired of hearing about Anna's lack of romance as Damian had been.

Anna unwrapped the red shiny paper and popped it in her mouth, as Rachel's attention was claimed by a hesitant-looking Staci.

Toni shot the author a smile—she wanted to include her and make her feel welcome like Serena had asked each of them, hence the invitation to the new couple tonight—but Staci held a sophisticated air that sometimes came across as intimidating. Staci's luxury brand-name bag and shoes were a world away from Toni's now-usual daily attire of flats and jeans and old tees. Added to this was the fact Staci was so smart. No wonder she'd landed herself a doctor.

"You okay?" Jackie asked.

Toni blinked. And realized she'd been staring at the couple like she had Anna's heart-eyes going on. "Yeah."

Jackie drew her attention back to Toni's painting. "You're so talented. I don't know how you get it to look so vibrant."

Toni shrugged. "It's just a technique with light and shading we use." Trying to explain the intricacies of chiaroscuro wasn't exactly riveting party conversation.

"Don't sell yourself short," Jackie gently chided. "You have a gift, which your new job obviously says you've earned."

Her new job! Her lips curved as a thrill rippled through her. God was a miracle worker, indeed, to have opened the door and allowed Toni—Toni!—to step into a newly-created role at the nearby resort of Muskoka Shores. A role that checked every one of Toni's passions: artistic expression, education, and awareness. Of course, Serena had been instrumental in Toni getting the job, basically talking up Toni's abilities when the resort's general manager had taken a liking to one of Toni's paintings Serena had hanging in her office. That initial conversation had led to the painting being incorporated into the resort's new logo and branding, and a job to establish and then run an art gallery at the resort, allowing Toni time to work on her own art, while also providing means to care for Ethan. Truly, a Godsend of a job, one her artsy friends back in Toronto hadn't believed when she'd told them. But then, Muskoka seemed to be a place where miracles could happen...

"Finally!"

Anna's whisper pivoted Toni's attention to where Joel and Serena had emerged, hand in hand, glowing with delight. Toni's heart grew soft. Oh, how sweet. Were they going to tell everyone? Joel scanned the room, eyes alighting on her, and she raised her brows which met with a lift of his own. She mimed a zipped lip, and he nodded, before bending to whisper to Serena.

"What's going on?" Anna asked.

A "nothing" wasn't going to cut it. Maybe she could feign cluelessness with an, "I don't know what you mean."

Anna's head tilted. "Are you sure?"

Toni bit her lip, glancing away only to meet Matt's gaze. He smiled, and after offering a small smile she ducked her head. Nope. She had no desire to encourage him.

A cleared throat swung her attention back to Joel. Serena stood beside him, almost sparkling. So, he was about to say something, after all?

She grew aware of a presence beside her, caught a whiff of something that smelled clean and fresh like the sea. Matt.

"Hey."

She glanced up, but didn't quite meet his eyes. "Hi."

"Your brother looks like he's ready to burst."

"Mmm."

She felt his gaze on her skin, but she refused to look in his direction anymore, her focus fully on Joel and Serena.

"Seeing it's almost the start of a new year, and that so many of our loved ones are here," Joel said, one arm firmly around Serena, "I thought it the best time to announce that"—

An excited murmur raced around the room.

"—that Serena and I are engaged!"

The room filled with cries of delight, cheers and applause, and Serena was instantly swamped with celebratory hugs from Anna, Jackie, and Rachel.

"I knew it," Matt said.

"You knew he was going to propose?"

He shrugged, shoved his hands in his pockets. "I might've had an inkling."

An *inkling*? What kind of man spoke like that? An old-fashioned one, that's who. But wait. Had he said—"You knew and you never said anything?" She placed her hands on her hips.

"Wasn't my news to share."

Matt studied her, his mouth hitched up at the corner, his dark-lashed blue eyes drawing her in.

Okay, she wasn't blind. The man might be way too tall and his voice way too deep, but she couldn't deny his handsomeness. Light brown hair the ends of which turned blond in summer sun, a square jaw and straight eyebrows and a mouth that was never too quick to smile. The man might suit a magazine cover, but he'd always been way too serious for her. Conscientious Man, she privately called him. Not that she was a fan of guys who proved themselves more worthy of the moniker of Mr. Irresponsible…

Her gaze swung back to the happy couple, and a moment later Matt left her side to join the congratulatory throng. Then she realized that her standing back here probably looked like she wasn't pleased about the engagement, when really, nobody here could be happier than her, other than the happy couple themselves.

Toni allowed herself to be swept into a group hug, as Anna and Rachel shrieked about weddings and venues and dates and all manner of things. Which was ridiculous, as Toni knew they'd only just decided—

"—hoping maybe near Valentine's Day," Joel said.

What? Toni's mouth fell open.

Serena leaned against his shoulder. "It's a fairly quiet time at the resort right now—"

No. No, it wasn't. Not when Toni was about to open the resort's art gallery space and needed Serena's help.

"—and Mom and Dad said they'd be back by then, so anyway, we thought it could work. Especially as John has already said he's free."

"But that's so soon," Toni blurted.

"Not soon enough," Joel said, eyes on his bride-to-be, before bending to kiss her in a swoon-worthy embrace, his deep affection obvious to all.

Toni's heart squeezed, and for a desperate second, she wanted to experience that feeling too. To have a man of Joel's caliber—he might be her brother, but she recognized a man of quality heart and character—regard her with that look of undying devotion, like she was his everything. What must that feel like?

She gulped down a stupid spurt of emotion, glancing up to meet Matt's intense gaze.

A shiver rolled through her. No. *No.* She was not going to get caught up in stupid emotions. She was glad, *so* glad for Joel and Serena. But just because they had found each other and were celebrating their love tonight didn't mean romance was available for all. She tossed back her dark hair. It didn't matter anyway. Ethan was enough—would always be enough—for her. Anything else was impossible. Even if she was good enough to have earned a shot at the love of a good man.

~

IT WAS FUNNY how on a night meant to celebrate a new year— meant to celebrate his best friend's engagement—Matt barely cared about the other partygoers here. Sure, he cared. About some more than others. About one very particularly.

Toni's dark hair hung in a straight line that swished when she turned quickly. He watched her go to the bedroom and was tempted to follow. Then thought better of it. Then second-guessed himself again. Or was it triple-guessed by now?

No matter. He'd been second-guessing Toni Wakefield since she'd first strutted into his awareness six years ago, back when he'd realized his best friend's little sister had grown up. Fast. Gone were the pigtails and bookworm tendencies. In was sarcastic sass and artistic expression, which saw everything over the past years from hair dye and piercings to darker and more pivotal decisions that had made his heart break.

But it didn't matter what she did, or how many cold shoulders she gave him. Toni held his heart, even as he wondered if she knew that. She held his heart, even if at times it seemed she had the power to make him nearly stop breathing. She was his person. That thud of recognition six years ago had been like—if he believed in such things—a giant jolt of cosmic awareness that she was supposed to be with him and he with her. Like God had ordained Toni for him and Matt for her. And while he'd hoped and prayed and waited patiently, and she'd given glimpses of hope she might one day come around—like at the Cranberry festival two months ago—each day that passed without him asking the question burning in his soul only increased his inner agitation. The eczema that had plagued his teenage years was making its itchy reappearance over a decade later.

"Matt?" A dark-haired man nodded—James, the new doctor in town Joel had asked Matt to befriend. He'd been happier to befriend him once he realized James and the author-lady had eyes only for each other. Men like James were way too good looking for their own good. Or for the good of other men's self-esteem. "It is Matt, isn't it?" His white grin was edged with apology. "Sorry, I'm still trying to remember names. You'd think I'd know more by now but my memory's been a little hazy."

Score one point for Matt. His memory had always been as sharp as broken glass. "How are you doing, James?" Was that a little pointed? Better soothe it with, "Are you enjoying living in Muskoka Shores?"

"Love it." James glanced around, taking in the conversations buzzing nearby. "I used to live here, and once thought I'd never want to return, but there's something pretty nice about living in a small town, isn't there?"

"Sure." Well, Matt imagined there *could* be. He'd always lived in the city. It was where he'd met Joel and Toni all those years ago. And while Muskoka Shores might be only two hours north of Toronto, it felt a world away compared to his usual breakneck speed of life. "Actually, to be honest, I'm not sure if I could cope with living at such a slow pace."

"What do you do again? I think Joel once mentioned you work in the city."

A ping of pride preceded his answer. "I work in investments." At one of the country's top pension funds companies. Any day now he expected to hear about his longed-for promotion, and the company bonuses. His bonus this year should be sweet.

"A money man, huh?"

Was that a bad thing? "Someone has to do it." And if it meant being an honest man in an industry known for cutthroat deals, then he was God's man for the job. "I like to think we're making a positive difference in the world." He'd always pushed for the company to invest in projects that would prove advantageous to shareholders and fund members while still holding an environmentally sustainable or community benefit. Even if not everyone else in his company agreed. Some, like Ray Weiner, seemed to care more about the bottom line than anything else. Ray's bottom line somehow always seemed to receive top priority.

"So how do you and Joel know each other?" James asked.

Matt explained about meeting in college and the past years of attending the city church where Joel had been a youth pastor for a number of years. "He's been like a brother to me." Even when his own hadn't.

James nodded, but said nothing more, Staci drawing his attention as the clock ticked closer to midnight. In that moment, Matt remembered Joel once saying something about James's older brother dying in an explosion in the Middle East.

Matt offered a weak smile and took the couple's low-voiced conversation as a sign that his talk with James was done. He pivoted, scanning the room but Toni was nowhere to be found. Joel and Serena were still talking with Rachel and Damian and

John and Angela McPherson. It didn't seem like their announcement had taken the pastors by surprise either. Joel hadn't exactly been shy about his feelings.

Unlike some people here.

Matt slowly exhaled. Was now a good time to go find Toni? Chances were she was checking on Ethan. Would she think it weird of him to find her there? Maybe. Probably.

But if he didn't ask her now, then could he really live with himself knowing another entire year had gone past where he hadn't manned up enough to ask her out for coffee, let alone tell her how he really felt? What had been that verse he'd read this morning? Something about faith not shrinking back but pressing forward, even as the new day approached.

Well, the new day—the new year—was coming in a matter of minutes now. He grabbed a meatball-on-a-toothpick and swallowed it for courage. Tossed the toothpick in the white ceramic bowl placed for such things. Prayed his millionth desperate prayer. And headed to the hall.

"Hey, man."

Matt's feet paused as he summoned a smile for Joel. "Congrats, dude."

Joel pulled him into another man-hug. More back-slapping. More grinning. "I can't believe she said yes."

"I can't believe you'd think she'd say anything but," he said dryly.

Serena hadn't exactly been reticent about her feelings for Joel, either, the two of them nauseatingly sweet even as they'd danced around each other for months. Now if only some of this could rub off on Matt and bring his own private feelings to the fore.

"Hey, have you seen Toni?" Joel asked, a slight crease between his brows. "She didn't sound like she was too excited about us getting married so soon."

"She'll be fine," Matt assured. "You know she loves you. Loves you both."

"Yeah, she's always seen Serena as the big sister she never had. Still." Joel's forehead puckered. "I don't want her to think this has to change things."

Now Matt's own forehead creased. "And how can it not? You're getting married, man. I'm guessing you and Serena will want to be alone and not have your sister and a baby around."

"Well, yeah. Wow. Okay. I've got some things to figure out."

"Apparently so."

Joel rubbed a hand along his jaw. "Hey, if you see her, make sure she knows it'll be okay."

"Will do."

Matt nodded, trying to tamp down his impatience. He would see Toni, and do his best to let her know that everything would be okay. That Matt would make it his personal mission to make sure everything was okay. That he'd like nothing more than for her to let him make everything okay in her life for the rest of her days.

Whoa. He blew out a breath. Best he not follow through with that last comment, or else she might go running for the hills.

The noise from the party in the living room was dying down, the karaoke contest from earlier having ceased at Joel's earlier news. Matt eased up the hallway, hoping he didn't look like a creepy stalker, that he was simply heading to the bathroom or something. But he wasn't. This was his time. He just knew it.

A soft humming sound drew his feet to a pause outside a yellow painted door that was slightly ajar, and had the name Ethan painted in curly letters on the door, along with a hand-drawn picture of a monkey.

Matt's heart grew soft. He'd never done the baby thing, but he could agree with Joel. There was something special about the little boy inside. And not just because of his mother.

"Hey, little man, it's time for you to go back to sleep."

From Matt's position here he could see Toni holding a blue-wrapped bundle. His heart gave a savage tug. Then, knowing it really would appear super creepy if she spotted him like this, he moved beyond, propping up the wall with a shoulder as he waited for her to exit. He fiddled with the leather strap of his Longines watch as he waited, waited...

The door opened. He straightened. "Hi, Toni."

"Oh!" She jumped, eyes wide, and placed a hand on her chest. "I didn't see you there."

No kidding.

"Did you, uh, want me for anything?"

Oh, yes. But the myriad of things he wanted—her attention, her time, her kisses—could only happen if he finally dared to say this one thing first. He swallowed. "I just, er, wanted to ask you something."

"Okay." She pulled Ethan's door shut.

From beyond he could hear the murmur as people called for party poppers. *Quick! Say it now. Before it's too late.* "I, um,"—oh, why couldn't he speak clearly, like he did at work presentations? —"just wanted to know if maybe some time you...you might like to have a coffee with me."

"A coffee?"

Time suspended. His blood hammered in his ears. *Please Lord. Please Lord. Please...*

Her brow knit. "You know I don't drink coffee, don't you?"

Oh man. Mental face slap. "I, um, meant a hot chocolate. Or a chai latte. Or tea. Or anything really." Yes. He was that desperate. Did he have a sign on him that said, 'Pathetic Guy'?

"Oh! Well, maybe."

Dreams that had fast been death-spiralling suddenly tipped their nose back in the air. *Yes!*

"I mean," her gaze dropped, along with his hopes, "sometime. Maybe. I suppose we could do like what we did before with Joel and Serena at the cranberry farm and go do something with them."

No. No, that wasn't what he meant. "I thought something more just the two of us," he dared.

"Oh."

Toni winced. She actually winced. And the last of his fast-shriveling hopes curled up with a whimper and expired.

She didn't want to go out with him. She didn't even want to have a hot drink alone with him. What kind of person must he be if she couldn't bear the thought of just having a simple hot drink?

A wave of something like dizziness washed over him. No. This was not what he'd prayed. Not what he dreamed. This manning up to finally ask her out wasn't supposed to go this way. But he couldn't admit the depths of his heart's ache. Wouldn't let her see that she'd crushed the breath from his lungs. With the last ounce of courage he lifted his head and pasted on a smile. "Don't worry about it."

"Sorry. It's not you—"

Sure it wasn't.

"It's just with the new job I'm going to be so busy, and now with Joel and Serena getting married—you know." Her smile was so small she might as well not have bothered. "I still can't believe you knew about this and never said anything."

He found a shrug he hoped looked convincing, even as a pitiful part of him gratefully clutched at her subject change. "I get things wrong, apparently."

Really wrong. Colossally, even.

His fingers clenched then he pushed away from the wall. Looked like he might make a swift exit. Forget staying the night like Joel had originally suggested. Matt had no desire to wake up tomorrow and have to somehow pretend indifference for the woman who plainly felt indifferent to him.

He had to leave. Drive two hours to his cold city apartment where he could lick his wounds in private. He pivoted, preparing to make his excuses—Joel would likely believe him if Matt said work had called with a situation that needed an immediate response. It wouldn't be the first time work had intruded on his personal time. And it wouldn't be a complete lie. It would be overwhelmingly hard work to stay here and try to stop caring about the woman who had no care for him. Who couldn't care for him. Not in the way he wanted, anyway.

"Matt?"

"Excuse me." He moved away, unable to look at her. He had to leave. Now. Each second in her uncaring company was sweet torture.

"There you are!" Joel said. Happy, sunshiny, newly-engaged-and-oceans-deep-in-love Joel. "Did you find Toni?"

"Sure did," he muttered.

"Everything okay?"

"Yep," he lied. His heart was dying.

"Tell her to come out here. The countdown is about to begin."

The countdown to the new year? The countdown he'd dared imagine might finally take him into a new year of love and promise? No, thanks.

"Hey, sorry." Matt held up his phone. "I'm gonna have to run. It's work." It was becoming stupidly difficult trying to keep it together.

"Are you serious? It's New Year's Eve, man. Who on earth would be calling at this hour?"

"You know how it is," he evaded. "Time zones around the world mean I'm always busy, busy—"

"Busy. I know. Dude, I think you need a different job. The hours are insane."

"Yeah, well, it's all I've got." Especially now he knew the woman he'd dreamed about for so long didn't want him. *Didn't want him.* His lungs felt like hanging strips of dried leather, at the mercy of life's fickle puffs. It was getting hard to breathe.

"Oh, here she is!" Rachel—the loud, slightly obnoxious friend of Serena's who seemed to like her cocktails a little too much—called. "Get yourself over here, girl."

Rachel dragged Toni to her side, shoved a party popper in her hand and placed a plastic silver crown on her head that said, "Happy new year!"

Toni acquiesced, her gaze darting to meet his, but he couldn't hold her gaze for longer than a second. "Matt, I—"

"Ten, nine, eight—"

His smile was going to fall off any second.

"—six, five—"

Lord, help me keep it together.

"—three, two, one! Happy new year!"

The living room exploded in a raucous chorus of cheers and congratulations as the sounds of Auld Lang Syne bleated from the TV.

His cheek was kissed—Serena. Joel hugged him. James slapped his back. Rachel kissed his other cheek. He fake-smiled through it all.

Then finally couraged up to face Toni, who looked like she'd been enduring the same. "Happy new year, Toni." His voice sounded stiff, even to his own ears.

"Happy new year," she echoed. She wet her bottom lip. "Matt, I—"

"Don't worry about it." His stomach roiled. His skin felt cold. "I'm going to go."

"You're leaving?"

Was that disappointment in her face? Oh, how delusional could one man be? Who was he kidding? That was relief, for sure. "I'll see you around."

"But what about the coffee?"

"You don't do coffee, remember?" How could he have been so dumb that he'd forgotten such a basic thing? "And don't worry. I won't ask again."

He swallowed, unable to cope with her stricken look. She didn't have the right to look stricken, not when she'd struck him in the heart.

Somehow he made his farewells. Somehow he stumbled to his car. Somehow he heard himself promise to call Joel when he got in. But he couldn't, wouldn't, look at Toni. He couldn't bear to see the woman who'd not only stolen his heart, but had apparently decided to trample it to the snowy ground. Especially on this first day of this anything-but happy new year.

CHAPTER 2

$$\sim$$

"*And* how do you feel about placing this one here?"

Toni stepped back, studying the placement of the landscape Chuck held at eye-level, the prime position for artworks in the almost-finished gallery.

Since the general manager, Adrian Jennings, had first welcomed her to the Muskoka Shores Resort, she'd been impressed by the energy and efficiency with which they'd managed to make this happen, the old sports office stripped, cleaned, and repainted, ready for its ugly duckling transformation into beautiful art gallery swan. Of course, it probably helped that Serena had been so vocal with her support, advising Toni on everything from which of Toni's paintings to include in the first exhibition, to making suggestions about finding lawyers who could ensure her images would be protected under copyright law for use by the resort in their new rebranding. This had led to a question to Matt several weeks ago, which had secured a city-based lawyer with expertise in similar artistic copyright cases. His fee had been surprisingly low, which had led her to wonder if Matt had negotiated a special deal for her. It would be just like him.

Her stomach twisted with regret about two nights ago. Why hadn't she just said yes instead of making a big deal out of things? Matt hadn't deserved her stupid comments about 'not drinking coffee.' She could've let him down way more gently than that. But in that moment of panic, she'd spurted out the first thing her brain had latched onto, leading her to say dumb things, to hesitate, to nearly have a panic attack when her "maybe" had drawn from him a look of pure joy. No. She wasn't supposed to be the one who made men look like that. She didn't even understand why he seemed to care for her that way. She wasn't worth it.

"Ms. Wakefield?" the resort's general assistant asked.

"Toni, please." Chuck had to be twice her age. "Um, yeah, that's fine."

Ugh. She probably needed to improve her vocabulary if she was going to pretend to know what she was doing here. It was one thing to be an artist, it was quite another to run an art gallery, and create a space suitable for "interactive artistic experiences" as the marketing copy read. Her mind had been in a whirl these past weeks. It hadn't just been a blow-off when she'd said no to a date with Matt. With all she'd had to learn and do in the past month, some days she really didn't have the mental or emotional capacity left over for anything beyond her son. Thank God Ethan was an easy baby. There was no way she could ever envisage doing this if he hadn't been.

She refocused, conscious Joel was looking after him at home —a slight sniffle meaning Ethan couldn't attend the employee-daycare here at the resort—and that on this cold and snowy day she had zero desire to be a second later than absolutely necessary. With Chuck's help, painting after painting—including the one she'd shown the girls at New Year's—was hung, their placement determined by the newly-installed spotlights and down-lights that showed each work to advantage.

It almost felt decadent, like she was a celebrity artist of the caliber of David Hockney or Erin Hanson, having so many of her works on display. But Mr. Jennings had advised this, saying that it was the perfect introduction to showing guests what kind of skills she would bring to the little studio that was part of this art space. The studio where she would both work as the 'artist in residence' and assist guests who might also be inclined to pick up a paintbrush and try their hand at an acrylic or watercolor.

She glanced around, pivoting on her heel. It might be a bleak, wintry January day in Muskoka, but there was still a surprising amount of good light pouring in from the windows. And while the light would make it good for the actual practice of painting, it also had the potential to harm the paintings on the walls. Which was probably why it was good to begin the gallery's exhibition with her own works, rather than ask another artist to display their paintings, only to have the light affect the pigments. This way, Toni could be the guinea pig, as it were, and they could reassess hanging space later, if necessary.

"What do you think of that, Toni?" Chuck asked, stepping back to join her.

She nodded slowly, narrowing her eyes as her perfectionist mind took in all the details. Simply framed, the acrylics and oils showed various scenes of Muskoka and similar environments, with everything from her signature maple trees to the blues and greens of lakeside scenes, with their ubiquitous wooden docks and red canoes. The use of trees in each painting was another nod to what could be seen out every resort window, a reminder of this beautiful region that guests could take home, and a subtle invitation to return, or so the general manager, Adrian Jennings had said.

"So it really works both ways. You'll profit by selling your paintings to guests with a special discounted commission rate for the resort, and we'll benefit by reminding guests that they need to return. Win-win, I say."

It was definitely a win for her. Being able to show her work in a dedicated gallery space for at least three months until she secured the next artist to display, was something few artists her age dared dream of. Then to know she and the resort would split the commission on any future artist's sales was another little bonus. Already the original Autumnal maple leaf tree painting that she'd given Serena last year had been commissioned by the resort for logo use as it rebranded, and Serena had agreed it could be placed above the registration desk so every guest would see her work displayed in prime position. Interested guests would then be invited to check out the special art gallery where more of the artist's works could be displayed. The offer was so generous—so obviously God-blessed—that Toni wondered whether she could one day suggest blessing other artists with a similar opportunity, by creating a resort-sponsored art prize, with such prime hanging space as part of the prize.

"I think the fifth one needs to be lifted a quarter inch on the right," she instructed.

"The one of the Muskoka chairs and sunset?" Chuck asked, shifting it up the required amount.

"Perfect."

He nodded, swiveling to take them all in. The art gallery was supposed to open in two days; the art studio would take another few days or so longer. Guests were being asked to register their interest in art classes via their hotel bookings, but Toni suspected that there would be walk-ins as well. The extra time allowed for her to build up her supplies of art materials. While she never envisaged anything more than five potential art students, Serena had suggested she supply herself with enough equipment to manage twelve.

"Twelve?" Toni had gasped. "There is no way there'd be that many people wanting lessons from me."

"I think you underestimate your abilities."

Something she'd been accused of all her life.

"And you know that part of the reason why we've been pushing to get this done now is the chance for the resort to offer something a little different over the winter months. It's not like the guests can go swimming in the lake when it's frozen, but I suspect there may well be a few people interested in coming to learn some skills that they might otherwise never get the opportunity for. And there's something special about being able to get away, to relax and unwind, and do things that you don't normally do."

"But art can take weeks, even months to perfect."

Serena had smiled. "You and I both know we're not talking about perfection here. You've heard of those paint-and-sip classes where people paint while enjoying a glass of wine, haven't you? People enjoy the chance to do something a little different. We're talking about some basic techniques that people can learn over a time frame that may mean half a day to two weeks. So much will depend on the guests themselves and how invested they are, but I think you'll find that word-of-mouth will see your classes start to sell out, and provide another nice little earner for you."

Was it any wonder this non-teacher was quietly freaking out? What if Toni's students weren't happy with what she told them, what if they couldn't apply the skills and wrote bad reviews? All of this she had discussed with both Serena and Mr. Jennings, and both of them had assured her that would not be the case. It was funny how often her insecurities shaped the way she saw the future, and while she knew she had to keep giving her past to God—that He'd already dealt with it—sometimes it was like her soul forgot. And it didn't take much for her to spiral back into questions and self-doubt.

"Oh, that's looking wonderful!" Serena's boots tap-tapped on the wooden floor as she entered the room. "Wow. I can't believe the transformation of this space." She looked at Chuck. "You've done a great job."

He shrugged. "Once the internal wall and those big cupboards were removed it was amazing how much lighter and brighter this space felt."

"And now it's painted white it just feels so fresh." Serena glanced at Toni. "I don't think I realized just how many windows are here. That won't be a problem for your work will it?"

"Not in winter, the sunlight will be too weak. In summer we may need to revisit, possibly look at installing drapes and more lighting, but that's down the track. We need to prove this will work first."

Six months, Mr. Jennings had said. All going well they would have covered the costs of the renovation by then and be turning a small profit. *Please God.*

"Oh, it'll work," Serena said confidently, turning the ring on her finger.

Toni's heart twisted. Mom's own engagement ring.

Joel had checked with Toni that it was still okay for him to give Serena that ring, like Toni had suggested a month or so ago in a moment of tease. And it was okay. Mostly. But it became yet another way that her mother felt lost to her.

"You okay?" Serena asked, drawing nearer Toni, her voice lower, as Chuck began collecting his tools.

"Yep. Just thinking about your wedding."

Serena's smile flashed. "I still can't believe we're rushing to make this happen so soon. But leaving things until later for the sake of convention felt wrong too."

"Your parents are happy?"

Serena nodded. "I think we're overdue for another soiree soon. Are you free this Friday?"

"Sure." Toni frowned. "I might need to see if Joel is able to babysit Ethan."

"If he can't, then you can bring him too."

"Who, Joel or Ethan?"

Serena chuckled. "As tempted as I am to say both of them, I think the girls would prefer the younger Wakefield man."

Toni nodded. "It'll be easier to talk about Joel if he's not there."

Laughter burst from Serena. "You'll need to be careful. I have a vested interest now in anything you might say."

"Like his favorite meals?"

Serena's smile held a degree of smugness. "I like to think I have a bit of a clue in that regard."

"So you know he's a big fan of eel?"

"Eel?" Serena's brow wrinkled. "Really? That's kind of gross."

"Which is why he never mentions it. But I bet he'd love you forever if you made it for him," Toni said, fighting to hold a straight face.

"You think so?" Serena's frown line deepened. "Can you even buy eel here?"

"Oh, no. It has to be freshly caught." Toni became aware that Chuck had stopped what he was doing and was listening in. "You're a fan of eel, aren't you, Chuck?"

"Love it," he said seriously, not missing a beat. "Tried some in Prince Edward Island once."

He had? Okay.

"I'm afraid I don't know much about eel," Serena said, her expression still holding a measure of distaste. "Can you buy it at a store?"

"Yeah. But I don't think this is the right season for them," he added kindly.

Toni bit her lip, hiding her amusement. "Summer might be better, eh?"

He dipped his chin, then moved to collect his things with a, "Let me know if there's anything else you need, Toni."

"Thank you."

Serena's brow still wore a pleat. "Wow. I can't believe I did not know that."

"There'll be time to discover all kinds of things. Just remember, once you say, 'I do' it gets hard to undo."

Serena nodded, as if she hadn't heard a million wedding services already. Her role as the resort's events coordinator was due to a recent promotion from a role that had overseen hundreds of weddings over the years. What was the bet that Serena already had a solid plan about what she wanted on her wedding day?

"Maybe we can discuss some of the wedding details on Friday," Toni suggested. "I bet Rachel and Anna would have lots of ideas."

"Yes." Serena's wrinkle between her brows deepened. "I don't know how many of their ideas I'd really need to implement."

"But it'd be fun to hear them all the same." Toni laughed. "We could play wedding planning bingo."

"What?"

"Wedding planning bingo. Where we write down what ideas we think the others will say, and see who gets the most right by the end of the night."

Serena grinned. "I can just imagine what will be on Rachel's list."

"Cocktails," they said in unison, before breaking into laughter.

"Just tell me what to bring," Toni said. "It'll be a nice way to celebrate the opening here."

Serena's eyes rounded. "Ooh! I know we were talking about just doing a soft launch, but that would be a great way to ramp up the publicity for the art gallery."

"Your soiree?"

"No! Doing a cocktail party or something like that. Oh! Maybe we could do an art auction, or one of your pieces of art as a door prize."

"Yeah, I think with all you have on your plate you're probably best off going with the soft launch idea."

"But it really wouldn't take too much to organize," Serena insisted. "And it would be a great way to publicize this."

"But when? There's no way you could have enough time to organize this before Valentine's Day, which reminds me. I heard some of the others talking about Galentine's Day. Do you know anything about that?"

Serena sighed. "Oh, I forgot. Yes, it's the singles event I've held the last few years, even when I was with Dwight." She made a face at the mention of her ex. "He never liked Valentine's Day —probably because it involved money—so us girls used to get together and it was a lot of fun. But I wasn't thinking I'd host it this year."

"Maybe we could tweak it to fit your bachelorette party or something."

"Maybe." Serena's smile could light birthday candles. "Or maybe Joel will have plans for us on that day."

D'oh. Of course. Well, with Joel there was no 'of course' about it. But there definitely *should* be if the man was planning to marry Serena in the upcoming weeks.

"We might need to mention that as well on Friday night," Toni said.

Serena's phone buzzed, and she read the message and winced. "Ah, that's Cherry." Serena's assistant. "She's got an issue with the conference we've got booked, so I better scoot. See you later." She moved to the door, her heels tap-tapping on the floor. "I'll message the others and let them know. Let's say seven on Friday?"

"Will you let Staci know?"

A nod. "She's nice, isn't she? I wasn't sure if she'd feel comfortable with us, especially knowing some of us slightly from when she was here at school before, but she seems to fit in well."

"I wouldn't be surprised if she and Dr. James are busy, but he might be on call."

"Anna's hot doctor." Serena's smile flashed. "Poor girl."

Indeed.

"One day her prince will come along." Serena eyed her. "As will yours."

"Yeah, I'm kind of too busy at the moment to worry about mythical princes coming to sweep me off my feet."

"What about handsome investment managers from the city?" Serena teased. "I seem to recall you and Matt having fun together at the cranberry festival."

"That was before…"

"Before what?"

Toni swallowed. For a work environment, there seemed to be an awful lot of conversation about personal matters. "That was before he let me know he wanted to go out with me."

Serena's eyes enlarged. "When did he do that?"

"On New Year's Eve."

"I didn't know!"

"Yeah, you've been kind of busy with other things."

"True, but this is important! Does Joel know?"

"I haven't told him. And Matt left before they had much conversation."

"Wait—I thought Matt left because of some work thing."

"That's what he said." But something inside had also wondered if maybe he'd left because of what she'd said. She tried to cover the disconcerting feelings with a shrug. "He's always been crazy busy with work, always at their beck and call."

"Mm, Joel has said that. I think he's concerned about his work load." Serena's head tilted. "Do you like him?"

"Joel?" Toni said, deliberately misunderstanding the question.

Serena looked at her, pushing up her eyebrows. "You do, don't you?"

Nope, not fooled a bit. "No. Matt is my complete opposite. We've got zero in common. He's way too serious for me."

"Mm, ever heard of opposites attract? Come on, Toni. He's a good guy. Christian. Handsome. Judging from the car he drives he can't be doing too badly for himself. And I've seen the way he looks at you."

Her stomach tensed. No. This was *not* the conversation she wanted to be having right now. "Didn't you have a conference emergency to sort out?"

Serena exhaled, pointing a finger at Toni as she retreated. "Don't think this conversation is finished. You and Matt could work. Maybe you should pray about it."

"Go. And if you think for a second that we're going to discuss this on Friday night then I think you'll find I'm going to be busy."

Serena's mocking laugh drifted down the hall as she disappeared.

But it was impossible, so not even worth bothering God by praying about. For how could the man she'd spurned now ever think of Toni kindly again?

~

FROM HIS OFFICE on the seventeenth floor of Toronto's highest habitable skyscraper he could just catch a glimpse of the gray sheathe of Lake Ontario. Winter wasn't his favorite season, but the dark days and cold felt appropriate for his mood. Not that he had much time to indulge in such things as moods. Especially when his new year had started off with a whimper that had quickly escalated into a roar.

"Dude, do you really think you're going to get the promotion sitting on your behind and staring out the window all day?"

Matt ground his teeth. He was pretty sure his dentist had funded several tropical island vacations from Matt's increased number of visits in the past two years, visits resulting from jaw pain and clenched teeth he could attribute to one man in particular. The man with the pink face and over-bleached teeth Matt was pretty sure would glow in a game of laser tag. Not that Ray Weiner seemed the sort to play games. Except with the company's money and by messing with other people's lives. *Ray, Ray, go away.*

"Yo, Matty V. I'm talking to you."

Sometimes Matt would really like to be the kind of person who could talk unfiltered. Who could just say what he thought without having to keep it all in. That was one of the things he admired about Toni, the way she just said what she thought and hang the consequences. If he was that kind of man then he would say, "Really, Ray? That's the best you can do at talking? I thought it was more your version of rapping. But with nothing of Drake or Jay-Z about it."

Or maybe he'd go with, "Just because you're talking, doesn't mean I care."

But—he swallowed a wry smile at that last thought, one he'd *really* like to say—Matt knew he wasn't that kind of man. And because he wanted this promotion he knew now wasn't the time to create trouble with the man who was a thorn in everyone's side. Ray was a pain but due to his connections with the company's chief executive officer they all knew they'd never see the back of Ray.

"Was there something you wanted?" Yep. That was more Matt's speed.

"Yeah. I want—and I'm gonna get—that promotion. Lee's just as good as promised it to me."

"Has he?" Matt hoped he'd conveyed the right level of disinterest in both his expression and tone. Ray wasn't the kind to overlook offense, so it was worth holding his true thoughts in check and adopting the mild-mannered pose Ray seemed to think all Christians should possess. "Well, if that's the case then you've got nothing to worry about from me."

"Wasn't anyway," Ray said with a smirk.

Okay. His bad start to the year was getting progressively worse.

Matt scratched at his left hand where the eczema was spreading between his ring and middle finger. If only there was a way to get rid of the itch that was Ray the pain.

He bent his head to his desk, studying the computer screen and using his mouse to open up the latest emails. He frowned, doing his best to ignore the problem man-child still hovering so close Matt could smell the garlic on his lunch, while he focused on the problem this latest email from Japan indicated.

Working as a portfolio manager for one of North America's largest pension funds meant constant high pressure and long hours. It also meant travel that some—like his parents and brother—seemed to think constituted first class trips, all expenses paid, and nonstop fun. And while there was some of that—the perks of constant business travel had led to some nice upgrades over the years—the fact was that it didn't seem to matter how many times he had explained it to them, his work involved many fourteen-hour days, the constant pressure of performance reviews, and the pain when he got it wrong. Thankfully, he hadn't been in poor Paolo's situation, recommending an investment in a company that had soon gone belly up, and seen Paolo fired spectacularly, departing the premises in a walk of shame and a blaze of tossed files and Spanish swear words. But this life of edging forward with next to no sleep made him feel like it was just a matter of time before it would be his turn. Well, except for the Spanish swear words, at least.

Some days it felt like it was just a matter of time before he imploded, as the stressful factors in his life seemed to notch up each day. It wasn't enough that Toni had rejected him. Oh no.

Now with a dream promotion within reach it was like his work colleagues had each decided to up their game and out-maneuver each other. Matt was used to this game, he could play it like other guys were experts at Xbox. But he hated the striving, the striving that just made him feel stressed, feeling like he was never good enough, that he would never win.

At least stressing at work meant he wasn't stressing at home.

He'd arrived at his apartment at 2 a.m. on New Year's Day thankful not to have encountered any police. They would've been well within their rights to book him for speeding. It wasn't something he was proud of, but sometimes the Lexus seemed to beg to go faster than what the traffic signs indicated. And he never sped when other cars were around, so he figured it was between him and his conscience. And he and his conscience were on such good terms most days that it didn't seem to matter too much to have this vice. Maybe it stemmed from a reckless streak that had never been resolved when he was a teen. But the adrenaline he felt was matched only by one other thing, and after that spectacular fail on New Year's Eve there was no way he was going back for round two of rejection. Nope, he'd tasted the bitterness and didn't want more. Besides, there was enough bitterness floating around these offices he didn't need extra.

He grabbed a sandwich and worked through lunch, reading reports, and answering email as he prepared for the research trip next week. He'd spent years cultivating some of these connections, and it felt good to know that Lee trusted him to make the call. His time would consist of traveling to meet businesses and those initiatives that Sage Investments was interested in potentially investing. Being too prescriptive meant possibly missing out on good opportunities, so Sage liked to partner with all kinds of operators in every asset class in North America and offshore. And a big part of that meant travelling to find those opportunities.

His phone flashed. Joel. He tapped open the message. *Can you be my best man?*

Some of the tight bowstrings across his heart eased. *Honored*, Matt typed back.

All at once his mind flicked to who the logical choice would be for bridesmaid.

His heart clenched. Toni.

But no, he shoved the phone away. He didn't need to torture himself with thoughts like that. It was far more likely that Serena would ask her sister, or one of her many other friends to help her on the day. But he wouldn't put it past them to invite Toni to be one of the wedding party.

Not that it mattered, anyway. She'd made her position clear, and he'd just suck it up and deal with it. Deal with it later, he frowned, when this report could finally be finished.

Two more hours passed, then, knowing he couldn't take another minute of Ray's presence, he left the building. The sun had long gone and sleet hung in the air. There was a hockey game tonight—Toronto versus Calgary—and while he loved the game as much as the next man, he didn't need more tension in his life. Besides, he still had about four hours' worth of work to complete before tomorrow.

He knuckled his forehead, digging deep to press the headache away. Man. He might not play pro-sports, but between his aching head, jaw, and broken skin, his body seemed to be wearing the abuse of stress and the rigors of his work as much as any hockey player's.

Thirty minutes later and the scent of hot food filled the ascending elevator, the other residents of this apartment complex eyeing the plastic bag like he might be holding nuggets of gold. The elevator door opened, and he stepped out, almost colliding with a woman with a hippie vibe and red hair. Sarah Walton wore a hockey jersey with her husband's number and carried a huge silver puffer jacket.

"Oh, that smells *so* delicious," she said, her Aussie accent drawing his smile.

Although it wasn't really the accent he appreciated so much as her wide-eyed enthusiasm. Since she'd married Dan Walton six months ago he'd come across the couple a few times. Matt had known Dan a little before, and his new wife's friendliness and buoyant spirits seemed to have charmed everyone in the building. Although sometimes he got the impression that she would love to have a baby like the one that lived across from their front door.

"If it's anything like the last dozen times, then it will be," he said now. "Are you off to the game?"

"Yep. I still can't get over how cold it is here, but I'm doing my best to adjust. This is my first January in Canada, and let's just say this is the opposite of the heatwave we're having at home. But hey, we don't get to see too many hockey games in Australia."

"Hope we win."

"Go Leafs!" She stepped into the elevator and grinned at him before the doors closed again.

Halfway down the hall, he keyed open his door and entered his apartment. For the first time since early this morning, stillness rushed to meet him. He closed the door, closed his eyes, and just stood, as peace nudged away some of the stress that threatened to overwhelm his life.

Sometimes it felt indulgent to have so much space for one man. But his job paid well, and he'd figured he might as well live somewhere he actually wanted to, rather than be forced into a stupidly long commute. And here, where there was a chance he might run into his favourite NHL player was a nice side bonus. He totally didn't have stalker vibes, no matter what some people in Muskoka might think.

Sighing, he opened his eyes and commenced the short walk to the galley kitchen, where he grabbed a knife and fork and snagged a bottle of water from the fridge, then moved to the square dining table with its view over the city. He didn't earn enough for an apartment with lake views—that was more Dan's domain—but the view here was pleasant enough. Not that you could see anything now, when it was so dark, and winter wasn't the best season anyway to showcase Toronto's beauty. But there was an element of escape in looking at the long roads that stretched north, that stretched toward Muskoka.

He exhaled, forcing his attention to the food, but even as he ate, trying to force himself to think about the work that still awaited him tonight, part of his mind toyed with what escape would look like. What *would* escape look like? His mind filled with images of lakes, peace, a quiet town, a caring community. He might know people here in the city, but so many of those relationships were just shallow, and the ones he wanted to strengthen his work did not allow time for.

Work.

It was one thing to think about the tantalizing promise of escape, but the fact remained that he needed to pay his mortgage, which meant working with colleagues he sometimes worried that he was fast starting to hate.

Ray had been extra painful today, like he'd never heard of the team part of teamwork. Ray was just hard work, and his long-standing friendship with the CEO just made life more difficult. In fact, tracking through the past six years of interactions with Ray, he couldn't think of one kind or generous thing the man had done, this despite Matt having turned the other cheek and doing his best to display Jesus to the man for years. What would Jesus do? Would he be a doormat or would he have stood up to the man who made life a misery for so many at the office? Matt rather suspected the latter. And if that was so, then what did that make Matt? The doormat he despised? He scratched the broken skin on his fingers, the persistent itch impossible to be rid of. Just like Ray.

A wave of darkness rolled through him, causing every single one of his muscles to contract. He gritted his teeth, hating the power the man had over him, stealing into his down-time. He bet anything Ray was off having fun, living his best life unfettered by a conscience, and not sparing Matt a single thought. And what was worse, Matt *knew* this was not the way God wanted him to be. Knew that frustration and envy and unforgiveness cursed him more than anyone else. He had to let this go. But letting go felt like letting Ray win, and the competitive part of him that still existed under layers of nice wouldn't, *couldn't* let go of things so easily. Maybe it was the same stubbornness that kept him yearning for a woman who wouldn't even have a coffee with him.

He pushed his food away, his agitation propelling him to his feet when he walked to the window and pressed his face against the glass like a little kid. His breath fogged the view and he tilted his forehead and gazed down, down, down to where he could see a couple of ant-like figures shuffling along the snow-strewn lit streets far below. He didn't envy anyone being out in this weather, battling the sleety conditions alone.

Loneliness washed over him, and for a moment he dared imagine a life where he had a wife, a child, and a family of his own. It was all well and good to be making money, but what was the point if there was no one to spend it on? His family were well off – his parents were leaving on an around-the-world cruise tomorrow – and his Vancouver-based brother lacked nothing. Matt gave generously to charities, and always did his best to pay for his friends when they went out, without making it look like he was richer than them. But a man could have all the money in the world and yet nothing could fill this ache inside that just wanted someone to love him. To care about him, and ask about his day like he bet Sarah asked Dan. Someone to hold and gaze out at this view together.

He sucked in a breath and slowly released, fogging up the

glass again. He really needed to get his head together, and get focused on the reports that the CEO had demanded just before knock off time earlier tonight. Maybe one day he'd find the courage to ask someone else out. If ever he managed to find time to get to know someone the way he'd gotten to know Toni. Or maybe he could just ask her again.

His stomach tensed. Had he been too quick to take her hesitation as a no? Maybe. But he had no clue when he would next be heading north. Work was taking him to England next week, a trip that would see him take in other countries like Germany and Denmark and Sweden before heading back to North America, New York, then Washington, and finally home. Once upon a time he'd found such travel exhilarating. Now the thought filled him with dread. So many planes, so many hands to shake, so many reports to memorize, so many things to pretend to care about when the only thing he really cared about lived two hours north of here.

He pushed away from the window. How pathetic was he? Maybe that was the special quality Toni had recognized in him that had resulted in a solid no. Anyway, all the moaning in the world wouldn't change the fact that those reports demanded attention. So he dragged what remained of his energy to deal with the reports the CEO wanted by tomorrow.

CHAPTER 3

"*A*nd so I wanted to ask you this before Staci gets here." Serena turned to Anna. "You've been my best friend since I first moved here, so I wanted to know, will you be my maid of honor?"

A squeal and a hug gave affirmation.

Serena laughed, pulling back from Anna's excitement, as she glanced at Jackie, Rachel, and Toni. "And we don't want a big wedding, but I wanted to ask if you would be happy if Toni was my other bridesmaid, and if you two read the Bible verses during the ceremony."

"Really?" Toni asked. She glanced at Jackie then back at Serena.

Serena nodded, and held out a hand. "I actually talked about this before with Joel, and he wanted you to feel involved, and this way we're not too big of a wedding party."

"It's only right, especially when you're the groom's sister," Jackie said generously. "Although I feel it only fair to warn you that I'm planning on giving little Ethan lots of cuddles while you do your thing."

"You know you're welcome to do so any time."

"Good."

Jackie might work at an old person's home, but sometimes Toni wondered if she'd prefer to work in a preschool. Her frequent offers to help with Ethan suggested a maternal side that neither being single nor working among the aged fulfilled.

The doorbell rang, and Serena jumped up to admit Staci while Toni helped Anna bring out some of the antipasto trays Serena had prepared earlier. This 'soiree' might be a little more low key than some that Toni had attended here, but there was still something special about gathering on a Friday night with the girls. Especially after the long week of art gallery prepping. But now, with everything ready for the first day of opening next week, she had the chance to relax, and enjoy time with these friends.

She smiled a welcome to Staci, and reclaimed the comfortable blue-and-white floral armchair that Serena had said once belonged to her grandmother, from whom Serena had inherited this cute two-bedroom house. Toni might like Joel's house, the four-bedder 1970s bungalow he'd renovated into the current millennium, but there was something about the quaint nature of Serena's place that called to her. Maybe it was the old diamond-paned windows, or the stone hearth fireplace, but this space had always seemed perfect for Serena. She wondered what Serena would do with it once she and Joel married – and what their marriage would mean for where Ethan and she would live.

Conversation carried on around her, and she dunked a homemade cheese straw in ranch dressing as she caught up to speed. Oh, the wedding. Of course.

"Okay, so I think it's only fair that we have special drinks at your reception," Rachel said. "You could call them, oh, I don't know, a 'Pina Joel-ada' or a 'Serena-ita' or something fun like that."

"You've clearly thought this through," Staci said, as Toni

swapped smirks with Serena. Wedding planning bingo was going exactly as she'd envisaged. Cocktails from Rachel? Check.

Rachel shrugged. "What can I say? I'm a fan of adult beverages."

"I'm not sure my parents will be up for that, though," Serena said gently.

Toni swished a carrot stick through French onion-flavored dip. From what she knew, Serena's parents were pretty strait-laced. They were currently finishing up a stint of time working as missionaries in India. She gathered from Serena's previous conversations they wouldn't view 'adult beverages' in a positive light.

"How are they getting on?" Jackie asked.

"They must be so excited," Anna chimed in. "I mean, I'm excited. I can't imagine how they feel, knowing that you're going to marry someone they haven't even met yet."

"Joel and my folks have met online a few times," Serena demurred. "Mom told me that Joel had asked for their blessing when they talked at Christmas, which was so sweet. I think it helped that Joel works as an assistant church minister."

Staci glanced between them. "Sorry, what does that have to do with anything?"

Serena explained about how her parents were rather conservative when it came to their idea of church ministry and what kinds of jobs Christians should have.

Staci winced. "Well, I don't think they'll ever really want to meet me then."

"Hey, you're not your past," Jackie said. "And didn't I hear you say at New Year's that you're writing different types of books now?"

Staci nodded. "Well, trying to. It's still a bit of a mess with my former publishers and all that's going on. My agent has been shopping my new manuscript around so we'll see if somebody wants to take a sweet and clean romance from me instead of the usual steamier version." She sipped her mulled wine. "I have to say, I never realized how nice it might be to write something where I don't have to worry about what others might think of me. I mean, James still gets a little concerned that I'm going to be describing his kisses in my books—"

"You could stop kissing him," Anna suggested, in a manner Toni wasn't exactly sure was meant as tease.

"I could. But I don't think he'd be happy about that, either." Staci's look of smugness drew laughter from the others, even a reluctant chuckle from Anna.

It was funny how Staci had managed to settle in with them. The awkwardness and sense of awe Toni had felt about an author whose books she'd read had mostly faded, and now Staci seemed more like one of the gang. Gratitude spurted again for the fact that Serena and the others had taken Toni under their wing. She knew how much it meant to feel included.

"So, back to wedding planning," Anna said. "What do you need us to do? It's only six weeks away or so, so you've got to be freaking out a little."

Serena shook her head in that calm way of hers. If ever a woman lived up to her name it was Toni's soon-to-be sister-in-law. "I discussed this with Joel and he's happy for me to plan things." Her smile flashed. "It's not like I haven't had some experience over the years."

"True, that," Rachel said.

Jackie dipped a celery stick in salsa. "So does this mean you've got things organized already?"

"Most things. I still need a dress, but I have some connections in the city that have promised to help me out."

"Ooh, dress shopping expedition!" Anna called, clapping her hands.

Toni mentally checked off wedding checklist bingo item two.

"You're looking so good, girl." Rachel raised her glass in

Serena's direction. "Sometimes I see you at church and I can't believe you're the same woman as six months ago."

"I look in the mirror and think the same," Serena confessed. "I still can't believe I let myself go like that."

Staci's look of enquiry drew Serena's murmur, "I've lost close to fifty pounds since July."

"Wow! Good for you." Staci's expression held respect. "I like to run, but I have a problem ankle so I don't fancy trying to run on snow. But I find if I don't exercise then I can pile on weight, especially seeing my day job keeps me in a chair for hours each day. I've noticed that exercise is good for my mental health, too."

"Exercise, schmexercise," Rachel groaned to Toni's silent Amen. "Now back to what's important. What else do you need us to do?"

"Honestly, there's nothing much. Between Joel's work and mine we pretty much have things covered."

"Yeah, I guess you didn't need to look far for finding a church and ministers," Jackie said. "Vows?"

"Just going traditional, so that's done too," Serena said. "And Alphonse has insisted on doing the reception in his restaurant at the resort, so I don't need to worry about that either."

"Cake?" Rachel asked.

"Alphonse is taking care of it. And Annette long ago told me she's doing my flowers, so that's pretty much arranged itself, too."

"You should at least let us throw you a bachelorette party, or do something fun," Anna said.

Toni smiled. Check!

"That's right! Ooh, we could do something really fun," said Jackie. "Like a movie marathon."

Seriously? Lame.

"What about a spa day and high tea at a resort?" Staci asked.

"That could be fun," Anna agreed. "But would you want to go to Muskoka Shores or somewhere else?"

"The spa at Muskoka Shores is good. Yvonne gives the best massages." Rachel's face took on a dreamy look.

"Or would you prefer to go elsewhere?" Jackie asked Serena. "Although it could get weird if it's too close by and you get recognized."

Staci frowned. "Sorry, are you a celebrity?"

Serena laughed. "No. I just probably need to be careful so it doesn't look like I'm checking out the competition at a nearby resort."

"Maybe we could do something in the city," Toni suggested. "You could combine it with your dress shopping day, make a weekend out of it."

"Ooh! I heard of this place that does axe throwing for girls," Anna said. "Wouldn't that be fun?"

Okay, totally not something on Wedding Planning Bingo. Nor something she'd ever expect Anna to say.

"Until you lose an arm," Rachel scoffed.

"What about creating your own lipstick or something like that?" Toni suggested. Paint-and-sip could even be an option…

Serena held up her hands. "I'm happy to do whatever. Surprise me. But I will have to plan to get my dress sorted soon, so I was thinking maybe in two or three weekends' time."

"You're hardly going to pick one off the shelf, are you?" Rachel asked.

"Actually, that was exactly what I thought. I've spent so much time organizing other people's weddings over the years that I know what I don't want, and I don't want a big fuss. I've always thought the best weddings are those where people are relaxed and happy to go with the flow."

"You could never be a Bridezilla," Anna said loyally.

"I hope not. So that's why I thought we could just keep things simple. John will do the ceremony at church, and we'll have the reception at Muskoka Shores. Alphonse has already told me he's got a special menu lined up, and I know whatever he cooks will be perfect."

Toni bit her lip. How lucky was Serena to be surrounded by people who wanted to help her?

"You should definitely check out Alphonse's," Rachel told Staci. "It's the best restaurant around for miles."

"I think James mentioned it," Staci said.

Toni caught the way Anna's face fell, as if she didn't want the constant referral to Staci and James's new couple status being rubbed in her face. Not that Staci was rubbing it in her face, but it wasn't exactly easy to ignore.

"I think those plans sound perfect," Toni said, getting the conversation back on track. "From what I've heard Joel say, he's so thankful that it needn't be a big fuss. Of course, that could be because he's a man and he's just happy to leave it all to you."

Amusement rippled around the room as Serena laughingly protested, "He's not that bad."

"Hmm, you haven't known him as long as I have. Talk to me in twenty-five years."

More chuckles, as Jackie passed around the platter of vegetables, cheeses, and dips. "John and Angela seemed pretty pleased."

"I think they are," Serena said shyly.

"*Everyone* is happy for you two," Toni said. "Especially Joel. He's always been a positive, glass-half-full kind of guy but now he's almost radiant. He's started singing around the house, Serena, and I blame you."

"I think he sings nicely," Serena protested.

"Love must be deaf as well as blind." Toni swapped smirks with Rachel.

"Well, I don't mind," Serena said. "It's nice to think I might make him happy."

She was always so modest.

Serena's eyes held a gleam as she glanced at Toni. "Anyway,

that's enough about me. I want to know what you're going to do about Matt. You know Joel asked him to be best man."

"Ooh, does that mean he's partnered with me?" Anna asked, her face brightening. "Okay, I am *totally* okay with that."

Toni's stomach tensed, almost like her body recognized that she wasn't okay with that.

"He's so handsome, isn't he?" Anna continued.

"Very hot," Rachel murmured, nodding as she ate a twiggy stick.

He was?

"Whoa. Spicy." Rachel fanned herself, then gulped the rest of her drink.

Toni stared at her, heart contracting, before realizing Rachel was referring to the spiced meat. Not Matt.

"Are you okay, Toni?" Jackie asked. "You look a little worried."

"I'm fine." She grabbed her own virgin mojito—she was driving—and sucked the straw vigorously.

"I think he was going to ask his friend Wade to be the other groomsman, which means he'll partner you, Toni," Serena said.

Awesome. Matt might be overly serious, but at least he supported women's lib. From what she'd heard Wade say before, she was pretty sure he still measured women according to their cooking and cleaning abilities.

"You don't mind, do you, Toni?" Anna asked.

"Mind what?" she asked, although she had a fair idea what she meant.

"Me and Matt. Being together."

Together. Why did that word make her feel a little nauseous?

From out of nowhere came a rush of mental images: Matt and Anna holding hands, Matt and Anna hugging, Matt and Anna kissing, Matt and Anna—

Something dark slithered inside, and she gulped. Shook her head in a vain attempt to get rid of these feelings. No. *No.* Why did she feel this way? Matt was only a friend. She had no claim on him. She didn't want to have a claim on him. She'd be very happy for him to stake a claim in someone else's heart. Really.

And yet, as the evening continued with more tease and plans and laughter, Toni couldn't help but notice the assessing looks she was getting from both Serena and Jackie. Almost like they could see something she didn't know. Or maybe they saw something she didn't want to admit. Matt and Anna? That didn't need to matter to her.

Not at all.

~

THERE SHOULD BE a law against working on weekends. Especially when he'd already worked a sixty-hour week. But the project that had kept him back in the office until nine last night had seen him start at seven this morning, in an attempt to contact London and Japan and somehow balance crazy time zones across the world.

And yeah, part of this was to prove to his superiors that he should win the promotion. Even if his brain felt foggy and his thoughts held as much clarity as the murky depths of the ice-strewn lake out there. But he had to plow on, he had to prove himself. Management had confirmed yesterday that the race was between Ray and himself and there was no way he'd ever want to be beholden to that man or be required to regard him as his boss. He'd sooner quit.

His phone buzzed. *Having a great trip!* Mom and Dad's picture accompanied the text message.

Awesome, he typed back. He'd managed to squeeze in a quick farewell on Thursday night before they boarded their flight to Seattle, from where they'd board a cruise ship that would see them travel across to Hawaii, Fiji, and Australia before heading to Asia and the Middle East, then the Mediterranean, Lisbon and finally England. He couldn't imagine three months at sea, but couldn't begrudge his folks the chance to see the world like they'd always dreamed. He'd upgraded their inside cabin to a balcony suite, sure that nobody should miss such sights as sunsets on the Pacific.

He'd already told them to enjoy themselves, to not feel like he expected them to report in too much, knowing their relationship was strong enough that it didn't need constant checking in. Or maybe that's just how he'd felt about things. Regardless, this chance to celebrate their fortieth wedding anniversary and Dad's recent retirement had been a long time coming. He only hoped their shorter cruises in the past had prepared them for so many days at sea.

He shot up a prayer for their protection then shoved the phone away, his mind tossing and turning over the figures. Propping his chin in his hand, his eyes started to glaze over as he studied the screen.

Some days he liked to imagine what it must be like to hold a creative career, one where the imagination was permitted to run free. What must it be like to write a book like that author he'd met at Joel's New Year's Eve party? What must it be like to be a painter and just create rather than be a stickler for the facts?

His mind flicked to a certain artist, and he shot up another prayer for her, before bending his mind to the reason he was in the office today. Nope. Couldn't think about her. He had to think about this instead.

Pressure rimmed his brain, banded his chest. He blinked, sucked down another of the energy drinks he'd started guzzling this week. Straight black coffee might usually be his friend, but lately it hadn't had enough kick. And the hours he was pulling demanded more.

The elevator pinged, and a second later opened. Who—?
Oh. No.

"You're here?" Incredulity lined Ray's voice. "I thought for sure the office would be free."

You thought wrong. He was tempted to reply with something that expressed the same as Ray's disbelief, but realized he didn't owe Ray any explanation. Apparently, his mouth didn't get the memo. "Just thought I'd catch up on some work before London next week."

"London?" Ray smirked. "Didn't you hear? You've been pulled and now Lee is sending me."

"What?"

Ray shrugged. "He told me he'd tell you last night."

"But it's all arranged. The tickets are in my name. I've been working these deals for weeks, and—"

"And now I'll be taking care of things."

Was that true, or was this just another example of Ray's version of the truth? Matt had never been a big fan of people owning their own 'truth'. Experience had shown him that one man's 'truth' often left out inconvenient facts. He couldn't believe Lee would just rearrange things.

"Go on, then. Call him."

Huh. Those didn't seem to be the words of someone who wasn't sure. Matt swiped his phone and soon his boss's name was on the screen. A couple of taps later and his phone was calling.

"Matt? Why are you calling on a Saturday morning?"

"Sir, I'm sorry to interrupt, but Ray is here and seems to be under the impression that you want him to go to London next week."

A swear word. "I was going to tell you, but things got crazy last night with my wife's work and the kids. But yeah, that's true."

Panic rose within him, and Matt ducked his head to not encounter Ray's folded-arms and smug face. "But I'm the one who's been working on this for months, sir. You asked me to arrange this and I have." He hated how his voice pitched up at the end like a little whiny kid. "Sir, I think you'd have to agree that I'm the person who's the best for the job. Nobody else knows the ins and outs of these potential contracts like me."

"I appreciate all your hard work," Lee said. "But this is how things need to be."

"But sir..." He gritted his teeth as Ray smirked and moved to lean against the door.

Matt wasn't a violent man, but right now he wanted nothing more than to kung fu hit the man away from his personal space.

The silence on the other end of the phone stretched. "Sir?"

"I have to admit I'm disappointed, Matt. I really thought you were more of a team player than this."

Matt got up from his seat and closed the door in Ray's face. "I am a team player, sir. That's why I've been working insanely long days trying to get this done in time."

"And we appreciate that, but it's come to our attention that your efforts could be better utilized elsewhere."

Panic crawled up his throat. "I beg your pardon?"

"Here at Sage Investments we believe it's important for all of our staff to have a well-rounded understanding of what portfolio management and investment actually means. And you are the one who has traveled to England and Europe the most. It's been pointed out to us that in order for others to learn the skills they need the opportunity too."

"You mean Ray has pointed this out," he said flatly. "Sir, I really feel I need to object in the strongest possible terms."

"Object to what?"

The fact Ray would be taking over his work. That Ray would be riding on his coat tails and claiming the deals Matt had all but already secured as wins of his own. Nausea rumbled through his stomach. His headache intensified. "I cannot see how it could be considered fair for him to receive the credit for all the work I've done these many months. You know that the

Scarborough project is basically a signature away from becoming ours. How is it fair that Ray is the one to see that happen when it's been my hard work and connections that have got this over the line?"

A sigh. "That is not the way to demonstrate you're a team player."

"Neither is being rewarded for stealing another man's work," he retorted, gritting his teeth.

He waited, waited. Had he said too much? Pushed things too far?

The silence on the other end of the phone spoke volumes. What did this mean? Was he being demoted? Right now it certainly didn't seem like a promotion was in the works. Well, too bad. Today was the day of plain speaking. "Sir, I can't help wondering why this is happening now. Is there anything I can say or do to convince you to not give this to Ray?"

"I'm afraid not, no."

Matt swallowed bile. And a swear word or five. "Then," his voice was shaky, and he clenched his fingers. "Then I have to wonder if there's any point in me going for the promotion when it seems apparent that you are preferring Ray to me."

"You know that we have a fair system in place. And to be honest—"

"I'd prefer that," Matt growled.

"—I don't like your attitude right now. I understand that you are disappointed, but you need to understand that I trust Ray—"

That made one of them.

"—to get the job done in a way that is most effective for our bottom line. I know you have done some good work for us in the past, but it's time for you to share some of that with others and not be selfish."

"Selfish?" Was Lee serious? "Sir, I don't know how you can possibly accuse me of that, but I assure you I am anything but."

"I'm afraid that's not how some others see it."

"Which others?" Matt demanded. He could feel his blood pressure escalating, his pulse pounding in his ears.

"You can't honestly expect me to answer that, can you?"

"I get the feeling that by not answering it, you are saying you don't value my work here."

"I'm sorry you feel that way."

"So, you really expect me to just roll over and let Ray take over my projects?"

"If you wish to keep your job, then yes."

Dizziness washed through him. "I think you'll find HR has something to say about this."

"I think you'll find that HR answers to me." A beat. "Look, Matt, you've been an excellent member of staff for a long time now, but I think it's time for you to consider other options."

Matt blinked. "Are you telling me to quit?"

"Nobody said anything about quitting," Lee said. "But you need to consider your results from the latest performance review."

"What about it? I did just fine."

"Yes, but 'just fine' isn't really what we expect from our employees here at Sage Investments. Perhaps it's time for you to take a break and consider your future."

"But I want to work here. Why do you think I want the promotion?"

"I'm sorry this is not the news you wanted to hear. Please give your reports to Ray and brief him on what he needs to know for the trip next week."

Was he kidding? Part of him wondered whether this was some elaborate ruse by Ray and it wasn't actually the CEO talking but someone whose voice sounded exactly the same.

"Do I have your word you'll do this?" Lee asked.

What option did he have but to say, "Yes"?

"He will be contacting me when he's got them. So please do that today."

Redness filled Matt's vision, and he stabbed at the phone to end the call, switching it to mute so when the CEO returned his call he ignored the vibration, throwing the phone across the room. He couldn't speak for a long moment as fury lodged in his throat. No. *No!* He hadn't worked this hard to simply give it all away.

Ray knocked on the door then opened it, not giving Matt a moment to compose himself. "Lee has asked if you've given me the documents yet. He said you got cut off." He eyed the phone on the floor and smirked.

Matt shoved his hands under the desk so Ray wouldn't see them shaking. He had no desire to stay here, to even breathe the same air as the man standing opposite.

"Well?"

He breathed through clenched teeth, willing himself to calm down. Then swallowed painfully. "Everything is there." He lurched to his feet. Jerked his chin at the neat pile of papers. Picked up the coffee cup and pen set his parents had given him last Christmas. Shoved them in his backpack. Bent to pick up his phone.

"What are you doing?" Ray asked, as Matt brushed past him, moving to the elevator.

He didn't answer to Ray. And it seemed the CEO wouldn't give Matt answers. He jabbed the down button, once, twice, three times.

"Where are you going?" Ray called.

"Elsewhere," he muttered. Anywhere. As long as it was away.

CHAPTER 4

⥲

*W*as it possible to burst from pride?

If Toni had been asked six months ago, if she ever thought she'd be hosting a solo exhibition in a high-end resort known through half the country, the answer would've been an incredulous laugh and a big fat no. God really had to be a miracle-worker to have made this possible.

Toni glanced around the white room, the paintings evenly spaced around the walls, each showcasing a unique aspect of Muskoka life. Water and trees were the main features, although scattered within were a fair amount of canoes, Muskoka chairs placed on wooden docks, and sunset vistas where blue bled into gold.

Her chest swelled. And to think, these paintings were all *hers*.

"It looks fantastic," Serena said, drawing closer. "Bravo."

"Oh, it couldn't have happened without your support and hard work," Toni demurred.

"And Adrian's green light."

"Did I hear my name?" The general manager of Muskoka Shores resort drew near, and smiled. "It's hard to believe this space just held old sports equipment for so many years. If I didn't know better, I'd think this place was designed to show-case art. It looks excellent."

He tilted his chin to the corner where her easel waited for her attention, part of the space she'd use as a studio as part of the artist-in-residence aspect of her role, while also teaching any interested guests some basics about art. "Have you given any thought to what your first painting will be?"

"I'm wondering about doing another maple tree, similar to the one that started this."

"That sounds like a great idea."

"I thought it might be a way of referencing the resort's new logo and inspiring people to think about the resort when they see it."

"Looks like we've got another savvy marketer on our hands," Adrian said to Serena.

Some of the other resort workers wandered in. Adrian and Serena had agreed to hold the official opening in spring, but this, the soft opening where resort guests and staff could come and find out what the mysterious painting and other construction work had been about, allowed time for Toni and Serena to figure out the intricacies of just how the art gallery could work.

Toni snuck a peek at Serena, who was chatting with her assistant, Cherry, as she waved a hand at another of Toni's paintings that was part of the same series as her initial maple tree that had become the symbol for the resort. How did Serena manage to juggle so many things? Maybe it had something to do with the multitude of lists and color-coded diaries Toni had seen. Whatever it was, she seemed to sail through life gracefully, whereas Toni often felt like a big mess. Toni's nerves had meant she'd spilled her morning coffee on her freshly-ironed white shirt, and had to go change. Then she'd gone to wake Ethan, and his howl at seeing her had only made her feel worse. Was this really the right thing to be doing? Chasing her dreams at the expense of time with her son? Although one of the—many—

perks of this job was that she would still be able to have him with her, whether here in the screened-off corner in the playpen during quiet periods, or in the daycare the resort provided for the workers. It wasn't like Toni was totally abandoning him.

She bit her lip. All of her nerves and questions and second-guessing meant she had only got out the door in time because Joel had promised to look after a grumpy Ethan today. She hadn't wanted to inflict her son on the workers' daycare, especially when there was so much else to get her head around.

"You're going to be great," Serena assured.

"Thank you," Toni said.

Mondays were usually Serena's day off, but she'd made an exception to be here this morning. Toni knew another surge of thankfulness for this woman who had opened doors and paved the way to Toni having opportunities few artists ever achieved. As for artists her age? Nada.

Toni turned to Adrian. "Mr. Jennings, you'll never know how much this opportunity means to me. I never would've dreamed of having such a chance as this."

He smiled. "I'm grateful you said yes. I'm sure Serena has explained to you the resort's focus on local and sustainable products and practices, so to have somebody on our doorstep able to offer such a service really feels like a Godsend."

A wave of emotion shuddered through her, causing her to swallow and blink. *A Godsend.* How funny that the rebel without a clue might now be considered in such a way. It was weird always feeling like she was the less worthy sibling, her brother's heart for God and focus on ministry from a young age meaning she'd always felt like the weaker link. His faith hadn't wavered, even when their parents had been killed several years ago, while she'd felt like her life had been thrown off a cliff. Too much grief had led to too many bad choices as she'd struggled to find her feet. And now, she barely recognized the girl she had been, could almost believe her wild years were a bad dream. Apart from the 'consequence' that was Ethan, of course.

For a moment, her mind flickered to that time, itching to wander down that path, before she shut it down again. Nope. No good came of that. John McPherson's sermons, and time spent with Serena, Jackie, and the others had long convinced her that Toni was forgiven, and that there was nothing to be gained from spending too long in the past.

As if God knew she needed a reminder to stay in the present moment, her phone buzzed, and she slid it open to see a message from Jackie.

Congratulations! Can't wait to see it after I finish work today.

Toni smiled and tapped back, *Thanks! It's pretty exciting.*

Jackie's reply consisted of a heart. Jackie's day job was as a nursing carer at a nearby old people's home, and her nights were often spent designing websites and more. She'd offered to help Toni with a website for her artwork, which had taken a backseat since the role at the resort. But maybe one day.

Toni pushed her phone back into the pocket of the nicest pair of trousers she owned. Most of her clothes were looser and more comfortable and practical for paint spills and dealing with a small boy sometimes prone to bouts of vomit and drool. Serena had advised that while Toni didn't need to lose her arty vibe, "Your aesthetic could be channeled into something slightly less casual for some of our less adventurous guests and potential clients." Reading this as code for "dress up or lose sales" she'd needed to enhance her wardrobe with a few items from the meagre selection at Merrill's, the best (and only) fashion boutique Muskoka Shores offered. These wool black trousers were warm, at least, and didn't make her look—or feel—like a 1980s housewife.

The trickle of people—mostly resort staff—cleared from the room, and she joined Serena at the table serving as a front desk.

A couple of signs, a ledger, and a portable point-of-sale device waited for customer orders.

"I still can't believe you think anyone would ever want to buy my work," she murmured to Serena.

"I still can't believe you can't think that." Serena straightened one of the signs. "You need to believe in yourself, my friend. God has good things in store for you."

Her eyes blurred for the second time in half an hour. She wasn't usually this emotional. Maybe she was about to get her period or something.

But then again… maybe God did have good things in store. He'd certainly proved himself faithful with the chance to do this. Maybe she could dare to believe Him for more.

"Now, is there anything else you need, or are you happy for me to leave you in peace?"

Toni surprised them both with a spontaneous hug. Hugs were usually more Joel's domain. It was no surprise he was so popular with the elderly ladies. "Thank you for all you've done. And for coming here today on your day off. You're the best."

Serena squeezed her gently, before pulling back and studying her seriously. "Honey, all I did was listen to the nudge I felt was from God. This is an opportunity, but it's up to you to keep it going." She pushed back a bang of artfully highlighted dark blonde hair. "You know we're excited about what this could mean, and whatever happens, Adrian is eager to use your works in the foyer. But it will require you to prove our faith in you is justified, and that the cost of the renovations will be repaid out of proceedings."

Toni nodded. The contract she'd signed last month had a clause indicating the thirty percent commission would be plowed back into the art gallery's financial kitty until the work done here was repaid.

"So, no questions?"

"I think I'm good." Well, not good exactly. More like sick with nerves.

"You remember how to use the device? Just link it to the app I showed you on your phone."

"For the dozens of sales I'm gonna make."

"Please." Serena's green eyes sparkled. "For the *hundreds* of sales you're going to make." She lifted a hand and departed, leaving Toni all alone.

Toni drew in a breath and surveyed the room. Drew in a whiff of that fresh paint smell. It probably was a good thing she hadn't brought Ethan here. Babies shouldn't be smelling toxic fumes, and although she'd made sure the paint used was child-friendly, it didn't hurt to be careful.

She pivoted on her heel and then shifted to the corner where she'd set up the easel and equipment for those times she'd do her own painting here and 'teach' classes. She swallowed a spurt of fear—she hoped this wasn't a stretch too far to think she'd have people willing to pay for lessons from someone who'd never formally taught before. But no. That was probably more of that negative thinking she needed to learn to squash.

A sort through of the art grade paper and thin canvases, a check of the paint brushes, charcoal and pastels, another check of the paints. The pads of watercolor pigments would probably get the most use, as they'd dry faster than acrylics and much faster than oils. But she'd keep some stock of acrylics and oils, as she thought people might like to try the differing types of medium, even if she didn't figure many guests would stay long enough to justify the oils.

Her phone buzzed again, and she drew it out, checked the message. Joel. *Hey, congrats! Do you have a secret stash of diapers I don't know about?*

She owed her brother, big time. When he'd first talked of moving up here to Muskoka she bet that never in a million years would he have imagined he'd be changing his nephew's diapers quite so often. And doing this today, on his day off? He might sometimes still be a doofus, but he was also the best brother ever.

She typed back: *There's a box in the cupboard in the laundry.*

Thanks.

Thank YOU.

She moved to the other corner, which was screened off to most of the room. Here she'd set up the portable baby change table, and the cot that could double as a playpen. A cupboard stored other necessities, such as wipes, diapers, and several spare changes of clothes. A basket of toys stood on top of it.

Everything was set up for Ethan to be safe and looked after if he was too unwell, or she just wanted to have him near. But the way she and Serena had set this up, he could easily be entertained here while she taught a class, or if she was simply doing her own painting, or looking after the gallery. Yet another blessing.

Silence ticked away. Beyond her, the big windows revealed gray skies and yet more snow. She shivered, and drew her scarf a little tighter.

Another phone buzz. She tugged it out again. Anna. *So proud of you! Can't wait to see it.*

A knot rose in her chest. Yes, she appreciated Anna's support, but she couldn't deny other feelings that tasted a lot like envy. So what if Anna was chief bridesmaid to Matt's best man? She'd meant it when she said she didn't mind. Except...

She kind of did.

Which was dumb. Which was so *not* mature. Which was selfish and greedy and wrong and just plain stupid because she didn't really care if Matt paid another girl attention. Really. She would be glad for him to spend time with someone else, and with all the extra duties demanded by their roles, they'd be sure to spend lots of time together, smiling at each other, laughing, talking, getting closer...

A shaft of something hot and green lodged in her chest. No. She *wasn't* jealous. Not at all. But she wouldn't mind if Anna and Matt didn't spend too much time together. Because if Anna was to discover just what a nice guy he was, and she managed to draw his attention away from Toni—

Oh, what was she *thinking*?

Thanks, Anna, she typed back, and pressed send.

The message swooshed away, and she tried to distract herself by wondering what else she needed to do. The room was all set up, but there hadn't been a visitor for the past hour, apart from a couple of employees who'd stuck their heads inside the door before quickly scuttling away.

What to do, what to do…

There were a million things she could do, like take pictures of her paintings and schedule them for Instagram and Facebook posts. She could finalize the wording for the other promotional material Serena was preparing. She could prep her canvas for when she started her next painting as part of the 'artist in residence' aspect of her role here. There were so many things she could do. But only one thing she really wanted to do.

She dragged out her phone and quickly called Joel.

"Hey, it's the famous artist. How many paintings have you sold today?" he teased.

She hoped it was tease. If he was genuine, he was about to be disappointed. "Exactly none."

A beat. Then, "Well, the day is young. Obviously all your rich clients are still waking up and plan to drop by later today."

"Obviously." Her tone could parch deserts.

"What do they say about Rome being built in a day? That's right. It wasn't."

"I was under the impression that it was more like 'Build it and they will come' from that Kevin Costner movie. That's what Serena seems to think, anyway."

"How is she?"

"Probably heading your way soon. She's been so great, Joel."

"That's because she *is* great. Which makes me great, because I recognized that first, and I get to live with her greatness for the rest of my life."

"Only if she can manage to cope with your great big head," she teased.

He chuckled. "Let me remind you just who is looking after your son."

"How is Ethan doing? Is he behaving?"

"He's been fine. I've been indoctrinating him on the fun of motor mechanics."

"I bet he loved that."

"You know it."

She smiled. "Can he talk to me?"

"You know he doesn't really talk, don't you, Toni? Besides, he's asleep right now."

"Oh." Disappointment creased within.

"But I'll be sure to pass that on when he wakes. Hey, go get 'em, Tiger. You're doing an amazing job."

"Will you come in and see it?"

"How is that even a question? Of course I'll be there. In fact, what time do you close?"

"Five p.m."

"Then I'll bring the tiny tacker and we'll see you just before then. Okay?"

Her heart eased. "Thanks."

They ended the call, and she was left to her own devices again. There weren't any other visitors for quite some time, which allowed time for her to get her laptop out and continue crafting the blurb for the promotional material. Writing her artist biography in third person felt a little pretentious, but she followed through on Serena's request all the same. Information about where she was born, where she studied, talking up the exhibitions and prizes she'd won along the way, even a quick reference to the fact that an NHL player had bought one of her paintings as a Christmas present for his wife last year. It was funny but looking back, she could see how God had used the challenges of her life to bring her this far. Building resilience was what some people called it.

The minutes dragged, and her resilience was tested as minutes dragged into hours, without a sign of a visitor. Her spirits sank. A person might think that on the first day of a new venture that there would be some more buzz than this, but while the room looked pretty it could do with some more visitors. Serena had said it would take some time, but Toni hoped it wasn't going to take too long. She'd hate to disappoint the resort, or Adrian's faith in her. She ate her sandwich and banana, then wondered if she should've brought mints to compensate for banana breath. Then added that in a note on her phone.

She'd just finished typing that in when her phone vibrated with another message. Rachel. *Congratulations! When can I come see?*

Any time, she typed back. *We're open from ten until five each day.*

She wondered if the office hours would prove too much and part of this initial phase was to figure out whether those hours would be manageable for her. This was especially important coming from a creative situation where she commanded her own day into something a lot more office hours-like in its structure. Would this prove a rude shock to the system? But the most important factor was ensuring Ethan could cope with a new routine. Because everything she was doing was for him. And if this couldn't work, then changes would need to happen to make it feasible for her and her son.

She put the phone back on the table she was using as a desk, and re-entered the world of social media, and was deep in the throes of figuring out how to schedule posts for the next two weeks when the door opened.

An elderly gentleman she'd never seen before entered the room. She straightened and smiled, and he nodded, before moving to the first painting nearest the door.

Nerves ping-ponged through her body. Okay, another thing to figure out. She'd never been a fan of those overly helpful store assistants who hovered too close and constantly asked customers if they needed help. But now she was in a similar role, she struggled to know what to do, what to say. She had no desire to appear pushy, but neither did she want a lack of interest to lose a potential sale. What was the best approach?

"Um, good afternoon."

He glanced at her and nodded.

Ah. Not the type to want to chat. "If there's anything I can help you with, please let me know."

Another nod, and his attention returned to her art.

Okay, then. Sometimes it felt hard to adult when everything within her wanted to run away. Dealing with people like this man with his elegant clothes and aloof manner was almost as intimidating as meeting her favorite author. And while she knew she didn't need to be afraid, something in her still craved the approval of people who looked like they were judging her work. Work which really was an expression of her soul.

Staci had talked about this a little on Friday night. How she dealt with reviews from readers who she was pretty sure hadn't had enough sleep or chocolate or caffeine or whatever and judged her books with unwarranted harshness. "Sometimes it hurts when people criticize," she'd said. "Especially when a book is a creation that stems from your heart. I imagine it's what it must be like when someone criticizes your baby."

"How do you deal with it then?" Toni had asked.

"I've learned to understand that not all readers are created equal, and that when they're judging my words it doesn't necessarily mean they're judging me. I'm pretty sure some are," Staci had said candidly, "but that doesn't mean that I need to let their opinions influence me. I figure there are people out there who are *my* readers, just like there are people out there who like Tom Cruise movies, although I've never really been able to understand that myself. But everyone is different and has different tastes and that's okay."

It *would* be okay. Toni knew that as she studied the man. He swung her a look, so she ducked her head and tried to make it look like she hadn't been looking. Not everyone would appreciate her work, and that was okay. It was just that this was the first time she really had so much of her heart on display, and that she was standing here with no other person around to be a buffer against whatever a critical person might say. She grimaced. Oh, how brave was she?

She shot the man another smile, and he seemed to hesitate. "Is there anything I can help you with, sir?"

He shook his head. "I've seen quite enough, thank you." And with that he exited the room.

She felt as if she had been splattered in the face with a ball of snow. Okay. So Mr. Elegant Clothes wasn't a fan, after all.

She hoped he wasn't one of the resort's board of directors or some influential person. How she hated feeling like she let Serena and Adrian down.

She spent the next hour trying to get her head back into the space where she could write about her paintings and the inspiration behind them, but it was like trying to write with maple syrup. Nothing was settling, nothing held substance. Hopelessness weighed on her. She pushed away the computer and propped her head in her hands, only lifting it when the door opened again.

"Hey, girl!" Anna and Jackie's sunny expressions drew an answering smile. "Wow, look at this!"

Toni had shown them her pictures but this was the first time they had been to this space and seen quite so many paintings in one setting. "Thanks so much for coming."

"It's amazing," Anna said, slowly taking it all in. "Wow. And this is where you'll do your art classes?"

"If anyone decides to come."

"Don't talk like that," Jackie gently admonished. "They'll come."

"Mmm. You two make the second lot of non-resort staff visitors today—"

"Is that all?" Anna interrupted, her face wearing a mix of surprise and what might be offense on Toni's behalf.

"I know it's early days, but I would've thought there would be more," Toni confessed. "I've started to have some doubts."

"That's probably very natural and understandable, but like you say, it's early days yet," Jackie encouraged. "And what did Serena call this? A soft launch? You haven't done any real advertising yet, have you?"

Toni shook her head. "We're still getting that information together, and I have scheduled my social media posts so hopefully we'll start to get some traction."

Jackie rubbed her arm. "Hey, it's probably a good thing you've been a little quiet as it gives you time to get your head around so many things."

True.

"Oh, and is this where you'll have Ethan?" Anna called from the other corner. "Oh, look, it's the tiny giraffe I got him for Christmas." She held a midget-sized blue toy aloft.

"He likes that one, so I thought it might be nice for him to have a favorite here."

"Smart cookie."

Her friends oohed and ahhed over her pictures, discussing which ones were their favorites, filling her heart tank with encouragement and good vibes until Anna said she'd need to leave, due to a training evening happening at her workplace.

"But I'm so proud of you." Anna squeezed Toni.

"Me too. It's awesome to see what God can do, isn't it?" Jackie said with a smile, before they departed with blown kisses and smiles.

The light outside was fading when Joel appeared at the gallery door, pushing Ethan in a stroller.

Toni's heart brightened, and she rushed to release her son from the straps securing him, pressing kisses to his forehead. "Hello, baby."

His gummy mouth widened into a smile and she opened her eyes and mouth wide to draw the giggle that enchanted her. She might never be proud of the way her son had come to be, but she delighted in his existence all the same. Ethan was like balm to her blistering soul, a soothing presence, even when it sometimes all felt too hard.

Joel laughed. "That never gets old."

"What?" she asked, eyes firmly fixed on Ethan's dark ones.

"Watching you make puffer fish faces. Maybe you should think about using one of those as your artist profile picture."

"You're funny."

He grinned and glanced around. "It looks awesome, sis."

"It still feels a little surreal."

"How do you think you'll go when this is your new normal?"

"I don't know. It really depends on what the day is like. To be honest, today has felt a little underwhelming."

"Because?"

"There weren't nearly as many visitors as I think Adrian and Serena expected, and I hate feeling like I might be disappointing them. Especially when they've given me this amazing opportunity. I don't want to let them down."

"You can't possibly think you're letting Serena down," he scoffed. "She is so proud of you and I think part of that pride is the fact that you've actually worked your butt off to make this happen. I bet there are some people who are presented opportunities who just let them slide past because it just feels too hard. But you're not like that." He gave her a hug. "I'm so proud of you."

She reveled in his affection, but knew he expected her to say the inevitable. "Get off me, you big doofus."

He chuckled, and squeezed harder. "I can't. I love you too much."

She laughed, and pushed him away. Only to see an elderly woman at the door, whose eyes widened before she went away.

"Oops." Joel winced, releasing her. "I hope I didn't scare a customer away."

"You can't help what others think," she said.

"True." He fished out a set of car keys. "Ethan has been fed and changed, he woke up from his sleep around three, so he'll probably be due for another one soon. But I'm heading over to Serena's for dinner so I'll need to grab the keys for my truck."

She nodded and moved to her bag. They'd swapped vehicles today, Toni driving Joel's F-150 while he drove her sedan with the baby seat. She fished out his keys and gave them to him. "Thanks so much for looking after him today."

"Hey, I love the little guy, and he was helping me with figuring out which flavor cake we should serve at the wedding."

"You fed him cake?"

"Only a crumb," he protested. "Well, okay, not even that. Ethan just pointed to the chocolate and said, 'That one.'"

"Did he now?"

"I know. I probably should've told you this first, huh? But hey, I was so surprised that he would choose the exact same flavor cake that I wanted that I didn't think to tell you that his first words were about chocolate cake and not Mama."

"And Serena's preferred cake flavor?"

"Will have to be chocolate too, obviously." He pressed a kiss to her cheek. "Hey, have you heard from Matt?"

Wow. What happened to a segue? "No. Why?"

He shrugged. "I've sent him a couple of messages and tried to call him, but there was no answer."

"Is he on another of his trips?"

"I think that's later this week." His brow furrowed. "Hey, if you think of it, pray for him. Something feels a little off."

"Sure." Her heart tensed. Something was off with Matt? He was the epitome of even keel, the kind of calm person she knew she could never be. Just one more reason why she and him would never work. There was no way he could ever cope with all her drama. But she shot up a prayer for Matt anyway.

~

MATT GLANCED AT THE PHONE. The screen read Joel. He let it ring out but made no effort to pick up. He didn't care. Even if he could care, he lacked the energy. Here he was, the first Monday in a long time when he hadn't gone to the office. He hadn't even bothered to call in sick. He had no energy to care about anything.

He hadn't gone to church yesterday. He hadn't answered when Joel had called the first five times. He hadn't even picked up when his parents called from their cruise. Maybe it was teenager-like behavior, but everything felt too hard and it was all he could do to keep on breathing, and occasionally shuffle his way to the toilet or the fridge.

His brain felt heavy, overwhelmed, like under twenty tons of snow, any thought beyond the immediate was too much. Tiredness weighted every limb so that even holding a phone was an effort. He'd barely moved from the sofa since exiting the office on Saturday. He'd thought it made a bold statement, having Ray yell after him, complaining he couldn't access Matt's files because he didn't have the codes. Hey, he could go ask Lee, his friend the CEO, for them. Why should Matt go out of his way to help someone who clearly wanted his role? Christians were supposed to turn the other cheek, but it didn't mean they had to lie down and be trampled over. And Matt sure as heck wasn't gonna invite Ray to wipe his feet on him in his scramble to climb the corporate ladder.

All the way home from the office Matt had contemplated what to do, fury at the man's arrogance fueling a need to do something, to do whatever he could to stop this from happening again. Words and phrases kept popping up, begging to be said. Why couldn't he finally say them? Why did he have to stay quiet? So as soon as Matt had got home he'd poured himself a drink, then written an email to HR outlining what had occurred. He then also copied in the CEO. Then blind carbon-copied everyone else in the company for good measure.

The email didn't just detail the incidents of that morning's stoush, but was a glorious email detailing the specifics concerning every bullying-like encounter in the past three years. Once Matt had started remembering the roll call of events, he'd been amazed at just how many problematic and unprofessional moments there had been. And been equally astounded at his complicity in allowing things to continue.

Had he really been so weak as to allow Ray to ride roughshod over him? The swearing, the undermining, the way Ray had spoken about other colleagues, the times Matt had seen colleagues in tears because of what Ray had said. Maybe it had been cathartic—he'd felt a vindictive sense of justice in exposing the man's sins—but it had felt *good* to finally have a clean slate. For one glorious minute, anyway. Until that moment when Matt had wondered whether he could accuse another of unprofessionalism when what he was doing checked every box in that regard. And then been astounded at his personal stupidity in sending it to everyone.

But he had. And all at once the shame of who he had allowed himself to become had been compounded with immense fear about what the consequences would be. It was Matt's word against Ray. And with Ray being friends with the CEO, well, it wouldn't come out well for Matt. He might like to believe the system dealt justly, but time and experience had shown this didn't occur nearly as often as it should.

Guilt had swamped him, leading him to question whether he should try and delete the email somehow, call in the cyber ops squad like in a Lincoln Cash action movie, or whether he should let the chips fall where they would and simply start looking for another job. Below this his stomach still churned with the injustice of it all. Why should Matt, the truth speaker, be forced to wear the consequences for another man's crimes?

He'd been half-surprised, and yet fully thankful that there hadn't been a response yet, but he put that down to it being the weekend. He'd checked yesterday, and earlier today, but still nothing. Maybe that was just as well, because he sure didn't have the energy to try and conduct a meeting face-to-face. And recognizing that his twitchy finger was all too ready to check his emails wasn't allowing him to get a mental break, he'd switched his email off and put the phone on silent, knowing he'd struggle with what to say, knowing that he didn't have the energy for anything.

His eyeballs felt like they wanted to bleed. His head felt stuffed up like he had a cold. His future, his bright and shiny future, seemed to have splintered into a million pieces, like a shattered mirror. And just like a broken mirror, he no longer recognized himself in the man he had become. He was used to working, to having energy for days, but now he felt like a shadow, unable to hold substance or anything of worth.

His phone flashed with another message. *Hey, dude. You okay or just off traveling? I've tried to reach you. Call me.* Joel.

He closed his eyes, his body tense as he waited for the reminder message guaranteed to arrive a minute later. Sorry, Joel. No can do. The only thing he wanted to do was to protect himself by hiding away here and sleeping for a thousand years.

Sure enough a few moments later his phone vibrated with the reminder message.

Nope. Still can't.

His phone beeped again, and maybe it was because he'd trained his eyes and ears over many years to pick up he glanced at the screen.

His heart pricked. Toni.

Hi. Just wanted to check if you are okay. I had my gallery opening today and thought you might like to see some pictures.

An image followed. Toni smiling at the camera, her artworks on display behind her, looking beautiful, looking professional, looking unattainable as ever.

His heart clenched, his eyes blurred, and he dropped the phone and squeezed his eyes shut. *I'm not okay,* he longed to say. *I need help. I need...*

You.

CHAPTER 5

"*H*ey, baby boy," Toni said, picking Ethan up from the cot. "Did you have a good afternoon?"

"He was very placid," Vera Walters said, smiling at them. The resort's daycare manager was a woman in her late forties with a maternal smile and who personified patience. "I think you could leave him with us for longer tomorrow, if you wish."

"Thank you. I'll have to see how we go. But it was certainly good to know we had the option today when he was a little unsettled."

"That age is a funny one, isn't it? They like their routine, and heaven help us if things aren't what they are used to."

"So true."

Toni had thought to see how Ethan would cope with spending time in the gallery today while she started doing some work on her painting. Her second morning of the open gallery had seen Ethan settled enough, but after lunch he'd been difficult to get to sleep again. She'd been almost at her wits' end when she remembered the daycare option for resort employees. A quick phone call later and she'd booked him in for the afternoon. It meant she'd actually managed to prime her canvas, ready for painting tomorrow as part of her artist-in-residence role, and felt a mix of relief at finally getting some work done mingled with guilt that she was relying on someone else to care for her son. Did all working mothers feel this way?

She collected Ethan's bag and made her way out to the hall, almost bumping into an elderly woman who looked a little familiar.

The woman's expression cleared. "You're the art gallery girl."

"Hello. Yes, I run the art gallery. I'm Toni Wakefield."

"I saw you yesterday, didn't I?"

Ah, that's right. The wide-eyed woman while Joel and she had been bonding in a brother-sister hug. "I believe so, yes."

"Is this your little boy?" she asked, smiling at Ethan.

"Yes, this is Ethan."

"He's very sweet." She touched his tiny sneakers. "You and your husband must be so proud."

"My husband?"

A faint frown crossed her features. "The man I saw you hugging yesterday."

Ah. Her heart tensed. Watch the judgement begin. "That was my brother. I'm not married."

"Oh." She pulled back, her thin lips flattening. "I see."

Yep, and so did Toni. Guess she wouldn't be seeing that woman in the gallery any time soon.

She pressed a kiss to Ethan's head as the woman walked away, her posture stiff. Okay, so maybe it was hypocritically judgy to judge someone for judging her, but really, in this day and age? Not that she was an advocate for single motherhood over a husband and wife welcoming a child together; of course she'd prefer to have done things differently. But it didn't help to feel a sense of worthlessness rippling underneath her skin about how somebody looked at her and made her feel ashamed.

Jackie and Serena might preach that Toni's shame had been dealt with by Jesus on the cross, and while she knew that was true, it was another thing to live it day by day. To have people look at her, look at Ethan, and make assumptions she could never fully explain. How could she, when she'd never even fully explained to her nearest and dearest exactly what had occurred? Joel might think he knew, but he only knew what Toni had chosen to tell him. An edited version of the whole.

For a moment, her thoughts flipped to *that man* once more, before flinging that door closed. No. He was part of the past and she didn't need to think about him impacting her future. He was nothing to her now, if indeed he ever had been.

She said her farewells to Chrissy and the reception staff, her heart jumping a little as she saw her painting above their heads. How amazing that a picture she'd once stored in a closet looked right at home there, the feeling as startling as one of Salvador Dali's melted clocks. She glimpsed one of the new brochures freshly branded with the same image of her maple tree. Surreal.

"Here you go." A doorman opened the front door for her, and she realized that as an employee she was probably supposed to take a different exit. Oh well, it was too late now. She pushed Ethan's stroller across that icy path to where her car sat amongst fresh fallen snow. Ugh. It was so cold.

In the parking lot, she saw Serena who hurried over and helped by holding Ethan as Toni unlocked the car. "Thanks."

"How did you go today?" Serena asked as Toni strapped him into his car seat.

Truth time. "It was much the same as yesterday." Barely any visitors. Not a single painting sold.

"I'm not surprised things have been a little slow lately. Winter can be our slowest time of year once Christmas is done." Serena's breath puffed white in the cold air. "But tomorrow is another day, right?"

"Right."

They exchanged hugs and farewells and Toni got in the car, lifting a gloved hand to Serena who was now in hers too. A minute later, she was passing the stone entryway and commencing the long drive to where the resort driveway met the main road. Her mind flipped to what would happen tonight. Joel had a meeting with his youth boys, and Toni would normally attend a Bible study with Jackie, Anna, and the girls. But she had already made her excuses about tonight, with the unknowns about what exactly what work would be like this week. And now, being so tired, she was glad that all she had to do tonight was to hop into her pajamas and eat some dinner and go to sleep. She hoped that Ethan would think this was a good idea too.

She drove into Muskoka Shores, slowing on the icy streets to admire the buildings along Main Street that were still lit up in Christmas cheer and twinkling lights in the evening darkness. The Coffee Blend stood next to Brandi's Books and Gifts, across the light-strewn road from places like The Nuthouse, Ice Creamery, and the vintage toy store, the last three all closed in winter until tourist season picked up again.

She could appreciate the fact that Muskoka Shores wasn't the place inundated with tourists in winter. Summer was when the lakes and festivals proved far more conducive to people wanting to stay rather than the time of year where snowfalls were biggest and the temperature hovered in the minuses. She turned into Poplar and soon pulled into the drive. Joel's truck was here, so he hadn't left for the boys' group yet.

Two minutes later she was clutching Ethan to her chest as she stomped snow off her Doc Martens and entered the front door.

"You're back." Joel wore a dish-cloth over his shoulder as a delectable smell drifted down the hall.

"Whatever it is you are cooking, I want some now."

"Ha. I'd like to claim the credit for the awesomeness that's in the crockpot, but I'm afraid you're gonna have to blame Angela MacPherson for that. Someone gave John a haunch of venison which she turned into this stew, so that's what we have for dinner tonight."

"Sorry, Bambi, but not sorry." She moved to the dining area and carefully deposited Ethan on a brightly-colored fabric playmat before dropping her various bags in her room and cleaning up. A quick change into comfortable clothes—and the ankle length Uggs Joel had given her for Christmas—and then she was sinking into a dining chair nearest Ethan as Joel asked her about her day.

"It was much the same as yesterday, not many visitors. But Serena says that will likely change when it's tourist season again."

As ever, Joel's face lit up at the mention of Serena's name. "She knows what she's talking about."

"Mmm." She eyed the grapes sitting in the glazed pottery bowl that she bought from an artist friend in Toronto. Sometimes her life in the city seemed so remote from what she did these days. She might have only lived here for six months but it seemed so much longer. But maybe that's what small towns did. They embraced you and made you feel like one of its own. Or maybe that was the effect of being drawn into a group of friends like Serena, Anna, Jackie, and Rachel. She had people she could relax with, people with whom she could be real. She sure hadn't felt like that in the city.

"So, you've got boys' group tonight?" She plucked a grape and ate it.

"Yeah." He sighed, and through the hatch she could see his brow had furrowed.

"What?"

"I've been wondering whether I should cancel."

"Is there another ice storm forecast?"

"Later this week, maybe." His smile was wry. "I know enough now to be checking the weather, don't you worry."

Because last year he hadn't, and he'd taken Serena out for

her birthday on the very day that Muskoka had experienced its first major snowstorm of the season. They'd been out all night after Joel had proved to not have the snow driving skills he'd apparently thought he had. But she got the feeling that neither he nor Serena had minded too much, even though it had caused her a night of worry and some comment when neither of them had shown up at church the next day.

"So, if it's not snow, then what's got you worried? Oh, I know. It's the cake. Serena is still eating healthy and doesn't want chocolate to lead her back into a life of sin."

His mouth curved but his eyes remained serious as he shook his head. "It's Matt."

"He still hasn't called you yet?"

"It's weird. I know he gets busy, but it's never been like this before."

"Are you sure he isn't just out of contact on one of his trips?"

"He never goes off the grid like this. I've known him for years now and I have never known him to be uncontactable. He's always got that phone switched on, always answers his emails. I've teased him that his phone is like his third hand and he'd die if he wasn't connected to it. I think he's so addicted to his job and the adrenaline rush of it that he'd not know what to do with himself if he lost his phone. And that's why I'm worried."

Her chest tensed. She exhaled, and told herself to not worry. "So is there anyone else you can call? What about his parents?"

"They're on an around-the-world cruise. They really are uncontactable."

"Does he have any other family?"

"His brother is in B.C., and there's no other family nearby."

"Well, what about his work? We both know he's addicted to his work. Can you call them and find out? Maybe he's been sick."

"I could." He chewed his lip.

"What about Wade? Or someone from his church? Surely there's someone in the city who could visit him and find out."

His expression cleared. "Wade. Yeah, I don't know why I didn't think of him."

"So go call him now and I'll serve up this food."

"Thanks."

She pushed to her slippered feet and made her way to the kitchen as Joel moved to the study to place the call. Joel had boiled potatoes, and she mashed these with butter and milk, then moved to the study. "Is it just us two? No Serena?"

He paused his conversation. "She's busy, so yeah just us two."

A minute later, two helpings of potatoes topped with hearty stew—one twice the size of the other, as Joel ate enough for two teenage boys—waited on the table. Joel returned as she poured two glasses of water.

"Wade's going to check on him."

"Check on him?" She paused, holding the glass bottle of water. "Do you mean to make it sound like a welfare check or something?"

His lips compressed and her heart constricted.

"Joel, come on. This is Matt. He'd never do anything stupid like hurt himself."

"Look, I'm not saying he'd do something like that. But he could be sick, or be lying in his apartment injured, and we'd never know. You've heard the stories of people who live alone who…" He swallowed.

Her mouth swung open, as fear squeezed her throat. "You don't think he's dead, do you?"

"No. Of course not. It's just…"

"Just what?"

"It's just so out of character for him, that's all. But hey, Wade will visit, all will be well. In Jesus' name." He eyed the food. "Hey, this looks great. We'd better eat before it gets cold."

He said grace, adding a prayer for Matt, then tucked in.

Her mind spun with awful possibilities, fear chasing concerns. No. Matt was a good guy. Their friend. Her friend. He couldn't be sick. He couldn't be...

She refused to even *think* that word. "How do you even know if he's there? For all you know he might've had a car accident like you did with Serena." She shivered. That had been a scary time. The storm, being home alone with Ethan as the house rocked under an Arctic attack. Wondering where her older brother was. Wondering if he was okay. Wondering if she should call the police or if he and Serena had stayed at the resort or made it to her house and were spending the night together. Stupid her. Her brother was as honorable as Serena was innocent. Neither of them had ever done anything like she once had.

"Hey, don't look like that. He's gonna be okay."

"You don't know that," she said. "And why is it okay for you to worry but not for me?"

He eyed her seriously, and she could almost hear his thoughts: *Because he's my best friend, not yours. Unless there's something you're not telling me.*

Which there wasn't. Because— "Matt is my friend too. And I'm allowed to be concerned without it meaning more, okay?"

He dipped his chin. But maybe her protesting had been a little too much, for she didn't trust that look he was giving her. It was a bit like a few months ago when Matt had visited for the cranberry festival and the four of them had gone out to a nearby farm. She'd enjoyed the first child-free day since Ethan was born, but maybe Joel had misunderstood and thought her pleasure was because Matt was there, rather than something less admissible. Who wanted to be the mom who admitted to being glad to be baby-free for a time? You might as well score an X in her forehead and vote her off the island.

"So, you don't think he's crashed his car?" she asked, as much to interrupt the spiraling negative thoughts as it was to refocus Joel on the most important thing.

"I don't think he was going anywhere. He said he had a huge weekend of work before his trip to London so I wouldn't have thought he'd be taking trips anywhere. And anyway, if he had an accident, you'd think there'd be news about it."

"I suppose Wade could always check, or get the building supervisors to check if his car is still there."

"Good idea." He drew out his phone and texted Wade then placed it back on the table.

She swallowed another mouthful of food but barely tasted it, only registering that it was hot. "Would he have gone to London early?"

"Maybe. But he usually sends me a message to say bye. And it's still out of character for him to not return any of my messages or calls."

Ethan whimpered, and she moved to cuddle him, like the living security blanket his cuddles always provided. His hand reached for her food, and she snatched his fingers away, kissing them, then swooping him up and gently placing him in the high chair he'd begun using a week ago. She strapped him in, then went to the kitchen for the container of pureed baby food that she'd made on Sunday. A swoop of the airplane-shaped spoon and his tongue pushed most of it out onto the plastic-backed bib with the handy scoop at the bottom to catch the mess. Sometimes she felt she could do with something similar.

Joel pushed his head into his hand and ate his food, his brow still wearing a crease.

She paused her feeding attempts. "Does Wade have a key?"

"A key for what?"

"Matt's apartment. In case Matt's inside and can't get to the door."

Joel scrubbed a hand over his eyes. "I don't know. Maybe. But I think I'm the only one with the spare key."

"So, do you need to go and see him?" Panic cramped her heart. "Joel? Do you need to cancel the boys' group tonight and go check on Matt instead?"

"Maybe." He exhaled heavily. "I don't know."

"You've got me really worried now."

"Matt's a big boy." But even Joel sounded uncertain.

"What are you going to do?" She encouraged Ethan to swallow another mouthful of food.

He glanced at her, glanced at his food, then closed his eyes. She could almost see him praying as his jaw clenched, then released, and his Adam's apple dipped as he swallowed. He exhaled, and met her gaze again. "Looks like I'm going to Toronto."

A THUD CAME at the door. One voice, two. His phone vibrated then instantly switched to black. Not surprising. He hadn't charged it since Saturday.

He pulled a cushion Mom had given him one year over his ears. Whoever it was, whatever they wanted, they could go away. He didn't care.

A louder voice, like whoever it was couldn't hear his thoughts and insisted on staying. Too bad. Let them shout and yell and carry on. He wasn't opening the door. He'd opened it for food delivery two days ago, the remains of which now littered the coffee table. He'd barely eaten any of it anyway, but he wasn't hungry. Sure, he felt a little woozy, and sometimes his stomach felt sore, but he barely cared what he ate or what he did anymore. Everything, everyone, felt too hard.

A different sound came now. A jangling, a scratching, then the noises, the voices, became louder.

"Matt? Matt, dude, are you in here? Where are the—oh, here."

Light flooded the room, and he closed his eyes.

"Dude!" Panic edged a voice he vaguely recognized, but whose it was he barely knew.

Hands on his arm, shaking him. "Matt? Wake up!"

Stop, he wanted to groan, but words seemed to have stuck to his tongue.

"Is he dead?" Another voice. Another man. "Do I need to call 911?"

"No, not yet."

Not yet? Not at all, thanks. He wasn't sick. He didn't need a hospital. He just needed out of here.

The first voice said something, then the sounds of breathing came louder. "Matt, it's Joel. We've been worried about you. Do you need to see a doctor or are you able to roll over and look at me?"

Rolling over was too hard, but he could pry open an eye at least.

His friend's form wavered in and out. Joel didn't wear his usual grin. "What happened, man? Have you been attacked?"

At work, maybe. If he even still had his job. What kind of idiot wrote stupid name-and-blame emails and fired them off to HR? And the CEO. *And* everyone else. He shuddered. "I'm fine," he mumbled.

"You sure don't look fine." Joel glanced at the coffee table, wrinkling his nose. "How long has this been sitting here for?" He sniffed a white Chinese takeout container. "Gross."

Matt watched as Joel—oh, and Wade was here, too—cleared the coffee table of takeout detritus and sat on it.

"What do you want to do? Have a shower?"

"You need it, man. You stink," Wade said.

"Wade is going to make you a coffee, then you're going to tell us what's happened." Joel frowned. "Are you positive nobody has hurt you?"

"Toni."

"Toni? Who's Toni? Do you need us to call the police?"

"Your sister."

"My sister hurt you?" Joel's eyes rounded. "Oh." He shot Wade a look, but Wade had moved to the kitchen. "We'll talk about that later. Right now, you need to sit up, and we're going to get you clean. Now, do you need me to help, or are you gonna be fine on your own?"

"I'm fine." He pushed up, the room spun for a moment then it cleared. His lip curled. Look at him now, successful investment manager.

"Come on."

With Joel's help, Matt managed to stumble to the bathroom, where Joel turned on the shower and threatened to come in if Matt hadn't showered in the next five minutes. Joel closed the door, and Matt slowly stripped before opening the shower door from which steam was already escaping.

The hot water revived him, seeming to simultaneously soak alertness into his limbs while also drumming his brain awake. He felt a little teetery, his movements lethargic still, but the knowledge Joel was coming in soon regardless of whether he was dressed or not made him focus on what needed to be done. Clean his hair. Clean himself. Done.

He'd just wrapped a towel around his middle when the door opened again.

"Good. Now brush your teeth, then go get dressed. I found some clothes. They're on your bed."

"Who made you the boss?" he grumbled.

"You did, when you scared us all by not answering our calls." Joel shook his head. "I can't believe you didn't even bother answering Toni."

Toni. His heart clenched. Just another failure in his long line of mistakes.

"She cares about you, man."

84

Matt shook his head. "No, she doesn't." He briefly admitted his spectacular New Year's Eve fail.

Joel's lips compressed. Then he exhaled. "Just because she shot you down once doesn't mean she doesn't care. She's worried about you. Now go." Joel's shove didn't feel too friendly. "Get dressed, then you've got some explaining to do."

Ten minutes later he was slumped at the dining table, hands cupped around a mug of black coffee as he faced the irate gazes of Joel and Wade. He'd shared some of what had happened, but the full extent of Ray's misdemeanors he couldn't admit to. Who wanted to own up to cowardice?

"So you mean to say you told HR and the CEO all that happened, and 'accidentally' copied everyone else into your email, and since then you've been hiding out here?"

He hung his head, avoiding Joel's gaze as he eyed the blackness filling his cup. Joel had given him the cup a few years ago, the joke 'I might look like I'm listening to you but inside I'm doing maths' one Matt had appreciated at the time. His brain had always been filled with numbers and plans, even if he could barely think now.

"Matt?" Joel prompted.

What was the question? Oh. Despair clutched at him again. "I don't know what to do. I'm exhausted, I'm so frustrated, I think if I was to go there and see Ray's smug face I might physically hurt him."

"So, have you applied for sick leave?"

"No."

"You've just not shown up?" Wade asked, sounding almost impressed.

"I didn't know what to do," he repeated. "Now Ray is basically doing my job, I have to wonder what they want me there for. But I don't feel like quitting. Quitting just makes it feel like they win."

"Well, if you don't show up and don't provide any explanation then they will be in their rights to fire you, I imagine." Wade said. He should know, being a HR manager himself.

"So what can I do?"

Joel's hands steepled. "Do you know any out-of-hours doctors? Is there anyone in the building who knows you and works as a doctor?"

A faint bell rang. Someone, somewhere... "Three doors down. Ramesh. Nice guy."

"Is he Indian? I think I met him before." Joel nodded. "If we can get him to sign a medical certificate that you've been sick then that might work out."

"Then what?" Matt closed his eyes as the others conferred in low voices again. All this thinking and talking after days on his own was exhausting.

"Then you're going to claim some days off as sick leave," Wade stated. "Knowing your hours, you'd have a stack of that waiting, wouldn't you?"

His chin jerked.

"And then," Joel said, "I'm going to take you back with me to Muskoka."

CHAPTER 6

"Good morning, Toni," Adrian said as she entered the staff common area the next day. "You're here early."

She nodded. "I've just put Ethan into the daycare for the day," because she didn't think she'd manage to deal with him while her emotions felt so frayed, "and get that all-important first hot chocolate of the day."

He studied her. "My wife tells me I'm never to say this, but you look like you're a little tired. Has Ethan started teething?"

She grimaced. "He's been drooling and more irritable lately, but there's no sign of teeth yet."

A look of sympathy crossed his face. "Ah, I remember those days. So, you're keeping up with things here? I know working here is a big change, but you're keeping well?"

"Yes. I just had a late night, that's all."

"Right, well, have a good day then."

She nodded and clutched the cup of hot chocolate closer as he moved on, stopping to talk to some other employees. Serena had said he treated people like this was a family. It wasn't any surprise he'd asked whether she was well. She knew she didn't look her best. A night worrying would do that to a girl. She'd been so thankful to get Joel's text late last night, then one again this morning. Matt wasn't well, Joel had said that he'd do better with some time out away from the city.

He can stay with us, she'd replied.

Thanks. I knew you'd agree.

That last comment of Joel's had made her wonder whether Joel had already asked and just assumed Toni would be okay with that. But it didn't matter. Not really. What mattered most was that Matt would be in a safe place with people who cared about him and he'd have the chance to get better.

Still, the knowledge of that had added a new churn to her day. Tension rode through her bloodstream, and had made her a trifle snappy and short-tempered with other drivers on the road to work today. *Lord, be with Matt, help him, heal him.* She didn't know what else to pray, not knowing any details, but this prayer at least seemed safe.

She finished her hot chocolate, glanced out the window and sighed. The snow seemed to have increased, and outside was so cold she'd been tempted to cancel and just stay home, snuggled up in bed with Ethan. But a girl couldn't very well not show up for work on her third day of the gallery's official opening. She supposed this was some of that discipline that Joel had said she would struggle with at times. It certainly wasn't the artistic free-for-all where she commanded her own hours and could follow the creative muse wherever it may lead. Those days had certainly fled with Ethan's arrival. But she'd determined to stay focused today, to spend less time worrying about whether the gallery was getting any visitors, and instead channel that concern into creating her art. At least then she'd have done something productive with her day.

She unlocked the gallery's doors, switched on lights, and stowed her bag. Her phone would stay close by today. She knew she'd be checking it frequently for messages to find out how Joel and Matt were getting on.

As the day stretched on with no word from Toronto she was sorely tempted to call Joel and find out where things were up to. But she refrained. She didn't want to distract or act like the needy girlfriend that she wasn't. She cared about Matt, as a friend. Anything more was out of the question, obviously. But something inside still itched to know how he was doing.

She moved to the studio space and prepared her materials, setting out the acrylics and brushes and water. A wrap of her apron over her good trousers and white shirt and she was ready. She flicked her phone to a music playlist of calming nature-inspired music—she figured it might be nice for any visitors to at least imagine outside was not always a frozen icicle-inducing place—and lifted her brush.

Soon she was lost in the place of creativity, stroke upon stroke adding color and vibrancy. She barely needed the photograph for inspiration, this picture of a tree was so clearly ingrained in her imagination she could probably paint it in her sleep. The canvas held the usual thirds of sky, ground and water, and there'd be room for reflections in the lake that constituted the picture's lowest third. She added some green, some yellow, giving the tree depth, then added a golden wash that gave her pictures their usual vibrancy. She smiled, took a step back, then realized from the gnawing in her stomach that she'd missed lunch.

She hastily ate today's sandwich while checking her phone. A message from Vera saying Ethan was having a good day. A message from Jackie with an encouraging verse. No message from Joel. She was super tempted to call him but hesitated. He was probably still busy. And he'd promised to let her know where things were up to.

Lord, be with Matt. Help him, heal him.

The door opened, and Serena walked in, and Toni's heart lifted. It was funny how some people instantly brought a sense of gladness, while seeing others made a person want to run for the hills. Serena was always the former. "Hey you."

"Hey yourself," Serena said, drawing closer to the canvas. "Ooh, looks like somebody has been hard at work."

Toni gave an exaggerated sigh. "Somebody has to be."

Serena laughed, and the air seemed to hold more joy. "Just so you know, I've spent the morning trying to figure out the rooming arrangements for three oil companies that hate each other when they're here together for a conference in March."

"Fun times." Toni threw the scraps of her lunch into the trash.

"You know it." Serena's smile held hopefulness. "So, um, any visitors today?"

"You're the first."

Serena winced, then seemed to quickly catch herself. "Well, I don't think God would've opened up this opportunity if He wanted it to fail. We'll keep going, and I know we'll see fruit one day soon. Oh, and I had to tell you that I have lined up a radio interview for you on Monday, and there's a city paper who is going to do a feature on the gallery next Tuesday."

"Can't wait," Toni deadpanned.

Serena's laughter rippled again. "I knew you'd be excited. But you might want to curb some of your enthusiasm. We do want people to want to come, and sarcasm might not be the best way to make people feel welcome."

"Can't wait!" Toni repeated, this time in peppy cheerleader tones.

"That's the spirit." Serena's teeth gleamed. "Hey, have you heard anything from Joel? He called me last night to say Matt was having a bit of a hard time and he'd be staying in the city for the night."

Her heart pinged. Huh. So the fiancée got a phone call and the sister got a text. Well, that was the changing of the guard, she supposed. And was how it *should* be, she told herself.

"Um, no. He only texted this morning to say Matt might stay with us."

Serena nodded, then glanced away. "Um, I don't know if Joel has spoken to you at all about what could happen with living arrangements once we're married, but," her gaze returned to Toni, "I thought I'd mention that you could live in my house, if that's of any interest."

"With you?" Toni teased.

"Well, no." Serena's cheeks took on a pink hue. "Joel had mentioned once we're married I could move in with you. But I know that could get tricky."

Especially since Joel didn't have the master bedroom. When they'd first moved to Muskoka he'd given the master to Toni because of all the baby paraphernalia, even though Ethan now had his own room. Ah, the awkwardness of conversations between brother and sister. No wonder he hadn't mentioned this to Toni.

"And please know I don't want to overstep my role, especially as there's so much else going on right now." Serena's cheeks were now very pink. "But I thought I'd mention it now, especially if Matt is staying there, if there's any problem at all, then you can know you're very welcome to come and stay with me."

"You'd really want me and Ethan to come and stay with you?"

"If it helps at all in the next few weeks, then yes."

Toni frowned. "Has Joel said that Matt is likely to cause a problem?"

"No. But if the man is struggling with unrequited love, then he might find it difficult being in the same house with her."

Toni coughed. "Excuse me? He does *not* think of me that way."

"Doesn't he? Oh. I must've mistaken those looks I saw last year, and again at New Year's Eve."

"I'm sure you did," Toni said firmly. "I've got zero interest in him, or in any man. The only man I have time for is Ethan. And he's hard enough work as it is. I think he's teething."

Serena winced. "Is that why he's been a little unsettled lately?"

"You've noticed? And you still want us to move in?"

"You know I love you. And Ethan."

Toni nodded. She did.

"The offer is there, teething and all," Serena said. "It wouldn't be hard to fix up the spare room at my house. But hey, everything might be fine."

"Okay, then I'll see how things go. I'll talk it over with Joel, too."

"Oh, and my friend in the city bridal boutique has time on Saturday in two weeks. Will that work for you to go dress shopping?"

Three weeks out from the wedding? For an organized person, Serena seemed to be leaving things a little late. "Does that leave enough time?"

"I know it seems a little last minute, but I've already teed up with her which type of gown I want, and sent her my measurements, and she's put aside some contenders for me. And I hoped you and Anna would be happy to pick whichever style and color of dress you think you'd like." She shrugged. "After years of seeing brides go crazy over every little detail, I'm determined to keep the main focus on the main thing. And it really shouldn't matter what I or anyone else is wearing. Not when the most important thing is that I'm marrying the man of my dreams."

Okay, so it was a little hard sometimes to see how anyone could regard her brother as a man of anyone's dreams, but then there was no accounting for love, was there? Witness the supposed attraction of Matt to Toni, something she still wasn't completely sure was genuine, even if he had made that awkward comment at New Year's. Hmm. If there was a repeat of that, then maybe moving to Serena's wasn't such a bad idea.

Serena glanced at her watch. "Okay, I'd better run. My lunch break is almost over."

"You could've phoned me with this," Toni said.

"And miss the latest Toni creation? No way. Anyway, I figure it's a great opportunity to get my steps in for the day, especially as I need to stay in shape for a certain wedding dress very soon."

"Something that taste-testing wedding cake is helping with, I'm sure."

Serena sighed. "I know Joel has a sweet tooth, and it was fun to see him choose the cake, but not so fun to have to sample every single flavor."

"Chocolate was still the winner, or so I heard. So original."

Serena's lips quirked. "No comment."

"And that comment says it all, really."

"Ha. Okay, now I really need to fly. Oh, and if you hear anything, please let me know."

"Will do."

Serena disappeared, leaving Toni to her quiet space, her painting, and her thoughts. If she was a more insecure person and didn't know that Serena had a good heart, she could almost regard Serena's offer for Toni to stay with her as a way to get Toni out of her hair. But because she did know that Serena cared for her she wouldn't regard it as an invitation to leave. More like some of that big sister-like concern that Toni had always appreciated. Having a brother like Joel was a real blessing, and him marrying Serena was gold. And even though nothing could truly compensate for the loss of her parents, Joel's marriage to Serena almost felt like Toni's family was being restored.

She returned her attention to the canvas, slowly working her way through the different branches, crafting, and creating the tree to approximate that which she saw in her mind's eye.

She was bent over her canvas when her phone buzzed. At last. Anticipation filled her as she glanced at the name on the screen. Oh. Angela McPherson. *Congratulations on your exhibition. Are things going well?*

Aw, that was nice of the pastor's wife to ask after her. She tapped out a reply, and tried to ignore the rising impatience to know what was happening in T.O. by refocusing on the painting. A careful brushstroke here, another feathering there.

The door opened, and Toni blinked. The elderly man from two days ago. She straightened. "Um, hi." Gosh, could she sound anything more like a teenager?

"Hello."

Should she ask if he wanted help with anything? She wrinkled her nose at herself. Honestly, what was she being paid for if not to do exactly that? "Can I help you?"

"So, *you* are the artist."

"Uh, yeah." Ooh, look at her with her sparkling teenage-speak. She wiped her hands on a towel and removed her apron. "My name is Antonia Wakefield," this elegant man seemed like he'd respond better to a refined-sounding Antonia than a mere Toni, "and these are my works."

He nodded, glancing around, eyes falling on the canvas. "Your current work?"

"I started it today."

"Today? You are a fast worker."

"I find I need to capture the moment while I can. I think creativity can be like..." What was the language this man would understand? "I think it can be like wine, and impossible to regather once it's spilled, so you have to make the most of it while it's flowing."

"And yet some wine goes stale or bitter if stored too long," he observed.

"That's true," she said, warming to her theme. "I find it's a tricky balance. Some wines age well, but others don't, and sometimes you just have to try it and see if it's ready." She didn't really like wine, but was pretty sure she'd once heard Matt say something like that. "Anyway, it's just like creativity. It can be ready, and delicious, but how would you know if you never uncork the bottle? I've learned to follow creative inspiration when it's stirring."

"Hmm." He studied her for a moment. "You might be just the person I need."

"I beg your pardon, sir?"

He glanced back at the paintings. "I don't know what it is, but I have found myself unable to forget the works here. When I saw the painting above the reception desk I immediately had to know who the artist was, and then they sent me here and I saw you and was positive you could not be the person responsible."

Good to see that judging others was no longer a thing.

"And so I left," the man continued, "but I couldn't quite forget. And now I see the numbers of artworks like the one at reception. I was interested in buying it, but apparently the resort is not selling as it belongs to someone else. So I wanted to know if it was possible to commission the same work. It looks like that's what you're doing here."

"It is of a similar series, that's right," she said cautiously. "I'm sorry, sir, but did you say you want to buy it?"

"My wife is an art enthusiast, but of greater enthusiasm than skill I fear. I thought I read somewhere that you were doing art lessons but it doesn't seem to be the case."

"It's the case, all right, but we haven't really been open very long and so this is still rather new," she admitted.

"Oh! Well, I suppose I have two requests then. Firstly, I would like to commission a painting that is very similar to the one above the reception desk. And secondly, I would like to book my wife in for an art lesson or two next week."

"Truly?"

"Truly." He smiled.

Oh, thank You God! She fought to keep her smile from split-ting her face. "I think we can come to an arrangement for both of those matters. May I ask how long your stay with us is for? And are you thinking of art lessons in the immediate or near future?"

The next half hour was spent discussing arrangements for classes and price, and talking about art and such. It turned out the man had visited art museums she'd only dreamed of seeing, in Europe and London and the like. His name was Alistair, and a repeat visitor at the resort, here for his wife's birthday. "We usually stay for two weeks although not normally in January, but sickness delayed us until now. And it turns out that might not be such a bad thing, considering it appears you weren't open until recently."

Huh. Maybe God did know a thing or two about timing, after all.

She organized to meet his wife on Monday at eleven, following the radio interview at ten, and collected his details so she would let him know when the painting was finished and framed.

And as she drove home, after collecting a weary but content Ethan, her heart overflowed with happiness. *Thank You God for this opportunity. Thank You God for Serena. Thank You God for Your mercy and kindness.*

She pulled into the driveway. Joel's truck still wasn't here. She checked her phone. Still no message. "Oh well." Chances were that Joel wouldn't be back tonight anyway.

She collected Ethan and went inside, flicking on the heater to send a fast stream of warmth to the house. She deposited Ethan on his playmat and switched on the kettle. A hot cup of tea felt very necessary, although considering she'd just about made her first sale, maybe she could pull out a soft version of one of Rachel's celebratory drinks.

Five minutes later she held a plate of cheese and an apple

juice mixed with lemonade with a slice of a Granny Smith decorating the glass rim. "Woohoo me!"

Ethan gurgled his approval, and she settled into the comfy chair near him as she grabbed her phone and texted Serena the good news.

Her reply was swift. *Awesome! See? I knew God was doing good things.*

A moment later there came a second one: *And this is only the beginning.*

Hope fluttered around Toni's heart. Maybe this did have a chance of working after all.

She ate her celebratory cheese and drank her mocktail and sent a message to the other girls. Their replies soon peppered notification dings through the quiet house: *Congrats! Well done! Here's to more!*

She was thinking about what to prepare for dinner when she heard the sound of the front door opening. She got up and ran to give her brother a hug as he entered. "Guess what? I sold a painting today, and I'm going to give my first art lesson next week. Isn't that awesome?"

He squeezed her. "That *is* awesome."

"We should celebrate. I wondered about reheating one of those casseroles your old ladies love to give you, then thought we can do better than that, right? Like go out somewhere for dinner, maybe?"

"Sure. But, uh…" Joel tilted his head behind him.

At the man whose wan appearance and obvious fatigue was so opposite to all she remembered that it drew a gasp. "Matt! I forgot."

∼

HIS HEART TWISTED. Way to go to feel like somebody cared.

"Oh, I didn't mean that," Toni said, wide-eyed, her fascinated gaze dipping down him like she couldn't believe her eyes. Which was fair enough. He'd barely recognized himself in the mirror either. His appearance had stunned his neighbors, too. Dan Walton himself had even asked if he was all right when he'd met them today in the apartment lobby.

Thank God for Joel and Wade, who together had gently batted away questions, assuring Dan and his wife that he was fine. Which was a lie, as anyone could tell, but it made Matt feel slightly less hopeless.

Joel had ushered Matt to Wade's car, and they'd visited Ramesh's clinic, securing a note of absence that Wade had then photographed and sent to Matt's work via email. Then Joel had driven to Muskoka while Matt slept most of the way, slipping between numbness and despair about what he'd done and what the future held. Wade had offered some helpful advice, but all of that seemed too large and hard for him to think about. Joel and Ramesh were right, and what Matt wanted more than anything was to rest. To get off the merry-go-round, out of the rat race, and just rest. He didn't want to think, he didn't want to make decisions, everything felt too nebulous and overwhelming. He'd barely been able to pack his clothes.

"Maybe you could get a casserole defrosted," Joel's voice intruded. "And we can have pie and ice-cream for dessert."

"Uh, sure." Toni offered Matt a small smile. "It's, uh, good to see you."

No, it wasn't. He knew his coming here was a mistake. She'd been shocked—had Joel told her Matt was coming too?—and about to celebrate something. "Congratulations."

Her face softened. "Thanks."

She hesitated a moment longer, then spun on her heel and disappeared in the direction of the kitchen. A minute later he could hear a microwave ping as he shuffled behind Joel to the spare room. Joel opened the door and patted the sofa. "Sorry, I should've asked Toni to make up the bed."

"S'okay." Matt slumped into Joel's office chair. He'd seen that look of pity she'd given him, and it made him want to shrivel up and die.

"Give me a moment."

In a normal world Matt would offer to help, but it was like all his strength had gone and it was enough to just sit here and watch as other people did things for him. How had it come to this? How had strong, independent him plunged to such depths that he needed to be treated like a small child? He didn't want to inflict his sorry self on anyone but it seemed he had little option. Joel certainly wasn't taking no as an option.

A few minutes later the space had been transformed from an office with a sofa into a bedroom. Joel muttered something Matt didn't hear and exited. Weariness leaked from his pores. He was too tired to do anything but get into bed. He craved sleep, not conversation.

"Come on," Joel said, returning to the room. "You can sleep in a moment, but first you need to eat."

"Don't want to," he mumbled.

"You need to, which is why you're going to have some of this deliciousness that one of the ladies from church has made. I think it was Rose. She's got this awesome Irish stew, and the vegetables and meat have got to be a heck of a lot better for you than what you were eating before. So, you're going to join us at the dining table, then you're going to have a shower and then you're gonna go to bed. If you go to bed now then your body sleep cycles will be disrupted, and you heard what Ramesh said before, that it's important to keep your body as healthy as you can with what you eat and how you sleep and by getting exercise."

"Don't feel like it." Man. He hated sounding like a whiny kid.

"I know. But that's why you're here with me. You're going to have some time out, get your life recalibrated again, and then you can think about what's next." Joel cupped Matt's elbow, forcing him to his feet. "Now, I want you to do your best to help Toni feel like she's done well. It's an important day for her and I don't want her to feel like we're putting a damper on her celebration."

"What's she celebrating?"

"She sold a painting today at the resort. Isn't that good?"

"Yeah."

Joel smiled. "Come on, man. You're gonna have to do better than that. Even if you don't feel like it, just pretend for her sake. Okay?"

Pretend? He was the master of pretend. He'd been pretending to not care about Toni for years, although at times he suspected he hadn't hidden his feelings very well. He certainly should've hidden them better at New Year's Eve.

He straightened and pasted on something that he hoped passed for a smile. "Better?"

"Better."

With a none-too-gentle shove, Joel propelled Matt into the room where Toni was slicing a breadstick. Matt watched her, her geometric top revealing her graceful hands, her elegant lines, her subtle strength, the way she multi-tasked. She glanced at him, her dark hair swinging with the movement. Her smile was small, like she didn't know quite what to do with him. Which made two of them. Being in the same room as her was torture. He could only lift his gaze to her mouth, not wanting to risk seeing more pity in her eyes.

"Hey, Matt."

Even her voice held pity. Still, he couldn't stand here like a mute. He should say something. But what? "Can... can I...?" Thoughts swam slower than a sunken log.

"Can you do anything?" she asked.

He nodded.

"I'm fine. You take a seat. I'll be finished in a moment."

Take a seat to where? Oh.

He obeyed, sinking into a dining chair, feeling like a zombie, being told what to do. But that was safer than trying to think for himself. Clearly when he'd last tried to do that he had stuffed things up royally. From here he could see the night-time lights glimmering on the ice-covered lake. From somewhere beyond came the murmur of Joel's voice, a clink of plates, Ethan's soft gabble as he talked a language only he understood. Sweet domesticity. A family.

An immense yearning for what could never be gripped him, and he clenched his hands, wishing he could suppress the thoughts, the ache inside. He might've told Joel he could pretend, but this was agony.

The microwave announced that it was done, and Toni stood. "Are you ready to eat, Matt? I think my brother has almost finished on the phone to Serena."

Serena? Who was Serena? Oh, Joel's girlfriend.

Joel pocketed his phone and carried several plates to the table before taking his seat. Toni joined them, carrying a plate of buttered bread.

Joel prayed, then they ate. There was little conversation, as if people didn't know what to say. What had Joel said before? That's right, this was supposed to be Toni's celebration. How he hated being the downer on her special day.

"You… you sold a painting?" he asked.

Her face brightened. "There was a man at the resort today who wants me to do a copy of the painting in the resort reception area. He's also asked me to teach his wife some painting skills."

"Congratulations."

"Thank you." Her smile was shy. "I've sold paintings before, but this was to a man who really seems to know his stuff." She turned to Joel. "He's traveled to Europe and seen the Louvre and the Rijksmuseum. I was pretty jealous when I heard that."

"You haven't been to Europe?" Matt's words still came out slow, sounding like they came from a non-English speaker.

"Not yet. But obviously I am going to have to go one day."

"One day," Joel said. He glanced at Matt. "Are you enjoying that?"

Matt glanced at his plate. He'd barely touched it. "Sure."

Joel chuckled. "I won't tell Rose you're not a fan."

That was enough to propel a spoonful of tender meat and gravy-soaked carrot and potato into his mouth. It wasn't bad. Actually, wasn't bad at all. He managed to eat all that was on his plate and a piece of bread soaked up the rest of the gravy. But just the effort of eating and of talking made him tired, and he was glad when Joel suggested it might be good to have an early night, have a shower and go to bed.

It would be good to go to sleep, when he could pretend this was just a dream. Not just his worst nightmare.

CHAPTER 7

"Thanks for being so understanding," Joel said, later that night after Matt had gone to bed.

Toni nodded, uncertainty stopping the many words and questions she wanted to say.

He scratched his head, weariness filling his own features, weariness that saw him hide a yawn behind a hand. "Man. It's been a day."

"How are you holding up?"

He sighed. "Honestly, it was kind of scary seeing him like that."

Like what? she longed to ask, but kept her mouth closed, not wanting Matt's privacy to be exposed. She could trust Joel to tell her what she'd need to know.

"Oh, that's right. Wow. Where do I begin? Well, you know that he wasn't answering his phone, so I asked Wade to check on him. Wade couldn't get an answer either, so when I got there with the key I went in." He shook his head. "The place was dark, he was lying on the sofa, and for a moment there I thought he…" His lips flattened.

Oh. No. Poor Matt. Her heart ached for him.

"I just haven't seen him like that before, you know? He's always so together, so organized, so on top of things. To see him like that was really hard."

"I bet," she said softly. Matt's haggard, bearded appearance here had shocked her. He'd always been quiet and intense, but neat and in command of himself. To see him otherwise made her want to cry.

"I don't know how long we'll have him here for. I hope it won't be too awkward for you. He, uh, mentioned that he asked you out and you said no."

She winced. "I didn't think he was my type. And I was so busy setting up the art gallery, and—"

"Hey, you don't owe me any explanations. You know I'm a fan of you both, and I want you both to find happiness. I just didn't want things to be awkward or inconvenient for you."

"It'll be okay." *Please, Lord.* "As long as he's able to put up with occasional tears from Ethan."

"You're a good sister."

"Yes I am."

His chuckle was loaded with weariness, something that reminded her of something else that had been said today. "Serena mentioned that I can always stay with her. In case things get tricky here," she added.

"That was kind of her."

"She, uh, also raised the question about the future." She studied her brother. "Have you thought about where I could stay after you are married?"

"Wow. That's another thing I hadn't really thought about."

"She suggested that Ethan and I could possibly move to her house once you two are married, but I guess all of that is dependent on what's happening with Matt."

"I can't imagine he'll be here that long." He shook his head. "No, he just needs a mental health break, and time away from the city for a while. I figured this is a safe spot where he is with people who love him, and he doesn't need to do much at all. I imagine it will be for a week, maybe two, but not much longer."

"What will this mean for his job?"

"That's the million-dollar question." He eyed her. "And I mean that, quite literally. He's poised to lose a lot of money if things go south with his work."

"What happened to him going to Europe?"

He hissed out a breath. "Apparently, his boss gave that role to the jerk who has undermined half the team. Our man Matt got so fired up he shot off an email to the whole staff outlining every misdemeanor this person has ever done, so I think it's a mix of exhaustion and revenge email remorse that he's dealing with now."

"Good on him for standing up to the bullies, though."

"Exactly. But sometimes the whistleblower is the one who bears the brunt of the criticism."

Poor Matt. *Lord, be with him.* "Has he been fired?"

"Wade was able to find a way to help him claim immediate medical leave, thanks to a doctor in Matt's apartment building. He's got three weeks off, and Wade thinks with personal leave he could get more, but beyond that we'll have to see what happens."

She settled back in her seat. "I don't know what to say. Except... I'm kind of impressed. I didn't think Matt had it in him to go out in a blaze of glory."

"I'm sure he'd love to hear that," her brother said dryly.

Okay, so maybe she would keep that to herself then. "Is there anything I can help with?"

"What you did tonight was perfect. He just needs quiet, and needs to eat good food, not junk food. The doctor wants to avoid medicating him, so advised that Matt needs to stay physically healthy so he can get the rest he needs to recover. I know tonight wasn't quite the celebration you wanted. I'm sorry about that."

"Hey, it's okay. We can celebrate another time."

"Wow."

"What?"

"Look at who is being so mature."

"Who?" She glanced around then placed a hand on her chest. "Oh, you mean me?"

"Oh, it was there for a fleeting moment, but now I'm not so sure."

Her lips lifted. "That's just mean."

"That's just honest." Joel's chuckle rumbled. "Although, that's not entirely honest. I gotta say, kiddo, I've been impressed to see how you've stepped up with all kinds of things."

"See? I can be impressive."

He grinned. "I think you need to tell me more about what happened today, and this painting you sold. But first I'll need to make you a celebratory cup of tea."

"Whoo! Nothing says celebration like honey, vanilla, and chamomile tea."

"Right?"

A few minutes later she was sipping her tea while filling him in on the details about her day, about the commissioned painting, the art lessons, and the radio and magazine interviews scheduled for next week. "I'm a bit nervous, but hey, things like tonight put things into perspective."

"That's for sure."

They smiled at each other, before a stirring from Ethan reminded her it was way past time for him to go to bed, which meant she should probably get some sleep too. She picked up her son and held him to her as Joel stood.

"Hey, come here." He hugged her, taking care not to squash Ethan. "It's going to be okay, you know."

"I know." Her words held more sound than hope. "G'night, bro."

"Good night, kiddo." He pressed a kiss to Ethan's brow. "And to you, squirt."

"Stop calling him that."

"What? I'm his uncle. Which means I get to call him whatever I like. And after that last diaper change—"

"Don't. You'll call him that when he's five and someone will ask and he'll never live it down."

"Then he should've thought about that before dousing his uncle who was only trying to help him."

"Good to see you've got that forgiveness thing working so well."

He grinned. "Sweet dreams."

"Yeah. You too."

And he pulled out his phone, like he couldn't wait to call Serena again, and ensure his dreams were sweet, and she put her son, then herself, to bed in a vain attempt to find sleep that might actually offer rest.

∾

SHE DIDN'T SEE Matt the next day. Or the next. Matt sleeping in she could understand, but when he didn't appear even when she returned from work, she couldn't help but feel like he was avoiding her. Which hurt her heart. Made her regret again her foolishness at New Year's Eve, and even wonder if that had contributed to his depressed state now.

Joel said Matt was exhausted, getting up at ten, eating, showering, sitting, not saying much or simply watching TV, before returning to bed. She did her best to keep Ethan quiet, even wondering aloud whether she should take up Serena's offer and move there for a few weeks. But Joel insisted that she stayed, that the doctor had said the sooner he began a normal routine the better. But she couldn't help wondering whether Matt thought the same.

Saturday arrived, and she heard the front door open and close. Probably Joel, doing some Joel-like thing. Maybe he was going to a men's breakfast or something. Although considering he'd pretty much canceled his other church activities and appointments this week maybe he wasn't. Regardless, she was glad she didn't need to go to the gallery today and could instead snuggle in bed with Ethan, until her protesting stomach insisted she eat breakfast.

She got up, got changed, changed Ethan then made her slippered way down the hall then paused at the entrance to the living area. It was one thing to spend half the week wondering and worrying over the man who'd spent the past three nights in their spare room. It was quite another to finally see him, t-shirt straining across his back muscles as he sat at the dining table eating cereal as he stared out the window, his head propped in one hand.

Toni swallowed. Somehow she had forgotten what having Matt here would mean. Had forgotten just how much space he took up. He was taller than Joel, broader too, and to see him sitting there in her space just felt a little… too personal.

Ethan grew restless, his grumble at being made to wait for his own breakfast drawing Matt to pause, then turn around.

She swallowed. Okay, so the man mightn't be her type, but with his liquid blue eyes and cheeks still covered in dark bristles he owned a kind of sexy appeal. Two words she'd never thought would apply to Matt. "Um, good morning."

"Hey."

Her stomach curled at the growl in his morning voice. She grasped Ethan's head as she hoisted him against her shoulder. "Did you sleep okay?"

"Yeah. Thanks." His face was wan, deeply shadowed. It was hard to tell if he was telling the truth or not.

"How are you?" She found a small smile. "I've barely seen you these past days."

His gaze, which still hadn't quite met hers, shifted away. "I thought you'd gone to work."

"Saturdays are optional, so I opted not to go today. Especially seeing Ethan's been a little sniffly."

His face softened. "Poor little guy."

Her heartstrings pulled tight at his compassion. "I, uh, just need to get the high chair."

"Let me." Matt pushed back his chair, retrieved the high chair from the wall and positioned it at the table. "This okay?"

"Perfect. Thanks." She carefully deposited Ethan in, strapping him in securely, before drawing on his scoop bib. "I'll be back in a moment, with your breakfast, okay?"

Ethan burbled his agreement, and she caught Matt's stare before he turned away.

Her insides clenched. She hurried to the kitchen, switching on the kettle as she grasped the counter top. She could do this. Just because the man was thoughtful in the midst of his own turmoil didn't mean anything. And just because he had some appealing qualities didn't mean her hormones needed to get carried away. He was Joel's friend. Her friend, too. She didn't need to start thinking of him in any other way.

"Do you need a cup of tea?" she called.

"No, thanks."

She made her tea, found Ethan's pureed apple, and poured out her own granola and milk. At the table she spooned in Ethan's breakfast, while juggling her own, her tea and awkward conversation.

"So, um, are you enjoying your escape to the country?" she asked. Then winced at herself. Seriously? She might as well ask him about the weather.

"It's good to be away." His gaze was fixed outside to the frozen lake. "It's pretty here."

"Sure is. I wondered at first whether I'd ever get used to a small town, but I love it here now." She was gabbling. Toni didn't gabble. *Rein it in, girl.*

In the past, silence between them had been normal, mostly because she'd been the one keeping him at arm's length. It felt weird to be the one trying to encourage him to conversation.

His glance finally veered back in her direction.

"So, um, is Joel here?" she asked.

"He went out for a quick jog."

Outside the window revealed a fresh drift of snowflakes. She grimaced. "I bet it was quick. I personally don't understand the appeal of jogging on snow."

"I hear you." He ate another mouthful, but his gaze didn't lift to hers.

Awkwardness filled the space between them again.

She snuck another look. At least he seemed more alert, his conversation holding less of the sluggish quality of that first night. Maybe being here meant he was finally getting better.

Ethan's protest drew her attention. "Okay, little man, let's get you out of there, shall we?"

She drew him out from the highchair and took him to the playmat. A sigh escaped as she thought of the week's washing to do, the cleaning up, and the fact that a big week was taking its toll. All with a little boy with a snuffly cold. Weariness gripped her.

"Is there anything I can do?"

∽

HER GAZE SWIVELED to meet his, and he finally saw deep into her eyes. Instead of pity, or alarm, he saw gratitude.

"I'd love it if you could sit there on the mat and talk to Ethan. That'd be a great help while I get a few things done."

"Okay."

"Thanks," she murmured.

He waited until she moved away, to the laundry, judging from the electronic beeps from what sounded like a washing machine. He was feeling a little better. Less like a zombie, at least. Those first few days here had been excruciating, tiptoeing out only when he was sure Toni had left so she didn't have to encounter his pitiful self. But now he felt a little more like himself, operating at five or ten percent, maybe. Conversation with her had proved he wouldn't die in her company. So that was something. And while he doubted he'd ever be the same man he'd been before his brain snap, at least he didn't have the relentless surging adrenaline, like he was bracing for a marathon to face each day instead of work.

He lowered himself to the carpeted floor next to where Ethan lay, gazing up at a fabric rainbow arch from which dangled toys that looked like a mirrored ladybug, and a toy spider with stretchy dangly legs. Ethan kept reaching up to stick the red spider feet in his gummy mouth.

"Hey, buddy."

Ethan cooed, his bright eyes shifting to Matt's face.

His heart clenched. The smooth pink skin was rounded into baby cheeks that pushed up into a toothless grin. Sometimes he caught glimpses of the beautiful baby Toni must've been. He never liked to think about the other person who contributed to this child's genetics. He didn't know who he was, apart from suspecting he'd been an art colleague. Matt hadn't dared ask, sure that if he knew then part of him would want to hunt the man down for desecrating Toni in this way. Sometimes it was best to not know everything.

Ethan was cute, though. He put his finger out and Ethan grasped it and then drew it to his mouth. Okay, he wasn't sure that was the most hygienic thing that should occur, so he gently tugged his finger away. "I think you're better off sucking on toy spiders than on me."

Movement drew his attention to Toni as she moved closer. "He loves that spider."

"It's pretty cute."

Her smile held tolerance. "I don't know if you remember, but I have an aversion to all things creepy crawly."

"I remember." A memory sparked. "Something about a summer camp and a toilet."

She shuddered. "Ugh. I can't believe Joel told you that story. That was something I hope I never see repeated. Can you imagine what that felt like to be minding your own business while doing your business and then have a spider fall on your head?"

"No."

"I think Joel thought it was funny to get Ethan that toy. But I was not amused."

His mouth curved partway, some of the tightness crowding his chest easing a mite more. "He's a cutie."

"If you're talking about Ethan, then yes, I think so, but then I am biased," she said, caressing one of Ethan's sock-clad toes.

"I think a mom should be."

She smiled at him, and more of the ice inside melted. "He's always been a good baby. Which is one of God's blessings, right?"

He nodded. God's blessings felt pretty far away from him right now, although he did recognize the blessing to be here. To have friends who cared. Even the blessing of sleep and quiet.

"He's been so good at work, but I'm grateful for the fact they have a daycare there for the kids." She tapped a fabric ladybug mirror toy and it swung from the arch. "I have a radio interview on Monday."

"About your exhibition?"

"Yeah. I've never done one before, so I'm pretty unsure of what to expect."

He'd done the occasional media spot in the past. "Is it live or pre-recorded?"

"I think it's live. Live means more chance to make mistakes, right? There's no second chances." She wrinkled her nose. "I don't want to embarrass the resort or myself by sounding like a fool."

"Just relax, be yourself."

"Easy for you to say."

She cut him a look that he wasn't sure what to do with. Did she mean he was not known for relaxing? Which was true, but he didn't think she'd point it out. Unless she hadn't meant it— Oh, this was too hard.

He ducked his head, refocusing on the baby whose bright eyes were fixed on him. He held out a finger and Ethan grabbed hold of it, tugging toward his gummy mouth again.

Matt grew aware of Toni watching him, watching them, and he wondered if he was supposed to say something more. But he had no idea of what to say without sounding like the doofus he'd often heard her call her brother. And his heart eased with relief as she soon scrambled up and away.

CHAPTER 8

"*A*nd can you tell us a little bit more about the inspiration behind this exhibition?"

Serena smiled at Toni then leaned closer to the phone. "It's been a wonderful opportunity that has stemmed from our love of the natural environment here. Here at Muskoka Shores Resort we love for our guests to feel like they can take a piece of their experience home with them, which is why we first asked Toni to come on board."

"And Toni, how do you feel about this all?" the radio host continued.

Toni shot Serena a nervous smile then drew in a breath and drew nearer to the phone. "I'm so proud to partner with Muskoka Shores in this new venture."

"It's certainly an honor for a young artist such as yourself."

"I am constantly amazed at such a privilege," she said honestly. "It's a dream come true."

The interview continued, the back-and-forth was straight-forward enough and the radio host was kind. It soon finished with the host asking for Toni to give the spiel for opening times.

"The art gallery is open every day from ten to five, with art lessons by appointment. We hope to see you there soon."

"Thanks, Toni and Serena. And thank you, listeners. Now for a word from our sponsors."

At the close of the interview, the radio host thanked them, there was a little more to-and-fro between Serena and the host, then the phone call ended. Serena sat back at her desk and smiled. "See? That wasn't so bad, was it?"

"Thanks for stepping in, especially when it's usually your day off. I didn't know he was going to ask about you too."

"I'm glad I'd already scheduled to be here. I know he's a little last minute sometimes, so I've learned it's important to be on your toes when interviews with him come up. But hey, publicity is important, which is why I wanted to talk to you about the magazine article. Now they should be arriving tomorrow around eleven, but because this is a Toronto-based magazine, you may find that they're a little delayed due to traffic. So just be prepared for that."

"Sure."

"They'll want to take photos of your artwork and the setup of the space, so it's good that you've got your canvas partly painted. I think they'll find that really interesting as an artist-in-residence is not something that's offered in too many places. Did I hear you mention something about having an art lesson today as well?"

"Yes. Mrs. Penham is due to come in soon."

"Okay, well you don't want to be late for that. Now you may find that they might want to take a photo of your lesson, so that's something you should raise with Mrs. Penham. If she's agreeable then there may need to be a media release statement so any photos can be used. I'll send you one via email that you can tweak. That's dependent on whether she's still doing the lesson tomorrow."

"You think I should push her to do two lessons?"

"Don't push her. If it seems like that's something she might be interested in you could mention it then. It wouldn't be hard for us to find somebody else who could step in and be a student for a few hours."

"You don't mind if they're not a genuine student?" Toni asked. "Wouldn't that be considered false advertising?"

"Mm, I would've thought it more like using models for a fashion shoot or in a resort brochure. But if you want to find somebody who can take a lesson so it is genuine then feel free. In fact, if you know anyone who might want to come anyway to help make it look like there's more than one student then that could be good too."

"It's all about the optics, right?"

"I don't like to say that, but because this is a new venture, and the magazine won't be releasing its article for a few weeks, then it would be good to project the image of what will be, rather than what currently is. I think going about it this way makes it more a faith statement rather than—"

"A realistic portrayal of current events?" Toni suggested.

Serena's lips tightened. "I didn't think you'd see it quite like that, but okay. If you'd prefer to not include the lesson component then I think you're missing an opportunity. Now I need to go and deal with some other matters."

A beat passed. Two. "Hey, you're not annoyed with me, are you?" Toni asked. "I don't mean to be difficult. I'm just trying to figure this stuff out."

"I know. I'm just trying to make things easier for you, and I can understand where you're coming from. However, I think it's important for us to do all we can to promote this. I won't be here tomorrow because I have a function of my own in the city so that's why I'm giving you a heads up now."

"I appreciate it."

Serena smiled, the moment of tension passing. "It's been a little crazy lately, hasn't it?"

"For sure."

"How is your new house guest doing? We missed you both at church yesterday."

Toni shrugged. "I'm sure he will feel more relaxed after a few more days. At the moment, I think he's still just finding his feet."

"Well, if he's looking for something to do maybe you could invite him to be your art student for tomorrow's interview."

"Yeah, I'm not sure if he's really ready for that just yet." Or if she was ready for it either. What would it be like to have Matt's handsome brooding self here? She shivered.

"Okay, well on that note, I suppose I'd better let you get back to your real student. Hope it goes well."

"Thanks. Me too."

Toni quick-walked her way from Serena's office to the art gallery, passing the gym and floor studios, the spa, the café, and the daycare. She smiled at the reception staff then noticed the woman standing outside the art gallery, glancing at her watch, one hand on her hip as if annoyed. Oh dear. Was this her student?

"Um, hello." Toni unlocked the glass doors. "Are you Mrs. Penham? Are you here for the art lesson?"

The elderly woman from the other day looked her up and down. "I was under the impression this place opened at ten." She sniffed as she passed through the door Toni held open. "I am not impressed at being made to wait."

"Please forgive me. I was involved in a radio interview that has only just concluded. And I thought your husband booked you in for eleven, not ten."

"Alistair is often mistaken about times."

Should she show the woman the appointment book or should she just get stuck into the lesson? She voted for the latter. "Well, if you'd like to come this way then, let's not waste any more time."

The woman's glance around at Toni's paintings drew a wrinkled nose, and Toni's misgivings. Why had Alistair believed this to be a good idea? "Here is an apron, and your easel. Let's get started."

~

THIS SITTING around staring out at a frozen lake felt kind of weird. He'd had the occasional day off before, but it had always been a rare thing. And during those times part of his brain had always been thinking about the next project, the next trip. Never since college days had he ever just stopped and done virtually nothing. And now, this sitting around for days, not knowing what to do with himself, was freaking him out a little. What did people do with themselves all day when they retired? Switch off their brains? No wonder things like those men's sheds for retirees that Joel supported were so popular. People needed to be doing, feeling like their life had purpose, like they were valued. He didn't feel any of those things anymore.

Maybe it was self-pitying to regard himself in this way, but he'd barely had the energy to fight it. He barely had the energy to do much more than stare at the lake and drink the coffee that Joel had brought back from The Coffee Blend café in town.

But maybe, just maybe, this sitting around was doing what it needed to. He was so happy to not have to think about his job or the city or the people he'd exposed that he was kind of glad to be hidden away here, to have nobody but Joel and Wade and Toni and Serena know where he was. He felt safe. Like no one could find him. And with his laptop in Toronto, his phone switched off and emails temporarily suspended, it was like the world could continue on without him, and he was learning he could still survive. In some ways that felt weird, almost disappointing, like he was way more of a non-entity than he had previously thought. And in other ways it was a relief, to have other people shoulder the weight of responsibility that he'd been carrying for years.

Was Dr. Ramesh right? Had Matt burned out because he didn't know how to take a break? He'd always thought that pushing, pushing, pushing to accomplish goals was worth something, was an achievement worth applauding. That's what people had promoted him in the past for, that's why people paid him so well, that's what everyone in his industry—in most industries—wanted: to achieve, to be successful, to be seen to have it all.

But what if Matt had been wrong?

Was there such a thing as too much striving? His body seemed to think so. The doctor seemed to think so. Joel and Wade agreed. But if he didn't do this, if he could no longer work in this profession, who *was* he? What was the alternative?

Matt wasn't small town. He could see its charm, could understand the appeal, and knew why Joel had moved here. But it wasn't for him. He preferred convenience, food and entertainment options, city lights, an apartment with a great view.

The wind rippled through the branches of an empty oak, causing snow to sprinkle to the ground. Okay, so maybe the view here was pretty. And maybe his work hours meant he rarely sought out entertainment—church was about it these days, if that counted as entertainment—and thanks to work he didn't do much more in the way of fun other than order in his food.

He supposed Muskoka Shores wasn't quite the backwater he'd always thought. True, he had no particular desire to visit a cranberry farm again any time soon, although the café food there was nice. But small town just felt so... small.

Quiet settled around him, seeming to seek out every nook and cranny within. It was like in the silence his thoughts got louder, his questions bigger, with no distractions to drown them out.

Who was he?

What was his life about?

What did God have for him?

He straightened, as that last thought slammed into him like a puck to the face. In all his planning, and working, and busy schedule, when was the last time he'd actually talked to God about what God wanted him to do?

What if God didn't want him to do this type of work anymore?

He reared back. No. That must be the meds talking. Dr. Ramesh had given him something to help him sleep, and he'd taken one that first night, which had knocked him out and made him virtually sleep walk through those first few days.

But now, with most of the brain fog lifted and he was thinking more clearly, maybe this was God's way of gaining Matt's attention and forcing him to look at his life again.

"Lord?"

His voice echoed softly in the empty room, and he closed his eyes, trying to still his thoughts, to refocus on God.

From somewhere deep within he felt assurance, that somehow Matt was still held within God's hands. He knew God loved him like he knew the sky was blue. But lately, all he'd been seeing was gray.

"Help me remember Your plans are good for me," he murmured.

Toni's comment on Saturday about blessings struck him anew. Matt *was* blessed. He knew that. And he also knew he could focus on the blessing or the pain; the blue skies or the gray. And whatever happened in his future didn't change the fact that God could still use it for Matt's good.

Which included whatever happened with Toni, too.

He blew out a shaky breath.

He'd been grateful to avoid Toni. Until Saturday. Then Sunday, when Ethan's cold had seen her stay home from church with him again. But it had been strangely nice, peaceful, even with Ethan's occasional cries. Being quiet. Studying the sculptural tree forms alongside the lake. Listening to chilled-out music. Breathing in the scent of fresh-baked cookies. Eating them. His foolish heart pretending they were a couple. Imagining this was his normal.

His hands clenched. "Stop it," he muttered aloud.

Trusting God with her felt like a battle, because every time he thought on her he wanted to cringe, hating to think how she must regard him.

He sunk deeper into his seat. Nope. No good would come of thinking about what she might be thinking. If she'd thought him a no-go before, he'd now be in leper-land. Untouchable. An outcast. A castaway. If she couldn't like him when he was successful there was no way she'd want anything to do with him now.

So, it'd do no good to think about Toni, or think about how beautiful she looked half asleep in the morning, with Ethan tucked up under her chin, his tiny thumb in his mouth. It did no good to think on them because she'd made it clear she wasn't into him, so yearning for what he could never have was a surefire way to load more frustration on his life. He didn't need to do that. He should probably stay away. Maybe he should leave…

No. He sucked in a breath and slowly exhaled. Nope. If Toni didn't want him, well, God was still in control. "But God, I really need Your help to let her go."

His prayers lifted and faltered over the next hour until the front door rattled and he turned to see Joel enter.

"Hey!" Joel grinned. "Still here? Haven't run away?"

"Don't tempt me."

"Look at that, Matt made a joke."

"Wasn't joking," he said, as Joel dumped his bag and snagged the nearby sofa. "It's killing me sitting here doing nothing."

Joel shrugged. "You heard the doctor. You need to avoid pressure-filled situations."

Matt maybe should've explained that being in Toni's general vicinity was a pressure-filled situation. "I can still do some things," he said instead.

"You're supposed to rest," Joel said kindly.

"I have been," he insisted. "I've barely done anything but sleep the past week."

And now trying to rest was simply making him more stressed. "How would you cope if someone told you to rest? And Dr. Ramesh didn't say I had to do nothing, just to take it easy, get away from my regular routine." He was pretty sure that's what he'd said anyway. It was hard to remember.

"Hmm." Joel's head tilted as he considered Matt, before giving a nod. "Maybe you can help me when I visit Golden Elms tomorrow."

"What's that?"

"It's an older person's home and retirement community. The most pressure you get there is trying to not squirm when an old dear says you remind her of her dead husband and can she have a kiss."

Matt almost smiled. "I bet you kiss them anyway."

"Yeah." He shrugged. "On the cheek, let me be clear."

"You don't want to make Serena jealous."

"That's for sure." Joel stretched his hands above his head, rolled his neck which produced two loud clicks. "So, what do you think?"

"About what?"

"About visiting Golden Elms with me tomorrow."

"I think I'll pass."

"How surprising."

"Shocking," he said dryly.

Joel grinned. "Well, no complaining then. You'll miss the opportunity to do such fun things as learning to foxtrot."

Matt blinked. "Are you serious?"

"Don't tell me you want to come with me now."

"Okay, I won't."

A chuckle erupted from Joel, and Matt's lips curved. One thing he'd always appreciated about Joel was his sunny nature. It was good to have a friend in his life whose optimism and enthusiasm balanced out Matt's own more carefully planned approach. Was it any wonder then that he wasn't coping with no schedule?

Maybe that was part of his problem. Maybe he was just too controlled, and now he'd proved to not be in control he was spiraling, descending into what felt like chaos. But did he need to be so controlled? His work demanded it. Work was all about conscientious check-the-boxes, schedules, deadlines, project management, meeting goals and objectives. That's what performance reviews were all about: had he met the company's targets or not? How could he do better? He couldn't imagine a job or a way of life that wasn't within these parameters.

"How do you do it?" he asked Joel.

"Do what? Let little old ladies kiss me? Well, I ask myself what would Jesus—"

"No, I mean how do you manage to do a job with no clear measurable performance indicators."

"Wow." Joel looked at him. "That's a question that needs at least one coffee to answer. You ready for another?" He peered at Matt's empty mug. "It appears so. Although, if you've already had your one-cup-a-day as prescribed by your new favorite doctor, then maybe you should try something softer."

"Not if it's one of those herbal hippie tea bags in there."

"Hmm. Sounds like someone's feeling a little aggressive toward poor chamomile. Does that mean you need to try some and relax?"

Matt shot him a sour look.

Joel laughed and moved to the kitchen. The sound of the kettle heating up was followed by a, "So, you really want to know about measurable performance indicators in the ministry, or do you mean any job that doesn't have a clear outcome?"

"The latter, I guess."

"Okay." Joel reappeared. "So how do I cope when I don't necessarily see a clear outcome? I guess I'm always aware that this is something I feel like God wants me to do, so I'm not too hung up on whether I see a certain number of salvations each week or not. I think God is bigger than what we imagine and is able to do way more behind our back than what we realize, so I trust Him to be working on people's hearts, and I trust Him to use me for His sake." He disappeared and the sounds of the kettle switching off and water being poured was followed by his reappearance holding two cups of what smelled like herbal tea.

"Thanks." Matt's nose wrinkled at the smell as Joel placed it on the coffee table.

"More than welcome. Don't knock it until you try it."

"Then I can knock it?"

"Sure."

Matt took a taste, and yep, it was as bad as he thought. "Yeah, happy to not pollute my taste buds with that ever again."

"But at least you tried it. Now, back to the question. Look, there are plenty of jobs in this world where you can't see a measurable result. A job isn't just about how many sales you make or how many deals you do or how many souls are saved. I think it's more than that. I think God wants it to be more than that, and He wants to use us wherever we are in whatever we do. And I guess part of that is asking ourselves whether what I'm doing is what God wants me to. If your job is causing you to lie, or to misrepresent the truth, or fosters an environment that isn't Godly or makes you sick, then is that something God wants us involved in, or is it something we can change? And if it's not something we can change and it's eating us up inside, then yeah, I think maybe it's time to look at something new."

Whoa. This discussion suddenly felt bigger than he wanted.

"I remember Serena saying something about her parents not understanding that God could use her in her role at the resort, and yet I see the difference she makes in other people's lives. Toni's work is similar. Some might discount it as only paintings, but there's a creativity and a passion that I think reflects God, and the way she can get people to pause and think about creation is a God-given gift. But it's not necessarily measurable, and it doesn't fit with what a lot of people might think as structured or check-a-box. But I think what she does is very much what she's meant to do in life."

"That's good to know," Toni said.

Matt's gaze swung up to meet her. "Hi," he blurted.

"Hi."

Her smile went straight to his heart, causing him to instantly avert his gaze. No. This wasn't good. Not good at all.

"So, what are you two talking about so intensely?"

Joel shot him a look, and Matt shook his head. "Just work stuff."

She groaned and plopped into the nearby sofa.

"Sounds like someone had fun today," Joel teased, before frowning. "Hey, where's the little fella?"

"I put him in his cot already. He had a big day so now he's going to sleep."

"Sounds like you had a big day too," Matt managed.

"Don't remind me. Actually, am I smelling my favorite tea?" She looked accusingly at her brother. "Are you drinking the good stuff?"

"Want me to make you a hot chocolate?" Matt asked.

She brightened. "Would you? With marshmallows?"

"Of course."

Her grin sent another shot of adrenaline through him, and

he escaped before Joel could give him an older-brother raised-eyebrows look. He made her hot chocolate and his, returning in time to catch Toni's complaint about her day.

"...I couldn't believe her. Everything I said to do she disputed, saying what would I know, but Maude must be three times my age and says she'd been painting before I even learned to walk. Which may well be true, but it doesn't mean that she knows everything. Not that I do, either, obviously, but you'd think that if her husband has paid for her to have a lesson that the least she could do is try. But she just didn't try. I almost felt bad taking Alistair's money, but he'd paid for it, and I've given her the time and the materials so it was justified. It was just a disappointing first lesson."

"I'm sorry," Matt said.

"Hey, there'll be others," Joel said. "Don't let her get you down."

"Ugh. That reminds me. Serena has asked me to find some people to be pretend students for when the magazine photographer comes tomorrow. I don't know if Maude will be back, and to be honest, I don't mind if she doesn't return. But Serena had said it would be good to have some people pretending to learn art tomorrow and now I have to find at least one person to be there and pretend to be my student."

Joel shot Matt a look, then glanced back at his sister. "Do they need to pretend, or can they be the real deal?"

"I don't care who they are. It would just be good to have someone else there so it doesn't look like it's a class with no students. Or only a super irritable one."

Uh oh. Matt had a bad feeling where this was gonna go.

"In that case, Toni, I have the perfect person in mind."

She frowned. "Who?"

Matt's heart double-thumped with foreboding.

"A person who was very recently describing just how boring

he was finding his time here, and his desire to push beyond his personal boundaries."

Wait—he'd never said *that*.

"Who?" Toni asked impatiently.

Joel waved a hand in Matt's direction. "Meet your new favorite art student. Matt Vandenburg."

CHAPTER 9

"Here, let me get that."

Toni glanced up at the man holding the resort's main door. "Thank you."

Matt dipped his chin, his gaze faltering then lowering to rest on Ethan in the stroller. She might consider herself a bit of a feminist, but she appreciated a man who could open the door. Especially when it was so cold outside.

They entered the resort's lobby and she smiled at Chrissy on reception.

Matt cleared his throat as he paused to look at the painting above the desk. "Is that yours?"

"Yes." A ping of pride exploded in her heart.

"It's amazing."

Yes, it was. It still took her aback to see her own work there. "The gallery is just across the hall there." She pointed to the glass doors. "But first I'm going to get Ethan into the daycare."

"Okay."

For some reason he seemed inclined to stay with her. "You could get a coffee in the resort café if you want to wait a few moments."

He shoved his hands in his pockets. "I will if you don't want me to come."

Aw, now refusing just made her sound ungracious. "I don't mind."

Although she kind of did. Having Matt here felt like inviting him into part of her life that she was still trying to come to terms with herself. It felt strange to have him with her for most of the day. But yesterday's announcement by Joel had again hijacked her plans, and after complaining about not having anyone to teach she couldn't very well refuse the man who had put up his hand and volunteered. Or at least been volunteered by Joel.

They moved to the daycare area where Vera greeted them with a smile and a subtle raised eyebrow glance at Matt and then back at Toni that she didn't have time to explain. Except to say, "Matt is a friend from the city here for the day."

The older woman nodded, her lips tipping up on one corner suggesting she wasn't entirely sure whether to believe it, but Ethan's gurgling chuckle at Vera's tickle allowed Toni to make her escape, with a kiss on Ethan's cheek, and a, "Have a good day," to Vera.

"You too," she called, with a sideways glance at Matt like she thought his company would instantly bring any woman immeasurable joy.

Toni settled for a tight smile and swiftly steered him from the room and back up the corridor to the main lobby area. She exhaled.

"What time does the magazine person arrive?" he asked, cutting off her insane desire to apologize.

"That's right. I almost forgot."

He looked at her curiously which propelled her to continue.

"She said they planned for eleven, but with city traffic and this snow they weren't sure."

He glanced at his watch. "It's almost ten now, so that gives a bit of time to settle down and get ready." He tilted his head at the cafeteria. "Can I get you a hot drink?"

"A peppermint tea would be great," and might settle her nerves, "but only if you're going there for yourself," she hastened to add.

"I thought your idea of a coffee sounded good." His mouth creased up, and his head tilted to the gallery. "I'll meet you in a moment."

"Sounds good." Sounds great, actually, she thought, watching him amble to the café. If he wasn't there, then she might have the chance to get her head straight. There was something about the man that was disconcerting, or distracting. Whatever it was, it left her feeling uneasy and unsure. She suspected she'd need way more than a peppermint tea to help her find a sense of equilibrium again.

But when she got to the glass doors it was to see Maude there, with Alistair, his face pinched in a concerned look.

"Ah, Antonia," he called as she drew near. "We're back, as you can see."

Oh, goody. "Good morning to you both." She unlocked the door, switched on the lights, and ushered them inside.

"Late again, I see," Maude said waspishly.

"Actually, dear, it's not even ten," her husband said. "How about you let the young lady have a moment before you launch your attack?"

Toni gritted out a smile. She'd be quite happy for a while longer than a moment if there was to be an attack. How about a couple of hours? Or a few days? Or at least until the magazine reporter had left for the day.

Alistair's smile pushed out his pink cheeks. "We'll give you a moment and Maude can look at her canvas from yesterday and perhaps find fresh inspiration."

"Great idea."

As they moved to the corner that was the studio space, Toni

took a moment to retrieve her phone and stow her bag. A deep breath. Hold. Release. She did this another couple of times, the sequence reminding her of the birthing process last August when Serena had coached her through the biggest physical pain of her life. But perhaps that was similar to what this was. Things that were good didn't tend to come easy, and there were challenges galore when she would need to remember that God was with her, giving her strength.

The couple's conversation drifted to her in muted tones. "...I don't understand why you're making me participate." Maude.

"I thought you'd enjoy this." Alistair sounded hurt.

"I don't think you understand the concept of what enjoyment is," she snapped.

Toni sighed. Perhaps the easiest thing would be for her to return Alistair's money. She didn't want the resort suffering from an unhappy client.

She forced herself to walk toward them as she pasted on a smile. "I'm sorry, but is there a problem?" she asked, looking between them.

"No indeed," Alistair said.

"Maude?" Toni prompted.

The elderly woman glanced at her husband then sighed. "No."

"So are you happy to have another lesson this morning?"

"I suppose."

"The reason I ask," Toni continued, "is that I'm expecting a reporter from a city magazine to be here soon who will want to take photos of what we do, so it would be extremely helpful if the people here look like they're pleased and aren't cutting across my instructions. Now I completely understand if this is something that you do not want to do—"

"A magazine?" Maude asked. "Which one?"

"*Toronto Living.*"

Her eyes rounded. "Oh! Well, in that case, I suppose I could be persuaded to spend a few more hours here."

"Do you need any other takers?" Alistair asked, in a tone that suggested he was joking.

"Actually, it would be good to have a few more people in attendance. I have another person who will be here shortly, but if you want to stay as well, that would be great."

He glanced at his wife then back at Toni. "That sounds good then. What do I need to do?"

She explained and spent the next few minutes setting up easels and preparing their supplies. She also set up an easel and supplies for Matt even if she wondered whether she should advise him to return home. His presence would be superfluous.

His return a minute later, bearing a cardboard tray holding two cups and a tentative smile drew a tightening in her stomach, and for a moment she could well understand why Vera had made her sly comment earlier. The man was attractive, she supposed, even if he didn't hold an ounce of the romance of a windswept raffish musician she'd long thought counted as the epitome of attractiveness. Matt had always been too clean-cut and serious for that. But now, with that hint of scruff on his jaws, and that air of vulnerability in his serious eyes, she found a new appeal. That, or maybe it was protectiveness for him. Or maybe she was simply suffering from sleep-deprivation and a jumble of hormones from her time of the month.

"Here's your tea," he said, placing it on a table near her.

"Thank you."

"Hmph. Is that from the café here?" Maude asked him.

"Yes."

"I didn't realize they had a delivery service. I'll have a cappuccino please."

"Maude, this is Matt, and he's not—"

"I don't care what his name is. A cappuccino for me, thank you. Half strength, skim milk, and two sugars." She peered over her glasses at him. "Do you think you'll be able to remember that or do I need to write it down?"

A muscle moved in his jaw. "I think I'll remember that."

Her gray bun bobbed up and down as she nodded. "We'll see, won't we?"

"I guess you will," he said easily, moving to the door.

Toni chased after him and grabbed his arm. "Matt, you really shouldn't—"

He stilled, glanced at her hand then up at her.

She released her hand. Swallowed. "She's a bully," she whispered. "And I don't want you pandering to her."

His eyes were intent on her. "If buying her a cup of coffee means she'll be kinder to you, then that's the least I can do."

Oh. For a second, emotion burned at the back of her eyes. She blinked, banishing the sudden blur. "You're very kind."

"Sometimes." His lips tweaked, then he paced back, turned, and disappeared.

She released a long breath, and slowly returned to the couple who both now had their aprons on.

"I didn't want to say this in front of him but I really feel like he should be wearing a uniform. Most unprofessional," Maude sniffed.

"Maude, he doesn't work here," Toni said.

"What?"

"Matt is my friend, and the other student in the class today. He doesn't work here at the café."

"Then what's he doing getting me a coffee?"

"He's a nice guy," Toni said.

Matt *was* a nice guy. Once upon a time she might've thought him boring and staid, but his kindness in overlooking Maude's rudeness spoke of his patience and generous heart. His goodness shone through even when facing challenges himself.

"Really, Maude." Alistair shook his head. "I better go after him and explain."

"It's fine, Alistair, really. I meant it before when I said he's a nice guy." Toni added softly, "He's not the only one around here who's nice, is he?"

He pinked, shot a look at his wife, then shrugged. "I'm sure I don't know what you mean."

It seemed she had embarrassed him. Aw, bless his humble heart. But time was ticking. Best to get this show on the road. "Well, let's get ready to do some painting, so when Matt returns we can begin."

And maybe in applying brush to canvas she'd finally have a chance to sift through these conflicting emotions.

~

THERE WAS a degree of torture in watching the woman he loved stand so close to others in a way he longed for her to do with him. Toni's lesson—the magazine person still hadn't arrived—had progressed through basic color theory, picture composition, and techniques with painting. At the start of the lesson he'd glimpsed Maude's work from yesterday—a rough sketch on her canvas with a couple of dabs of paint—so the fact her canvas now held a layer of paint across the top third indicated she'd already completed more than the entire day yesterday. Maybe the cappuccino—for which she'd been almost pathetically grateful and apologetic for— had proved the fuel she needed to paint. Or maybe she'd decided to try a little harder, seeing her husband was working alongside her. Alistair—who had murmured his apologies over his wife's behavior—had the room's greatest enthusiasm for Toni's task. Toni had pinned an enlarged photograph of a vibrant maple tree to the board, and their task was to sketch out the tree's shape onto their canvas. Matt had found the actions strangely therapeutic, even as he carried a sense of tension that had nothing to do with the art, but everything to do with the artist.

He watched her again as she moved to help Maude.

"Now, Maude, if you can please just hold the paintbrush like so."

He felt, rather than heard, Maude's sigh, and bit back a smile. The woman was as cantankerous as his own grandmother, with a bite to her words bigger than a bear's, but that also suggested she was frustrated in her own life, just as his own grandmother had been.

Toni glanced up, and their gazes connected, and he smiled.

She blinked again, and hastily ducked her head, giving soft direction about which colors might best approximate those in the photo.

Alistair cleared his throat. "So, how long have you and Antonia been friends for?"

Antonia. It felt funny to hear her called so. So much more formal than the sassy, sarcasm-prone woman he knew. "For several years now. Her brother is my best friend."

"That's often the way."

Huh?

Maybe his confusion showed because Alistair winked. "I can tell you have a soft spot for her."

Great. So if strangers could see it, then Toni must be writhing inside to have the man she'd said no to here with her today. Maybe that's why she'd suggested he get a coffee earlier. She didn't want him around. Pain reared, and he leaned over his palette, taking his time to recover a neutral face as he swirled paint colors together. He should call Joel and get him to collect him. Man. He rolled his eyes at himself. How much like a six-year-old did that make him sound?

A drift of something sweet, like honey, scented the air and made him still, just as he had when she'd clutched his arm before.

"I like the colors you have chosen," Toni said softly.

He glanced up, his gaze drowning in hers. *I like you*, his heart roared. He ducked his head.

"May I?" she asked.

He nodded, and the space between them became very still, very quiet, as she leaned close, her arm stretching along his. Then she touched his hand.

His fingers jerked, splattering paint on the canvas. "Sorry," he muttered.

"No, that was my fault," she said.

Sure was.

She grabbed a damp cloth and carefully dabbed at the excess red marks until they'd disappeared. "There you go. No harm done."

He nodded, not trusting himself to speak. No harm done? This was hopeless. The woman had stolen his heart and he'd sooner die than admit his feelings again. So much harm had been done, he suspected he'd never be okay again.

"I'M SO SORRY I'm late!"

He glanced up at the visitor.

The brunette in her early thirties hurried forward. "I'm Leanne, from *Toronto Living*. I missed the turnoff and found myself in the town where I came across a really cute coffee shop —The Coffee Blend, I think it was called? Anyway, it was next to a bookstore, which looked so inviting, as did so many of the stores here. I gotta say, if it's going to be a pig of a day with the weather, then it's lovely to see the main street all lit up with twinkle lights. I might have to see if I can do a feature on the town one day. But first things first. I'm here now, and we've got an interview to do."

Toni moved to the chatterbox with an outstretched hand. "I'm Toni Wakefield. Thank you for coming all this way."

"My pleasure. Well, shall we get started?"

He tried not to make it obvious that he was listening as the two women talked about Toni's training, the inspiration behind the art space, and Leanne oohed and ahhed over Toni's paintings. That was obvious, as was Toni's lack of confidence, something that made his heart ache. How could she not see that she was talented? But he knew she had scars in her soul that might make it hard to trust not just her talent but to trust another man. Joel had mentioned something about an art professor of Toni's, and he'd never dared ask her. He'd rather be the recipient of her confidence and hope she'd one day trust him enough to tell him about this episode of her life herself.

"And can I ask what brought you from the city to Muskoka Shores?" Leanne asked her.

"My brother's work." Toni adjusted a painting.

"You're close, then?"

"Yes."

His ears pricked at the note of constraint in Toni's voice, and he glanced up.

Toni glanced away. Huh. Had she been watching him?

"Okay, then. So, these are some of your students," Leanne said, drawing closer. "Hi," she said to him. "Oh, that's looking good."

Hmm. He wasn't sure if she was mocking him or not, because all he had on the page were some rough pencil drawn sketches and some blobs of dull red paint. He managed a "Thanks" anyway.

Leanne moved to Alistair and Maude, admiring Alistair's painting while Maude fished out a lipstick from her bag and repainted her lips. She caught Matt looking and he gave her a thumbs up, which scored a glimmer of a smile before she ducked away. Vanity, thy name was Maude.

Toni trailed behind Leanne, offering answers to the questions the reporter shot at her as Toni plucked nervously at her own sleeve. Finally, Leanne drew out a large camera. "Okay, so I wanted to take some photos of you all, but first I needed to check if that's okay." She fished some forms from her messenger bag's side pocket. "These are some waivers saying you're happy to be photographed and have your pictures included in the magazine. If you can sign and date it, that'd be great. We're not promising that your picture will appear," this was said with a glance at Maude, "but it may, so it's good to be prepared."

Toni hurried to gather and distribute pens, handing one to him.

"Thanks." She smiled and was about to move away when he whispered, "You're doing great."

"You think so?" She glanced at Leanne then back at him. "She's just so intense," she said in a low voice, "and talks so much that I can't even be sure that what I'm saying is making any sense."

"Everything I've heard you say makes sense to me," he assured.

Her eyes held his for a long, sweet moment, as if his words of encouragement had seeded hope.

Click!

"Oh, that's perfect," Leanne's voice intruded.

His head swiveled to see her holding her camera positioned at them. "Now, maybe if we could get one for you Toni, looking like you're helping—I'm sorry, what is your name?"

"Matt," he mumbled.

"You've signed the waiver, yes?"

He scrawled his name and dated it. "Have now." He shoved the paper at her.

She snatched it up and stuffed it in her bag's pocket. "Okay, now I want you two to move in close together."

The soft, sweet scent of honey drifted over the sharpness of acrylic paint as Toni shuffled closer.

"That's it. Now, Matt, I want you to hold the brush against the canvas like you're painting," Leanne instructed.

Which he had been up until now, but whatever.

"And Toni, could you reach across and point as if you're showing where he could paint next."

"Um, like this?" Toni asked, stretching a slender arm across, three inches in front of his face.

"Yes!"

Click, click!

"Oh, that's good," Leanne said, checking her viewfinder. "Now, just talk normally as you were before, and I'll get a few more candid shots of you both, then of the others, and the room." She smoothed a hand down her sleek ponytail. "You have some professional shots of your paintings, I expect?" she asked Toni.

"Yes."

"Okay, then. Keep talking, smiling, look like you're having fun."

He faked a smile as he wondered what would happen if he was to shift and wrap Toni in a hug like he'd seen the ever-affectionate Joel do with his sister a million times before. Probably get sued for sexual harassment, that's what. But still, the fact she stood so near that he could see the curly tendrils of her hair below her ears, tendrils he longed to touch, only increased his yearning for her. But even though she was so near that he could hear her breath hitch as he leaned forward, closing the gap, she'd always be too far away. And some might say it was better to have loved and lost than never to have loved, but right now this gnawing inside made him wish he'd never been ensnared by those entrancing amber eyes.

"Matt? Can you make that smile look a little more genuine, please?" Leanne called.

Toni glanced at him. His heart quickened.

"That's it!" *Click, click!*

"How long do you think this'll take?" he asked Toni through gritted teeth.

Her lips tipped up into amusement.

Click, click.

"Yes! That should do nicely," Leanne said, with another glance at her camera. "Okay, let's get one of all of you. Toni, want to come out to the front now? Maybe you could hold a paintbrush at your easel here and look like a teacher."

"You're a good sport," Toni murmured, gently squeezing his bare forearm, before moving away.

His skin sizzled, like her touch held the sun.

He grasped the now-cold remains of his coffee from before and chugged it down, wanting, needing to do something to stop the slow combustion he could feel building inside. He might've felt frustration with his work, but this connection between them was growing way too hard to cope with. A phone call to Joel sounded necessary right about now.

"Matt? Can you make it look like you're paying attention to Toni there?"

Oh, sweet torture. Like he didn't pay attention to her every single day.

He resumed his painting pose, pasting on a smile he hoped looked genuine enough as his ears tuned into the other conversations.

Maude was asking when this feature might be published, as Leanne took several more pictures.

"At the start of next month, I expect," Leanne said, as she lowered her camera. "Now, let me just check if I have quotes from you all. Maude? What would you like to say about Toni's class?"

Toni stiffened, as if she too was unsure what the volatile Maude might say.

"Oh! Well, if it's a quote from me you want, well, I'm more than happy to oblige. Let me see. I guess you could say, 'As a talented artist herself, Maude Penham has found the lessons useful to fine tuning her already considerable skills.' There, would that do?"

Leanne looked like she was trying not to laugh. "Excellent. Alistair?"

"Antonia is a patient and talented artist," he said.

"I can see that," Leanne nodded. "Matt?"

He glanced at Toni, and knew a sudden urge to encourage her. "Toni brings art to life, infusing a canvas with vibrancy and hope, and helps her students do the same. This class can take a basic beginner and make him believe anything is possible."

"Wow." Leanne's eyebrows shot up. "That's a quote and a half."

He shrugged, conscious the others were looking at him, and Toni wore a soft expression on her face.

Waves of… something… passed between them, and he glanced down, breaking the connection and drawing in a breath. This room might be light and bright, and cool and airy, but it seemed way too warm to him. As soon as Leanne left he'd be making that six-year-old's-like phone call for Joel to collect him.

"Okay, and one last thing." Leanne pulled out the waivers again. "Let me just check I have these names right. Maude and Alistair Penham?"

"Yes," Maude said, preening.

"And Matt Vandenburg, correct?"

"Correct," he said.

Leanne's head tilted. "Do I know you from someplace? Your name is familiar."

He shrugged. "I've lived in the city."

"Hmm. Well, I'm sure it'll come to me." Leanne turned to Toni and held out her hand. "Thanks for today. This has been fun."

"Would you like to stay for lunch? I hear the café makes some nice soups."

"Thanks, but I need to get back, and if I leave now, I might have a chance to check out the stores in town. And if I'm super quick, I'll have time to grab some pics that I can use in another article, so I'd better go. I'll probably need to send you an email with the copy just to make sure it's accurate, okay?"

"Sure."

"And I'll send the resort several copies once it's printed."

"Thank you," Toni said.

"Okay. Well, see you around." Leanne lifted a hand, stared at Matt hard for a second, shrugged, then smiled and walked away.

Toni escorted her to the door then closed it gently. It seemed as though the room took a collective breath.

"Whew!" Alistair said, wiping his brow. "She sure was a fire-cracker. I don't know if I have heard a woman talk so much before."

"Do you think she'll use our picture?" Maude asked, her forehead pleated. "It seemed she was far more interested in taking photos of you two than of me."

"I think *Toronto Living* is more aimed at a younger demographic," Toni said kindly, shooting Matt a glance as if to say *Please don't disagree*.

He inclined his head. "That's what I've heard."

"Oh. How disappointing. I wanted to show off to our friends," Maude said with a pout.

No surprise there. Matt managed a half smile then bent his attention to his canvas. The paint outlining his tree had dried in the time it had taken to do the photograph posing and answer the reporter's questions.

Toni's sigh cut his gaze her way again. Now the reporter had gone, he could see the weariness, the fatigue that her vivacity—and her makeup—had hidden before. "Do you need a break?" he asked her. "That was fairly intense. We could probably all do with some time out for lunch, if you think that would work with the schedule."

Her expression held relief. "That sounds good if Alistair and Maude agree. We could take half an hour, seeing that I know the interview interrupted our time quite a bit more than I expected."

"I, for one, could do with stretching my legs, followed by some of that soup you mentioned," Alistair said. "Come on, Maude. Let's take a break."

They followed Toni's instructions about washing their paint brushes in water or wrapping them in plastic wrap until they returned. Toni seemed inclined to linger, and he was reluctant to leave her, knowing she had to be more tired than the rest of them.

Alistair glanced at Matt. "Coming?"

"I'll be there soon." He waved Alistair and Maude on, catching the older man's wink which drew fluster again and hurried him to return his attention to Toni. "Are you okay?"

She nodded. "It went better than I expected," she admitted. "She seemed nice, if a little pushy."

"You mean about the photos?"

"Of you and me, yes."

You and me. How he wished that was a thing. "I didn't mind." Too much.

"To be honest," she said, eyes steady on him, "I didn't either."

His mouth dried. Some might think him a man of no imagination, but when she said things like this his imagination soared. Did she mean to suggest that she liked being near him?

"I, um, I just didn't want it to get awkward."

What did she mean by that? Hopes that had been sprinting stumbled to a pause. Did she mean he might be thinking more of it than he ought? "Well, there's no awkwardness as far as I'm concerned," he lied.

She bit her lip, as if she wasn't sure.

"And I'm positive the article will be fine."

Toni's shoulders relaxed, prompting him to assure, "You don't need to worry, okay?"

She nodded, then smiled.

"Right. Well, I guess I'll meet you back here in half an hour."

Toni pushed her hair behind her ear. "Unless you wanted to have lunch together?"

CHAPTER 10

*W*hat was she doing? Having lunch with Matt in the resort café would be like inviting the whole world to stop and see. But it was like her mouth had been on autopilot and leaping ahead of her brain.

Something that a vain girl might think was hope flickered in his eyes then died. And that sight drew a renewed desire to make him believe her. "Please?" She smiled. "I don't think I could go in there and face Maude's complaining about the lack of photos of her and her painting."

His mouth pulled out wryly. "So you want me to be your protector."

Her heart thumped. The idea of someone so kind and good willing to go out of his way to protect her caused a fuzzy feeling in her heart. His consideration and forbearance today had drilled deeper into new levels of appreciation, finding depths that felt a little like affection. But all of this she couldn't say, so settled for a simple, "Yes."

The corner of his mouth flicked up briefly, as if he was amused by this, then he shrugged, and gestured for her to lead the way.

But all through lunch and during the afternoon she grew conscious of a new awareness of him. Like how the air seemed to heat when he was in her space. Like how the grave depths of his eyes held an intense regard that made her skin prickle at his perusal. His subtle scent of sea and spice. His classy watch. His beautiful hands. Hands she'd never noticed before, but now admired the shape, the clean nails, the play of tendon and bone. Hands she now wanted to draw. Hands she now wanted to hold.

She reared back. No. Uh uh. She wasn't going to let herself get carried away. But despite the constant pep talks, she couldn't stop noticing him. How his hair held subtle blond tints. How he rubbed his neck so she wondered if he was sore. Wondered what it must be like to touch him. To massage—

"Toni?"

Heaven help her. "Yes, Maude?"

"I do not understand why my tree looks so flat. Can you help me?"

"Sure."

Toni spent the next few minutes back on task, helping Maude with her technique before checking with Alistair how he was going. The man possessed more energy than talent, but she applauded his efforts all the same. Then she turned to the other man in the room, and hesitated, before figuring this was her class and it would be rude to ignore him, just because she was starting to have feelings she'd never experienced before. It didn't mean she should ignore the man. He was her student after all. "How about you, Matt? Do you have any questions?"

His gaze met hers, and again she felt that strange connection pulse between them.

She swallowed, hoping for moisture to ease a sudden dry mouth, and moved beside him. His tree looked a little flat—not as flat as Maude's though—and she gently coached him in how to get the leaves to look more leaf-like.

"May I?" At her gesture he handed her his brush, and she

commenced a tiny flicking motion. "See how these tiny strokes give the leaves a sense of movement? Maybe you could try that." She handed the brush back to him, and their fingers touched.

Her skin felt scorched, and she heard his breath hitch, and she jerked away. No. This was inappropriate, and not how an art teacher should feel about a student. Even if she'd known the student for half of forever.

She crossed her arms as he attempted to follow her direction. His flicking motions were too big, the resulting brush strokes too wide. "Do you want to make it look like a willow? Here." She grasped the brush. "I think you might find it easier if you hold the brush this way."

Her fingers slid down over his, and she felt him freeze, heard his breath catch, as she leaned close and gently flick, flick, flicked the bristles in tiny motions. Holding his hand, her fingers on top of his, drew new recognition of his latent strength, and how in this moment she could control it. And that as tempted as she was to hold his hand longer she really shouldn't play with fire. So she let go, and moved back.

"There." Her voice sounded breathy, even to her. "See how those leaves look more defined? You have a go."

He nodded, not looking at her, and she silently exhaled, hoping her fluster didn't appear so obvious to the others in the room. For it was obvious to her that this man who she'd long thought was too serious was actually fast becoming the first who might be able to warm the scared, scarred spaces of her soul.

AWARENESS OF HIM lasted all that afternoon, and then later that night at dinner, when she pushed food around her plate, wondering why each time she looked at him she felt simultaneously shy while wanting to memorize every detail on his face.

It only increased the next morning when she'd knocked on

the spare room door to retrieve more painting supplies from the closet and at his call of enter she'd gone in to see him shirtless.

"I thought you were Joel," he'd said, before hastily dragging on a T-shirt—inside out, her detail-brain noticed—before noticing the way it clung to the contours of his chest and abs.

She'd apologized, cheeks burning, and took what she needed back to her room.

But later, when she'd spied him playing with Ethan and making her son chuckle, deep gratitude and admiration wove through her again.

It continued through the remainder of the week, and now she was in church on Sunday, seated between Matt and Serena, pretending to listen to Joel's sermon, but only really conscious of Matt's hand, an inch from hers, curled around the edge of the wooden pew, and she wondered what he'd do if she was to touch him. Temptation grew, and her little finger twitched, itching to touch his. Agitation rose. How much longer would Joel talk? She felt, rather than saw, Matt turn to her.

"You okay?" he whispered.

He was always doing that. Always checking on her, asking about her. A lump grew in her throat. He'd always done that, too, for as long as she could remember. He cared about her, even when she stayed aloof, even when she'd gone astray. Matt *cared*.

Her hand moved of its own volition and grasped his, and now she could see his whole body pivot to her in shock. But she stayed focused on the front, wondering if Serena had noticed, hoping Joel couldn't see her, that he'd stay oblivious in his talk about the prodigal son while she, who so often had felt like the prodigal daughter, clutched the hand of the man whose care for her echoed that of the prodigal son's father. Patient. Trustworthy. Ever-hopeful.

Her fingers slipped over Matt's, gently pushing past his

knuckles to slide between his until their fingers were threaded together. His breath caught, and the sound snagged her stomach, and she shifted a fraction closer.

"What are you doing?" he murmured.

She barely knew. And even if she did know, she definitely couldn't explain it right now here in church. All she knew was that she now recognized this man was rare, that he was a man she could trust. Impulsive her had once thought she could trust her emotions. Had once thought she could trust a man. And then she'd been proven very, very wrong. But now she had a feeling—no, a *knowing*—that she could trust Matt, and with him she'd be safe.

His hand twisted under hers, then their hands were palm-to-palm, fingers interlaced, his grip strong, like he couldn't believe this either, but had no intention of letting her go.

"Toni," he whispered.

"Shh. He's finishing." She nodded to the front, then as Joel prayed, she closed her eyes.

And thanked God for this unexpected moment. Thanked God that in Matt she had a friend. Thanked God that, just like Joel had preached about, God who knew a person's paths could lead them astray could also lead that stray home. She thanked God for His vast reservoirs of forgiveness, forgiveness that flowed through his followers to people like Joel and Matt. God was so very, very good.

"Amen."

Matt's deeper echo drew open her eyes, and she smiled at his dazed look before releasing his hand as Joel resumed his seat next to Serena.

Breath escaped as John McPherson closed out the service, followed by a round of misgiving. What had she done? Was she raising hopes of a future she hadn't thought all the way through? Whoever she sought to date had to be aware of the long-term consequences. She'd learned that the hard way. Of course, Matt already knew that a future with her meant a future of being Ethan's dad as well. So, this was big. This was huge. This was like a monumental shift in all she'd ever known.

And Matt was one of the good guys. In fact, he might just be the best man that she knew. Solid, trustworthy, caring, kind. So she couldn't lead him on just to drop him. This wasn't something she could let go if it got too difficult, so she would have to work hard to make this work. She needed time to think, they needed time to talk, but as soon as the service finished, she was going to have an already-agreed-to lunch at Serena's. Of course, Joel and Matt would be there too, but so would others, and after her big week, conversation would be centered on her art, not matters of her heart. And right now, knowing her heart—and Matt's—seemed to be the only thing that mattered.

～

FRUSTRATION KNIT with wonder at what had occurred in the sermon before. God forgive him, but his attention hadn't been on Joel's words, but on Joel's sister's actions. Over the past few days he'd noticed a new tension in Toni, the way her gaze seemed to veer between in-depth ponderings of his soul, and times when she'd blush and glance away. You'd think a man who had known a woman for so long would be better schooled in understanding, but she still perplexed him. Some days he thought he'd never understand the depths of Toni and what made her tick. Why had she held his hand?

"So, Matt. How long do you plan to be in Muskoka?" Rachel asked from the comfort of Serena's blue-and-white sofa.

She of the quick and at-times ribald wit, and sharp eyes that reminded him of a red-tailed hawk, looking to select her prey. Which might be doing her a disservice, but previous interactions had proved her comments tended to pick awfully close to the bone.

"I'm not sure yet. My leave was for three weeks, and it's only been ten days." Dr. Ramesh had been kind enough to give him two days post-dated sick leave, which, added to the week and a half he'd spent here meant he'd been absent from work for ten days. He should by all rights have another week off, but where he spent that had been up in the air. Until Toni had held his hand.

He glanced at her, seated across Serena's living room, and Toni's lips curled up one side, lifting his heart, too.

"Matt has been taking painting lessons while he's here," Joel announced.

Serena's glance took him in then veered to Toni. "Is that going well?"

"Yes."

"Is he a good student?" Anna asked, studying Matt.

His smile dimmed. She was the one Joel had once said was on the prowl for a man. The one he'd been paired with at the wedding. He wished she could switch with Toni.

"He's come a long way," Toni said, her gaze intent on his, her smile angled in a way that could almost be described as flirty.

His heart skipped. Did she mean he'd improved with his painting, or in her estimation as a man?

"Muskoka Shores is a great place to get away from it all, isn't it?" Angela McPherson asked. The minister's wife didn't seem privy to some of the undercurrents flowing here.

"I didn't realize just how good it could be for creativity," the author woman—he'd forgotten her name—said. She eyed her doctor boyfriend. "But maybe it's got something to do with the people."

"Maybe," Anna said.

"Especially if someone's a romance author who has found romance," Jackie said dryly, from next to Toni.

He fought a smile at her words. He could understand why Toni liked Jackie. Not only did Jackie seem to have an affinity for young Ethan—even now the baby was nestled on Jackie's lap —her faith in God and practical common sense appealed too. Would appeal to a man who shared similar values, if that man hadn't already been possessed of a passion for a certain creative brunette.

"What can I say? I think James is inspiring," author-woman said, with all the hearts-eyes.

Matt caught Anna's roll of eyes and stifled a laugh within a cough.

"So how are things going for your wedding?" Anna asked Serena, seemingly determined to change the subject.

As Serena answered, he caught Toni's gaze and tilted his head to the kitchen. The open plan design of the home didn't allow for much privacy, but apart from locking themselves in a bathroom or bedroom—not gonna happen, especially after the hormone rush of having Toni see him half-naked yesterday—it was the best they could do.

She dipped her chin, and eased up from her chair. "Who else needs a cup of tea? Serena, you don't mind, do you? No, don't get up. Matt can help me."

"Sure." He smoothed the smile from his face and followed as nonchalantly as he could, leaving the conversation behind as he rounded the corner.

Toni eyed him uncertainly, as he drew closer to where she stood in the kitchen's far corner, near Serena's kettle. "Hi."

"Hi," she said, then dropped her gaze.

He waited—patience was his forte—and drank her in. The glossy dark hair that begged his touch to see if it was as smooth as it looked. The creamy skin with six freckles across her nose. Her peach-colored lips that filled his dreams. She'd always been beautiful to him, even in her nose-pierced, purple-dyed hair, Gothic-makeup days. These days she was softer, as if Ethan and life had smoothed some of the hard edges. Which only made her more appealing.

But at her hesitation, his worries began to mount. What was it she was finding so hard to say?

Finally, she peeked up at him. "I think I like you."

Well, he wasn't expecting that. "I know I like you."

Her mouth curved in a sweet little girl-like grin. "I don't know why."

Neither did he, sometimes. But other times, it was as clear as day. Like that verse which talked about deep calling unto deep. It was like something in him recognized something in her and knew it was meant to be. Which might sound fatalistic, and God knew that Matt had tried to pray it away, but the stubborn hope had remained, and had grown even stronger over the past years. He reached out a hand, and she took it, threading her fingers through his in another heat-inducing encounter.

"So, why do you only think you like me?" he asked before wincing. "Sorry. That makes me sound so arrogant, doesn't it?"

"It would if somebody else said it. But because I know you, I know you're not arrogant."

He gently squeezed her hand. He was holding her hand. He was *holding her hand!* "So, what are you saying?"

"I… I guess I'm saying that I think that you are one of the loveliest men I know, and if you were to ask me to have coffee with you again like you did at New Year's Eve I would say yes."

His heart soared. He tried to rein in the smile sprouting over his face. Couldn't. "Are you saying what I think you're saying?"

Her head tilted, her look was coy. "It depends on what you think I might be saying."

"That you'd go so far as to drink coffee with me?" He grinned, and inched closer.

She laughed, and fresh pleasure filled his chest. "I wouldn't go that far," she murmured. "Let's just say I like you enough to go out for a hot chocolate."

He chuckled. The kettle switched off, the rumble of boiling

water drawing attention to what they were supposed to be doing. Neither of them moved.

"So, when do you want to go have a hot chocolate?" Tomorrow? Today? Right now?

"What are you two talking about in here?" Anna asked. "I heard laughter and—" Her eyes widened as she saw their entwined fingers. "Not you too."

Toni instantly released his hand, and she hurried to her friend. "We were just talking."

"Yeah, I bet I know what about." Anna's flat lips mimicked the line in her forehead.

He didn't want to get into the middle of whatever insecurities Anna had. Not when he might finally be finding a way forward to overcome his own. "How many are we making coffee for?"

Toni hurried from the room and asked the question while he busied himself with collecting cups and mugs from the overhead cabinets, as much to be helpful as to be busy and avoid Anna's accusing stare.

"Five coffees, three black teas, one chai and one green tea," Toni said. "That is, if you two are having coffee."

He nodded, but now the thought of remaining here at Serena's a second longer than necessary was anathema. He wanted nothing more than to take Toni away and finally have the conversation he'd been waiting years to have. Did she really like him? Could they find a way to make this work? What did the future hold? *Lord, what do You want?*

The next hour passed in an agony of hot beverages, conversations, and trying to hide his impatience—and the fact his every sense was tuned into everything Toni said or did or when she moved. *I think I like you.* Those five words held a world of possibility. And his every hope hung on the chance they might finally be able to have that conversation. And have it soon.

. . .

Joel veered around the corner, and shot Matt a look from the driver's seat. He was dropping them back at his house before returning to spend time with Serena. "So, have you given any more thought about what you plan to do?"

Right now? He wanted nothing more than to speak with Toni and then see about—

"With work?" Joel clarified.

Ah. That. His sky-high anticipation at having time with Toni plummeted back to earth. "I guess I should look at the work emails. See what's hit the fan."

"It mightn't be too bad," Toni said encouragingly from the back next to Ethan's car-seat.

He shot her a smile over his shoulder, but wasn't so sure her confidence was well-founded. Tension grew in his gut.

"Hey, Dr. Ramesh said to give yourself time, so if you're not ready then you don't need to look at it. You don't need to worry, okay?" Joel said.

In that case— "Maybe I'll give it a few more days."

"I would," Joel said bluntly. "You might as well make the most of your time away. You'll have to face the music one day, but that needn't be today."

Sure didn't. "Happy to postpone it until next weekend." When he'd arranged with Joel and Wade to go suit shopping. He could revisit his apartment and learn the truth then.

Joel pulled into his drive and Matt helped Toni with a sleeping Ethan and the various pieces of baby equipment. They entered the quiet space, waved goodbye to Joel, then closed the door. Looked at each other and smiled.

"So."

"So," she said, her smile widening. "I might see if I can get this sleepy boy into his cot."

"That sounds like a good idea."

"Then I think I might need to see if we could have a talk."

"That sounds like an even better one."

She smiled. "Maybe you could put the kettle on? Then I could have a hot chocolate."

"Didn't you just have a drink?" he asked.

"Not the drink I really wanted."

The way she studied him left him with that flutter of uncertainty again, just like before when he'd wondered what she'd meant when she'd said something about Matt 'improving.' "I think I'll go switch the kettle on."

"I think that's a great idea."

Her smile chased him around the corner to the kitchen where he exhaled. He so wasn't used to moments heavy with flirtatiousness. He made two hot chocolates, almost jumping as he turned to see Toni standing at the kitchen entry, her shoulder propped against the wall. "Hi."

"Hi." Okay, he officially loved doing this banter with her. "One hot chocolate for mademoiselle."

"With marshmallows?" she said.

"*Naturellement.*"

"Hmm. I think I like it when you speak French to me."

"See, I would do more, but then you preface all these sentences with 'I think,' and while a man doesn't like to admit that he's insecure, when it comes to you, Antonia Wakefield, I'm very insecure."

"It takes a secure man to admit he's insecure."

"I'm glad you think so."

He followed her to the living room, placing his cup on the coffee table to attend to the fire. A few additional pieces of wood managed to bring it back to the dull roar he figured better suited an atmosphere appropriate for this conversation. He collected his cup, hesitating as he wondered where to sit. Then Toni moved to the end of the couch and smiled.

Okay, he might be a newbie at this romance thing, but he recognized that move as an invitation.

He sat, half a meter separating them, which enabled him to shift so he could face her fully. "So."

She grinned, recognizing this game. "So."

"Ethan is down," he said slowly. "You and I are alone."

She nodded.

"So you want to talk?"

She sipped her hot chocolate, her eyes not leaving him. "This is really delicious."

"Some might even say skillfully made."

"I'd definitely say skillfully made," she murmured, her eyes lowering to his chest and moving up again.

He almost choked on his drink. "Do you mean to sound like you're flirting? Because I can't help but hope that what you're saying is stuff you actually mean."

"Are you asking me if I think you're hot?"

"No!" Maybe. "No, I just meant—"

She laughed, a sound that brought ease from his confusion. "I don't know if I should be taking this much pleasure, but I have to admit that I never thought I would be attracted to my brother's best friend."

Did she just say what he thought she said? "You're attracted to me?"

"Maybe. And not just because I saw you without your shirt on, although that was very impressive."

He felt his cheeks heat.

"I don't know why I never paid too much attention before, but now I can't help but see all these wonderful qualities."

"Like my abs?"

She gave another joyous chuckle. "See? You're funny."

"You mean you don't like my abs?"

"And so sweetly insecure. I might hate the word adorable but honestly, it's kind of adorable."

"It's not so adorable on this side of the fence," he grumbled. "You could help a man out by just saying what you mean."

She exhaled heavily, her expression turning serious. "Fine. Matt, I like you. And even though it feels weird, I'd love to think this," she gestured between them, "is something we can explore."

He barely dared breathe as she continued.

"I think—no, I *regard* you as my friend, and I wouldn't want to do anything to jeopardize that. And because of Ethan, I don't want to get too attached to someone who is going to break my heart."

"I won't break your heart," he promised hoarsely.

"You say that, and I'm pretty sure you never would, but I guess my real concern is that I'm far more likely to break yours. And I could never forgive myself for hurting you in that way."

The atmosphere which had felt so buoyant just moments earlier grew weighty. He placed his cup on the coffee table and picked up her hand. "Toni, I like you, and I suspect you know that I wanted to explore this," he gestured between them, "for years. You know me. You know I'm a patient man, and we can go as slow as you like."

"No six-week engagement for you then?"

"I'd marry you in six minutes if I could," he admitted.

Her eyes widened. "You don't mean that."

Maybe not. It might've just been a rush of blood to the head. But— "I would like a future with you, and I'm happy to take it slow. We don't have to kiss, or do anything more than hold hands if you like. I know things with Ethan make it a little more challenging, but that doesn't mean it's impossible."

Her gaze fell to their joined hands. "So you could cope with being the father of someone else's baby?"

Wow. So they'd reached this point at last. "I could. I'd more than cope. It would be a privilege. Ethan is so sweet, a reflection of you."

"I'm not sweet," she muttered, still not looking up. "I did things I shouldn't have."

He squeezed her hands, willing her to push aside the unworthiness he knew she'd struggled with in the past. "You know God has forgiven you."

She nodded.

"You know I'm not perfect either."

Her gaze lifted. "Sure you're not."

"Okay, I'm pretty close"—she laughed, as he'd hoped—"not."

"See? You're so nice, and I just go around thinking mean things all the time."

"Well, it can't be all the time because you've said some pretty nice things to me today."

"Some people make it easy."

"That's true," he said, looking deeply at her.

She pinked, but this time held his gaze.

The world had shrunk to just the two of them. Nothing else mattered. And his world felt like it teetered on whatever she might say next.

"Did I ever tell you about Bryant?"

His mouth dried. "No." But he suspected he knew who this was.

"Bryant… is Ethan's father," she said in a low voice. "I don't know if he knows he has a son. I never told him, and his name is not on Ethan's birth certificate."

His breath held as she bit her lip and looked down again, and he prayed for her, and that he'd cope with whatever she'd say next.

"Bryant was an art professor at my college. He was married but he told me they were divorced. I don't know what it was, maybe it was the fact my parents had just died in that car crash, or the fact he seemed to like my art, that he liked me, and he was my ideal of what a handsome man should be, but whatever. I fell for him, and thought he'd fallen for me."

His heart ached for her, and truth be told, for himself as well. If only she'd seen Matt's own liking for her. If only he'd fitted her idea of what a handsome man should be.

"When I told him I was pregnant he wanted nothing to do with me. I felt so unworthy and unlovely, then people at church made comments, then Joel got the job here and we moved." She released his hands and flicked away a tear. "But through it all, you stayed by my side, you've always been so encouraging and kind and patient, even when I've treated you so badly." She glanced up, her eyes were red. "I'm sorry for not seeing you when I should have."

"Hey, it's okay."

She shook her head, wiping her cheek. "Oh, I hate crying. I love Serena like a sister, but man, she's so emotional all the time."

He shifted closer to her, repossessing her hands again. "You don't ever have to be embarrassed with me. You can cry or not cry, it's okay."

"See? You're so good to me and I don't deserve it."

"You do," he assured. "You are special. You've always been special, Toni."

Her eyes welled, and he couldn't help but open his arms and draw her close.

The feel of her, tucked here under his chin, her curves against his hard chest, made him draw her closer still, as he smoothed a hand over her soft hair while he continued to pray for her. To pray she'd find healing, wholeness, peace, and that she would know—really *know*—God's forgiveness that meant she could forgive herself too.

Her confession felled other long-burning questions to the floor. He didn't need to know how many times, whether Bryant had been her first, or anything else. She was repentant, she'd been forgiven, and although some might not think it his place, he'd forgiven her too.

He closed his eyes, leaned his cheek against her fragrant hair, and savored this special moment. Life might have knocked them both around, but there were pockets of peace to be treasured too. And this was a moment he'd never forget.

He didn't know how long they stayed there in each other's arms. Long enough that the skies grew dim, and the fire grew low, and eventually Ethan made his feelings known.

Toni sighed, and eased away. Her face wore peace, contentment he'd prayed to see. Her smile was weary but still held tease. "Are you sure you want to get involved with us?"

"I'd like nothing more," he assured. And lifted her hand and pressed it to his lips.

CHAPTER 11

The next five days passed in a whirl of happy disbelief. She could barely comprehend what had happened last Sunday, that her impulsive hand-holding had led to this new sunshiney promise of hope for the future. This week had seen a carnival of shared meals and conversations and hand-holding amid more art lessons and the thrill of painting sales. And now, Toni and Anna accompanied Serena as she drove to the city to organize dresses while Jackie minded Ethan. Joel and Matt were driving in a separate car to find suits with Wade.

She glanced across at Serena, wondering just how much she knew. Toni didn't think that Anna had said anything about the hand-holding, but maybe Serena already suspected. If only she could be brave enough to tell her brother the truth. He'd been in his own happy whirl that she couldn't be sure he'd noticed the lengthy gazes and smiles shared between his best friend and his sister.

Serena grinned at her, before glancing at Anna in the back-seat. "You doing okay there, Anna?"

"I'm fine."

Her voice didn't exactly match her words. Apparently,

Serena thought so too, as she exchanged glances with Toni before asking Anna, "Are you sure?"

"Look, I'm happy for you. Really, I am," Anna said, her voice wavering. "It's just hard, you know, to watch everyone falling in love around me, where I'm stuck feeling all alone."

"You're not alone," Toni reassured.

"Yeah, it always seems to be the paired-up ones who are saying that."

"Paired up?" Serena glanced at Toni, one eyebrow raised.

Darn. How to explain…

"Are you and Matt together?" Serena asked.

"No." Not *together* together, anyway.

"But I thought I saw you two holding hands," Anna objected.

This immediately swung Serena's attention back to Toni. Ouch. Now it sounded like she'd just lied. "Look, we're friends, and I, uh, well, might've started to see him slightly differently, and enjoyed spending time with him. But it's not like we've kissed." A kiss on the hand or on her hair didn't count.

Was it her imagination or did Serena's shoulders ease like she might be a mite relieved?

"Would it be a problem if we had?" Toni asked.

"He's a good guy," Serena said. "He just has some things he's working through at the moment, so it's probably not the right time."

"I thought Matt was on sick leave," Anna said. "Although he never actually looked too sick to me."

"He's, um, had a bit going on lately," Serena said, with another look at Toni.

Toni nodded. "He goes back to work next week, so he's actually going to be staying here in the city." She glanced at Serena. "So I appreciate your kind invitation to stay at your house, but it won't be necessary just yet."

Serena nodded. Wait, that definitely was relief washing over her features. Was she that worried about Toni? Uncertainty stabbed at her. Did Serena expect Toni to have another 'moral failing' after giving birth to the proof of her prior lapse? Her heart, her chin fell. She should have expected it. Her previous church here in the city had been full of people who had judged Toni for having a baby outside marriage. She bet they would've judged her more if she'd had an abortion. But it was funny how some sins always seem to earn more judgement than others. Rare were those who judged others for gluttony, while drinking alcohol and smoking always seemed to get a bad rap. One of the problems with sex outside of marriage was that it sometimes led to a consequence you couldn't hide away too easily. Although some might say the same about over-eating. But the way she read her Bible, sin was sin, and everyone had fallen short of God's standard. But the Bible also promised that forgiveness was forgiveness, so when she'd repented, God had restored her relationship with Him. But while forgiveness was available for all sins, the consequences were not uniform. And she suspected dealing with gluttony by losing weight might be a lot easier than dealing with the lifelong consequence of having a child…

"Are you okay?" Serena asked Toni. "You got awfully serious-looking just then."

"I'm fine." She pasted on a grin. "Just thinking about today."

They soon arrived at the boutique, and the morning passed in a glittering distraction of dresses and trying on outfits. Victoria, Serena's friend, and wedding dress boutique owner, had received very precise specifications about what Serena wanted in a wedding gown, but when she took in Serena's new measurements she was alarmed.

"Girl, you have to stop losing weight. You've only got a few weeks until the wedding so don't go losing anymore, okay?"

Serena laughed. "First time in a long time that I've been told to stop losing weight."

"You are eating though, aren't you?" Victoria asked.

"I've had a bit going on with work and wedding arrangements," Serena admitted.

Including helping Toni with all that had needed doing with the opening of the art gallery. Guilt wove between Toni's sips of water. Was she supposed to have checked that Serena was doing okay? She was doing okay, though. Wasn't she?

Later, while they enjoyed lunch at the Gaugin, a restaurant in a mock Tudor building that specialized in high teas, Anna glanced at Toni. "If you wanted, you could always partner Matt. I'm sure Serena and Joel wouldn't mind."

Toni cut Serena a look, saw the surprise, which only solidified her response. "It's okay." She had no desire to make things any more complicated for Serena than she already had. "I don't want any changes made for me."

"I don't mind," Serena said after a pause.

Misgiving struck with that pause. Yeah, 'I don't mind' was very different to 'if Anna doesn't mind then I'd love you to consider it!'

"I'm very happy to keep arrangements as they are," Toni said firmly.

Call her crazy, but it seemed Serena relaxed a little more. Her stomach tensed. The vibe between her and her soon-to-be sister-in-law seemed off. Or was that just paranoia speaking?

Insecurities continued to eat into the afternoon, so the day wasn't as wonderful as she had hoped, and by the time they met the guys for dinner that night things seemed to have spiraled even further out of control.

It wasn't helped by the fact that Wade had brought his wife, which left Anna at the table without a partner. It didn't help either that Anna made several references to her single state throughout the night, including bemoaning the fact that there probably was no point having a Galentine's dinner if everyone was coupling up.

This comment immediately brought Joel's attention to Toni,

and he glanced between her and Matt, his eyes widening. "Are you—? No. Really?"

Was that shock or gladness in his voice? "We're friends," Toni insisted, with a sideways glance at Matt. Anything more than that could not really be assumed. Not until he kissed her. And she didn't really want to be pressuring him into a situation he might feel uncomfortable with. Especially now she knew some people had misgivings about Toni's morality.

"Okay, well, if that changes, then you need to let me know, okay?" Joel said.

Matt's gaze was heavy on her skin, and her stomach twisted at the confusion she saw in his eyes. She'd just need to get a moment to talk to him about this, to explain. She was suddenly very glad they'd decided to take things slow and keep things on the down-low.

Toni caught Wade's speculation, the way his wife leaned close to him and whispered in his ear, before glancing at Toni and offering a little smile. Toni's returned smile felt as fake as a Kardashian photo, and she ducked her head to pretend interest in her food again. But she had no real desire to eat. She was only hungry to talk with Matt, and somehow try to explain away the words that seem to have caused the hurt look in his eye. She didn't like being someone who upset him.

Wade settled back in his chair, slung an arm around his wife. "So how are you feeling about next week and going back to work?" he asked Matt, as Anna talked with Joel and Serena.

"It'll be what it will be," he said, shrugging.

Toni offered Matt a reassuring smile, which ticked one corner of his mouth up. She was tempted to reach under the table and hold his hand to encourage him.

"Hmm. Well, I'm glad you've had Joel to babysit you."

Toni blinked. What had Wade just said?

Matt's lips had flattened. His gaze was on his plate. He pushed it away, his hands clenched into fists.

Regrets gnawed, coupled with offense on his behalf. "I think you mistake the matter, Wade." Ice was in her voice. "Matt is extremely capable."

"Whoa." Wade looked amused. "Calm down."

Calm down? What was it about a man saying that to a woman that made her want to scream? "Excuse me?"

"Look, I'm not disputing that Matt is capable," Wade protested.

"Weren't you? It sure sounded like it to me." By now the conversation at the other end of the table had ceased, and she grew conscious that everyone was listening to her.

"Toni? Are you all right?" Serena asked.

"Is everything okay?" Joel asked.

Toni glanced at Matt. He didn't look at her. Her heart dropped.

Toni pushed back her chair. "Excuse me. I just need to go powder my nose."

She collected her bag and made her unsteady way to the bathroom, locking the cubicle's door before sitting down on the toilet lid. Okay, this was getting ridiculous. She had no desire to start a conflict about stupid things, but everything was making her feel antsy. What was wrong with her that she was feeling so quick to find offence and pick a fight? Matt was a big boy. He could take care of himself. And he might not like her stepping into his own battles. Maybe after the last few weeks with all its highs and lows she needed to have a big sleep. Like for several days. Or weeks. Then maybe she'd stop misreading things.

She exhaled, stood, and slowly opened the door, coming to an abrupt pause at the sight of Serena standing opposite. "Hi."

"Hi." Serena's brow knit. "Is everything okay?"

Fake smile. "Yep!"

"You've just seemed a little, I don't know, a little distant, and I wanted to make sure that we're okay."

"I'm fine," Toni said, with perhaps a tiny excess emphasis on the *I'm*.

"Are you?"

Are you? She wanted to ask Serena, but figured she'd done enough to cause tension on the bride-to-be's day that she didn't need to add any more.

"I wanted to ask before, but not in front of Anna or Joel. Um, are you and Matt a couple?"

Toni swallowed. Admitting this to Serena when she hadn't even admitted it to Joel felt a little weird. "Like I said before, we're friends and we're taking things slow as we get to know each other more."

"That's wise," Serena said, with a smile that was more like the big sister expression Toni knew her for. "I want you to be happy, and I think Matt would be a great husband—"

"Wait, we're not talking about that."

"But if you're willing to take this step, surely that's got to be the next one."

Whoa. This conversation had suddenly gotten way too real and serious for a restaurant washroom. "I'll let you know if anything changes," she promised. "But I've been here so long I'm pretty sure people will start thinking I've got tummy trouble if I stay any longer."

"Hmm. Okay. Well. If my tummy could look as good as yours after a baby then I'd be a very happy woman."

Yeah, but she hadn't seen the stretch marks that decorated Toni's skin. "But Victoria might not be," she countered, as they returned to the table.

Conversation continued over dessert, but Toni couldn't help but notice Matt's smile seemed less frequent and had dimmed. He seemed to have pulled into himself again, not holding her gaze, not holding eye contact with anyone for very long. Her heart hurt for him.

The night seemed to be winding to a close, and still she

hadn't had a chance to get him alone and see if he was all right. But with Anna, Serena, Joel, and Toni having a two hour drive ahead of them she knew she had to do it soon. But how to do so without causing more unnecessary speculation?

She waited, watching him, until his gaze flicked up to meet hers again. She smiled, tilting her head toward the bar area, where she had noticed some couches next to a long fish tank. She raised her eyebrows and put some extra curl into her smile.

His lips curved on one side and he nodded.

"Well, before we go, I'm going to check out the cool fish tank I saw near the bar."

"Since when do you like fish?" Joel asked.

She pretended not to hear him, hurrying away, hoping that Matt had understood her invitation. She reached the bar and found a leather sofa, sinking onto it as her fingers tapped the cool leather as she waited, waited...

"Hey."

She glanced up, smiling. Then her smile dropped away.

Before her stood a man. A man she'd hoped she'd never see again.

Bryant.

~

"I'll be back in a moment," Matt muttered, choosing to over-look Wade's snigger and comment, "Do you think he likes fish too?"

He hurried to the bar area, thankful to finally get the opportunity to talk to Toni. Today hadn't been as much fun as he had hoped. Between Wade's pointed comments and Joel's distraction, Matt felt unprepared to return to his normal life. He didn't want to return to work. He didn't even want to have to think about work. But Wade had barely let up about it all day.

And maybe it was immature of him to want to put it off, but

time in Muskoka Shores had helped him see things in a different light. And he didn't want to be the man he had been before, consumed by work, his life controlled by email and text messages. Having time to sit, to think, to create, to feel, had revealed this life he would soon re-enter would be way more challenging than he'd imagined before.

He drew close to the bar area then pulled up sharply as he caught Toni with a man. A man whose black man-bun and raffish air screamed of tortured artist or rock musician. His heart thudded. Her ex?

Toni pushed up from her spot on the sofa and brushed past the man, who turned to watch her, then seemed to notice Matt watching him. He raised his thick eyebrows in a "You got something to say?" look then turned away.

Matt pivoted to follow Toni but she'd been swallowed up in their crowd which had apparently decided to leave. Wait. He still needed to find out who that guy was. And to clarify what she'd really meant by the 'we're friends' comment. Had she told Joel the truth about their relationship? They'd discussed this, and Toni had said she needed time, but now it felt a little like she wasn't sure anymore. Which left him dangling in the wind, filled with uncertainty. One minute she was standing up for him with her fiery defense in front of Wade; the next she was avoiding him. And it had been so long since he'd had any kind of real relationship with a girl that wasn't just in his head that he didn't really know what to do. And now, with everyone surrounding them, it wasn't like he had a chance to talk to her, let alone give her the goodbye he'd imagined before they'd part for a week until his return to Muskoka next weekend.

"Hey," he moved beside her amid the hubbub of conversations, "we need to talk."

"I know," she said, glancing around. "But it's a bit hard now."

Their wedding-party huddle was moving closer to the door.

"Are you okay?" she murmured, touching his hand.

Electricity sparked between them. "I'm fine," he fibbed. "You?" *Who was that man?* he longed to ask. Didn't.

"I'm good," she murmured, before farewells began.

He was being palmed off to Wade, who would take him back to his apartment so he could face the fun of three weeks' worth of missed emails. Emails he had zero desire to deal with. And after Wade's 'babysitting' comment, had little desire to be with him either. Wade mightn't have meant it to sound like a slur, but Toni's reaction had shown Matt wasn't the only one offended. Which led him to hope she felt more deeply than her lack of eye contact tonight had indicated.

"It's been great getting to know you more this past little while," Serena said, giving him a hug.

"Thanks for letting me steal some of Joel's attention," he managed, before turning to Anna and offering her a hand. But no, she apparently wanted her own hug too, which he hurried through, before Joel clasped him in a bear hug.

Hugs weren't really Matt's thing. His mom always used to say physical touch wasn't Matt's love language, whatever that meant. But he'd endured it with Joel, knowing that was part of his best friend's touchy-feely personality.

"Thanks for all you've done," he muttered.

"Any time," Joel said, pulling back, eyeing him seriously. "And I mean that."

"I know. I appreciate it."

Joel nodded, which left one last person to say goodbye to. One last person who he'd barely spoken to all night, despite her being the only one he'd wanted to. He hated how this made him feel like such a wuss, even if she was the one who'd insisted on taking things slow. But now, after having Toni agree to his dreams, his heart plummeted at the thought he wouldn't see her tomorrow, wouldn't be able to take her hand, meet her smile.

He opened his arms and she hugged him. Okay, so hugging might not be his love language, but hugging Toni certainly was a language he wanted to explore. Touching her sent his nerve endings into a frenzy, like he was ice and she was heat and he might melt completely. "I'll miss you," he whispered as he bent to her ear.

"I'll miss you too," she murmured, her hair ticking his chin.

He wanted to hold her forever, but five pairs of eyes were watching, and no doubt wondering, so he had to pull back. "Thanks for teaching me to paint."

"Thanks for being a great student," she returned, with a smile that might just hold a touch of sadness.

"Say hi to Ethan for me."

"Will do."

He exhaled, as she was ushered away toward Serena's car. Conversation at dinner had revealed that Toni would drive Serena's car back to Muskoka and take Anna with her, while Joel would drive Serena to her house so they could spend the two hour drive together. So, if Toni was driving that meant it would take even longer before Matt could call her. Or text her. Or FaceTime her. How did people cope before digital technology?

"You like her," Wade observed, as they waved goodbye to the two vehicles.

"Like Serena?" he asked, purposely choosing obtuseness.

Which apparently didn't go down too well as Wade rolled his eyes. "Toni."

"Well, yeah," he said, veering onto another tack. "Don't you?"

Wade gestured to his own vehicle, a late model Mercedes. "Well, yeah. She's nice and all. But you need to be careful, man. You don't want to get hurt by letting yourself get mixed up with someone who's got a lot of baggage."

"Baggage?"

"She's got a kid. Do you really want to be daddy to another man's baby?"

Was that the man he'd spied at the restaurant not an hour ago?

"Well?" Wade prodded.

"I like Ethan and I wouldn't ever want to hurt Toni by making her think I was judging her."

Wade's breath hissed inward, and Matt realized he'd said that last bit aloud.

"Hey, look, I don't think you need to worry about me and Toni. Like she said before, we're friends, so let's just leave it at that."

"Huh. The fact you feel the need to explain says it's way more than just that, but okay. Anyway, you need to get your head back into thinking about the future and about work."

Work. His spirits sank again.

Wade dropped his wife at home then accompanied Matt to his apartment. It felt strange to be back after so long. He was used to it after some of the longer trips he took, but the last time he'd taken time for a vacation was nearly a decade ago. No wonder his mental health had struggled.

But even though this building might be sought after, with a doorman, good security, and parking, it didn't feel like home anymore. Instead its height and breadth seemed to overwhelm him, like he was in some kind of prison.

He got in the elevator, and he and Wade reached the seventeenth floor. They got out and he saw Dan and Sarah Walton exit the other elevator. Judging from the hockey jersey with her husband's name on it, Dan had likely been playing in a game. Judging from their smiles, the Leafs had won.

"Matt!" Sarah's smile took on an extra layer of delight. "How are you? We haven't seen you for a while. Has everything been okay?"

He nodded, murmuring something about being in Muskoka, which drew her sigh. "I can't wait to go back. I just love Muskoka. But I bet it's cold though, huh?"

He smiled at the Aussie. "It's summer back in Australia, isn't it?"

"Yes. And perfect beach weather." She shot her husband a grin. "It's a good thing there are *some* things I love here."

"Just as well," Dan said, before unlocking his door. "Good to see you, Matt." He nodded to Wade. "See you around."

"Have a good night," Sarah called.

Matt nodded, and unlocked his own.

The space was dark, and had a musty odor from being shut up for so long. He flicked on lights, and Wade moved to the dining table where his laptop had stayed switched off these past three weeks. The reality of what he was about to face knotted his stomach, chasing the light-hearted encounter of moments ago far, far away. Would it be a demand from his bosses to face up to a disciplinary committee? Would he be discharged for violation of firm compliance policies?

"You ready?" Wade asked, as Matt retrieved his phone.

He studied it, this device he'd once considered as essential as a second brain. While he'd had his phone in his possession over the past weeks, Joel and Wade had ensured he'd turned off all notifications. Switching it back on would be the first taste of all that he'd missed. He went to settings, switched on notifications, and winced as 621 new emails pinged for attention. Winced again as he saw new messages, missed calls. Weight crashed onto his shoulders, sending him to his couch. No. He didn't want to open these. He wanted to be back in Muskoka, back with Toni, back where life was easy and he felt free.

"You all right there, bud?" Wade asked.

"There's over six hundred emails."

"Six hundred? That's insane."

Maybe not so insane if every employee had replied. Coupled with the usual plethora of work and other things meant six hundred might be tame. He glanced through, wincing at the subject lines.

"Want me to take a look?"

"Please." Matt handed Wade the phone. "I'd love it if you deleted anything that doesn't look essential."

Wade's head tilted to the computer. "Are your emails synced?"

"Yeah."

"Okay. Then let's do this."

Matt spent the next few minutes with his head in his hands, gazing out at the night time city view. Every so often Wade's breath hitched and Matt wondered what he'd just read. His spam filters were usually pretty good but who knew what had slipped by in the last few weeks?

After what seemed an age Wade looked up. "Okay, I think we're down to just over a hundred."

"Awesome."

Wade chuckled. "You're a popular man."

"Anything that's really important?" He braced. "Go on. Hit me with it."

"Okay," Wade sighed. "Your boss and HR person wish to see you ASAP. Some guy called Michael wants you to call him. And there were about a dozen messages from a guy called Ray."

"Were?"

"I whittled them down to two." Wade grinned. "You can thank me later."

He nodded. "So, from what you read, does it seem like I still have a job or has that ship sailed?"

"I think the sick leave certificate from Dr. Ramesh bought you some time, but it appears that if you don't show up on Monday then there are threats of legal consequences."

Hmm, Matt had a feeling that legal consequences were about to get extremely messy. There was no coming back from the email he'd sent to all employees.

"I'm sorry it's not better news."

"It's okay. It's better than what I expected, which was a termination."

Wade's features pulled to one side. "Yeah, judging from what I read you might need to be aware that that still seems like an option. So, what do you want me to do?"

Rewind the clock twenty-one days? But if he did that, then Toni and Matt might never have had a chance…

He pushed back his shoulders. "Hey, you've gone over and beyond in helping me. I don't want to ask you to do more."

"Dude, you're my friend. Of course I'm gonna help you."

Stupid emotion tickled the backs of his eyeballs. Thank God for Wade's friendship – and his experience in HR.

"And hey, you may well find that it's not as bad as what you thought. The company still has to be seen to be acting professionally, even if some of the employees are not exactly professional. I wouldn't think this is necessarily a case of automatic termination," he said kindly.

"No, they're probably going to wait until they can 'restructure' the company and then make my position redundant." Matt had seen that happen before. How to get rid of the underperforming team members: Tell them to improve X, Y and Z or face the consequences as part of the performance management, or look for a way to restructure which meant telling a team member they were consolidating roles and their role was superfluous at this time, only to create a new role several months down the track. They might deal with ethics, but there were still ways of skirting around the truth.

"Do you want to keep working with Sage anyway?" Wade asked curiously.

"I don't know. I don't like how they've managed this, and I don't like feeling like I have zero down time, and the company owns my life."

"You know they don't," Wade said.

"That's the other thing. I hate that I haven't created the

personal boundaries that I need, and I feel like if I just go straight back into it, those boundaries between work and home life are just gonna erode again. And that just makes me feel even more weak."

"Hey, you're not in this by yourself. God is with you, remember?"

He nodded.

Thank God it was Sunday tomorrow. He'd need a day to be refueled with faith before facing the challenges of work on Monday.

CHAPTER 12

"Come, let us take a moment to pray."

Toni bowed her head as John McPherson prayed, his words a soothing balm over the stinging ache within.

Ever since yesterday morning her heart was a playground of chaos, confusion, and questions, her insecurities piling up and tumbling over each other. And that was all before she'd seen Bryant. Shock had meant she'd barely said a word to him, that she'd barely said a word to Matt even though she could tell he was as confused as she was. She hadn't even admitted to Joel that she'd seen Bryant, either. Secrets, the past, the way memories had been stirred, kept reminding her that she would never be good enough for Matt, and that it wouldn't take much for him to know the truth about Bryant. Then this brief moment of happiness would be snatched away.

She needed God to help her.

"...and so we give our concerns to you, Lord, and lay them at the foot of the cross, and we thank You that You are trustworthy and Your love for us is real. And just like it says in Philippians 'that in everything, with prayer and petition, with thanksgiving, we present our request to you. And the peace of God that transcends all understanding will guard your heart, and our minds, and the knowledge and love of Jesus Christ'. So we thank You for Your peace, and assurance that You have our paths in Your hands. Amen."

"Amen," she echoed, keeping her eyes down.

That's right. God didn't want her carrying her burdens. That was what Jesus had died for. And following Him meant trusting Him, which meant laying down those things that got in the way.

The service continued, as did her worries, but now, each time they taunted and teased she committed them to God, praying for Him to deal with those situations. There was so much that was simply impossible for her to manage, but she knew that with God all things were possible.

Joel nudged her as the last song began and she joined the congregation in standing and singing the words of faith and devotion. She noticed the song was by Sarah Maguire, the singer who'd married Dan Walton last year, who had bought one of her paintings. Her heart beat a little faster, like God was reminding her of His faithfulness. *See?* The song seemed to be saying. *You might be worried, but I am the Lord, and I'm still your provider, able to open doors to employment, to friendships, to finances, able to do all kinds of good things. You can trust Me.*

She *could* trust Him. She knew that. God had proved his faithfulness time and time again.

She joined in the words of the song: "And we can trust Him, we can trust him with it all. Yeah!"

The words became a prayer Toni sang aloud, her words matching those penned by Sarah for this song, the "yeah!" at the end emphasizing their trust like a musical Amen.

John ended the service, encouraging them to be a blessing to their world. The bands across her chest had eased, her heart feeling lighter as the crowd broke into groups of chatter on the way to the hall for coffee and snacks.

"So, how did things go yesterday?" Rachel asked.

"Yesterday? Oh, dress shopping? Yeah, all good. I got one, and shoes."

"Details, please. What's your dress look like?"

"Peach-colored, satiny. It has a bow on the shoulder."

"Ooh, sounds classy. Can't wait to see it."

"I bet you'll look amazing," Jackie said.

Toni studied her. Jackie really was one of the most generous-hearted women Toni knew. "Are you sure you're okay about me being a bridesmaid when you're not?"

"I'm totally okay," she assured. "Really, Anna was always Serena's best friend through school, and you're like Serena's little sister, so it makes sense for you to be a bridesmaid. Anyway, if I'm honest, I'm not a fan of the spotlight, so I'm glad that all I need to do is a Bible reading and not have to try and look pretty all day."

"Because some people don't have to try?" Toni teased.

Jackie's lips quirked. "And hey, if it means I get to hold Ethan, well, I'm a fan."

It was funny how Jackie rarely talked about her love life, or lack of, unlike Anna, but she seemed so eager to have a family of her own. "Would you like to have a baby?"

Jackie shrugged. "One day. But you need a man for that, and there aren't too many on the horizon, so I'm content being Aunty Jackie for my friends." She grinned. "Plus, that means I get to hand them back at the end of the day."

"You know I appreciate all you do with Ethan."

"I know."

They soon found the others, and it turned out that Joel and James had arranged to visit Golden Elms together, which left Staci at loose ends. "You could all come to our place for lunch," Toni offered.

"Oh, but you have your baby," Staci objected.

"Yes, which is why it'd be good for him to have a quieter day at home before he goes back to the resort daycare tomorrow."

"How is that going?" Rachel asked.

"It's great. Vera is lovely, and really good with him. The job is such a blessing."

"You have Serena to thank for that."

That was true. What had been going on yesterday that made her doubt Serena's friendship? "Serena is the best."

"Did I hear my name?" Serena asked.

"We're talking about you, not to you," Rachel teased. "And we want to hear all about yesterday's dress hunt, so we're going to Toni's for lunch."

"We are?" Serena asked.

"We are," Toni confirmed.

"Want us to bring something?"

Toni thought about what was currently in their fridge and pantry. "Yeah, maybe if everyone brings something to share, we'll see what we end up with."

"Ooh, like a pot-luck," Staci said. "I'm still getting used to how small towns work."

"I don't think this is just a small-town concept," Rachel objected.

"And it doesn't have to be home-cooked. Just grab something from the grocery store, that'll do." Toni put up her hand. "I'm the first to admit I don't have Serena's hospitality skills, but it would be fun to gather together."

An hour later, the house she shared with Joel was filled with noise and laughter, the sound she hadn't heard since New Year's Eve. It was good to have the distraction, to have the comments and queries flying around as a reminder that the world was bigger than the questions that resided in her head.

They caught up, sharing about the last few weeks. Staci was writing another book: "It's my first real foray into Christian romance, and I have to say, it's pretty awesome to include the God stuff, like prayers and things that are important to me, too."

Rachel's boys and Jemima were back in school, leaving

Rachel free to help with the financial side of things with her husband Damian's construction business.

Jackie was keeping busy with her part-time job of creating several website designs for local businesses. "Which is awesome, because I love supporting stores in Muskoka Shores."

And Anna was—as ever—focused on boy troubles. "I hear all your stories and I just don't think there's any point in doing a Galentine's event this year."

"Galentine's?" Staci asked.

Jackie explained about the event for single ladies to celebrate on Valentine's Day.

"Oh. Yeah, I've been to a few of them in my time," Staci admitted, "but we called it something different. But why couldn't you still do it?"

"Because it'd only be me and Jackie."

Staci's gaze slipped to Toni. "Have you got a boyfriend?"

"Me?" Who else here didn't know? Judging from the curious looks, it would seem most of them. "Not really," she mumbled.

"Not really?" Anna asked. "What about Matt?"

She shrugged. "We're friends."

"Friends?" Anna snorted. "Yeah, I sure wouldn't mind a *friend* who looked at me the way Matt looks at you."

Serena had stilled and was watching Toni carefully. "I thought you said…"

"We're just friends," she insisted. "And now he's moved back to the city, and I'm here, and that's that."

"Long distance would really suck," Staci murmured, her brow lowered, as if she was imagining her own situation with James.

"See? So, there's no reason for anyone to start imagining things. And if it wasn't for me having to look after Ethan I'd say you could probably count me in for a Galentine's Day event as well."

Because Matt wouldn't really want to come all this way on a

weeknight, would he? Not if he had to turn around and return to the city for work the next day. Besides, they'd agreed on only holding hands. Doing something like Valentine's Day suggested a depth to their relationship she didn't think they were at. Yet.

That last word swirled butterflies through her stomach, as she imagined just what it would be like to be secure in a relationship with Matt. To know his kiss. To know his love. Her breath caught.

"You okay?" Jackie asked her.

"I'm fine." She pasted on a smile. "Now, who's ready for a cup of tea?"

LATER, AFTER THE OTHERS had gone home and she'd switched on Netflix to watch a mindless romance, her thoughts kept swinging to Matt. How was he getting on? How was he feeling about going back to work tomorrow? The speculation raised by the girls only increased the concerns already residing within her heart. Oh, why was this so hard? She could just text him, and stop the cycle of worry.

Hey, just thought I'd see how you are. How was church? How are you? How are you feeling about tomorrow? She pressed send.

A minute later her phone pinged its reply. *Good. Great. Okay. Nervous.*

She smiled at the characteristic reply, her heart snagging on his last word. Joel might be openly affectionate, but he wasn't one for admitting his nerves. In fact, she'd rarely seen him be vulnerable. She sensed this wasn't something Matt admitted to many people, if at all.

The fact he was on his phone, and she was on hers, but they were only messaging, not talking spurred her to press his number. Then smile as he answered the call.

"I was wondering how long we'd text before deciding it's just easier to call," she said.

"I'm always happy to talk with you," he said. "Especially after the past two weeks when it's felt like we've talked so much."

"Right? It feels weird that you're there and I'm here. I... I miss you."

"I miss you too."

His voice held a rasp that drew new warmth inside. Judging from that rasp, it seemed he did.

"So, what happens tomorrow?"

He explained about Wade helping him sift through his emails to find the most relevant ones. "So I'm about to sort through those, but then you messaged, and to be honest, I'd much rather talk to you than deal with them."

"I'll be praying for you, that it goes better than you think."

"Thank you."

Silence throbbed between them, as she wondered what else to say. How to explain about her weird behavior at the restaurant last evening?

Maybe just say it. "I, uh, I'm sorry I didn't get much of a chance to talk to you last night."

"Hey, it was hectic. I get that."

What should she say? 'I bumped into my ex and was so shocked I didn't know what to say about it.' Was it even necessary to say something? Matt could ask if he really wanted to know. Couldn't he?

"Do you think you'll be heading up this way again?" she asked instead.

"I'd like to, but I probably need to see how things go at work this week," he said, his tone holding apology.

"Of course. And I totally understand if it means you're really busy there for a while. Not that I don't want you to come and visit us, but I don't want you to feel pressured, or add any more pressure to your life."

"You're really thoughtful."

Not really. But she'd take it. It felt strange to have a man she admired compliment her.

"So, you'll let me know how things go at work tomorrow?"

"For sure. I imagine there will be quite a lot to sort out, and it might take quite some time, so if I take a while to get back to you, you'll need to forgive me."

"Of course. Like I said, no pressure. And if you don't get back to me tomorrow then that's okay too."

He sighed.

"What?"

"You make this very difficult."

"Make what very difficult?"

"This not seeing you. You say things like that, and all I want to do is hold you and hug you, and…"

She swallowed her suddenly dry mouth. "And what?"

"And kiss you."

She closed her eyes, as her imagination leapt into a fantasy where Matt was kissing her, holding her, his lips on hers as he—

"Matt," she whispered.

"Toni."

"Don't stay away too long."

"I won't."

Ethan's cry rent the air. "I'd better go, but I'll be praying for you regarding tomorrow, okay?"

"Thank you."

They said their goodbyes, and she went to pick up Ethan from his nap, holding him close to her chest, as her heart and mind twirled with the possibility of Matt's lips on hers. Oh, yes. *Please, God.*

⁓

"MATT. THANK YOU FOR COMING."

Matt nodded, and took the seat in Helen Welkin's office. The head of HR—or the 'company culture' office, as they liked to call it here—was not without compassion. The way she'd filed his mental health break under sick leave was proof of that.

"I'm just waiting for Lee to get here." She gestured to the fridge which contained bottles of water.

Matt shook his head.

"How are you?"

"You mean after my brain snap and near breakdown?" He shrugged. "I don't know. It was good to get away, it really helped clarify some things, but a lot depends on what happens now."

She nodded. "Where did you go?"

"Muskoka. Spent some time with a friend who lives in Muskoka Shores."

"Nice part of the world."

"For sure."

Small talk turned to business as Lee Drake walked in. Matt rose, shook his hand, and settled back straighter in his chair.

"How are you?" Lee asked Matt.

The man was businesslike to a fault. Best Matt answer accordingly. "Better."

Lee nodded, steepling his fingers. "I probably don't need to tell you how unprofessional your email was."

"No, sir."

"Or that it appeared to be a vindictive attack against me."

"I'm sorry, sir. I know that doesn't cut it, but it's all I have."

"Is it?" Lee snapped. "That's disappointing. I'd hoped for something more."

Like what? His soul?

"I apologize for the embarrassment I have caused you and the company," Matt said.

"Hmm." Lee studied him, two horizontal lines creasing his brow.

Matt scratched at his fingers. His skin, nearly healed in his stay in Muskoka, had flared with eczema again since his return.

"I probably don't need to tell you just how disappointing and frustrating this whole scenario has proved."

"No, sir."

Lee sighed. "I know it may surprise you, but taking Ray to London was not actually an indictment on you. Putting Ray in that situation was a test for me to see whether he actually is producing anything of value himself, or if he is a bad manager who just makes a lot of noise."

What?

"You look surprised. But I'm not unaware of what's going on, despite some people obviously thinking otherwise."

This was said with a sharp look that prickled concern inside.

"And while I've had my concerns, I also have to admit his transactions over the past five years have on the whole proved generally beneficial."

Maybe in a monetary sense for investors, but at what price to his workmates?

"I see you still don't look convinced, but I was looking to see if he would be able to close the deal in a situation I know you worked hard for."

"But why?"

Lee leaned back in his seat. "Because I wanted to know if he was coasting on other people's hard work or able to initiate opportunities for himself. The fact he produced nothing more than what you'd done showed his true colors. Having said that, hiring a portfolio manager is a costly endeavor, and booting a good manager is even more costly." He leaned forward. "What you did was unprofessional, illogical, felt personal, and frankly, was stupid and reckless. I didn't think you were so petty."

Matt inclined his head. Apparently he was that petty.

"You've worked here for how long now—eight years?"

"Ten," Helen said.

Wow. Ten years.

"You were one of our top portfolio managers," Lee continued.

Were being the operative word right now. Matt fiddled with his watch as he braced for more.

"I considered you a trustworthy member of our team, and so for you of all people to do this in such a way is just, quite frankly, staggering. A real stab in the back."

Was he supposed to apologize again? "I'm sorry." *Lord, help me.*

"Over my many years of working here I've never come across the like. It's not like a simple case of fraud when you would automatically be fired. You're not a bad actor we need to get rid of. And Helen has informed me that this is not a breach of firm compliance policies, so you won't be fired."

He wouldn't? An ocean of relief washed over his soul. "Thank you, sir."

But while Lee said that, Matt wouldn't put it past him to instigate a restructure that would mean the end of Matt's role here.

"I've been thinking about what to do with you, because it won't look good to the rest of the team to see you come back with no consequences. I don't care," he held up a hand, "about mental health stresses and the like. We're all under pressure here. You're just lucky that your years of excellent service mean that we all know that you are one of the hardest workers here. In fact, it's probably a good thing you're known as having an issue with putting boundaries in your life, as we can make some allowances and perhaps spin it that way. But the real issue is that people will likely feel that you are a loose cannon and can't be trusted, and trust is everything in this business."

Like Ray's total fail. He bit back the words he wanted to say.

"What is it?" Helen asked him.

He shook his head.

"Go on," Lee said. "What?"

"You talk about trust, but I'm sorry sir, Ray has proven himself untrustworthy time and time again. How can you call me untrustworthy and unreliable when you've now seen in my email the many instances of his failures?"

"This meeting today is not about Ray, it's about you."

He nodded. He'd expected that, hence the need to bite back his words before. Even if this meeting felt like a direct result of Ray's machinations.

"We will be dealing with some of these allegations you've made soon. Others of them have already been investigated."

They had? Well, hallelujah.

"So that's something your little stunt has achieved. But why you didn't speak to us in person is something I still find it hard to understand."

He figured that pointing out his boss's own tendencies to overwork probably wouldn't be helpful right now. Nor his friendship with Ray.

"Well?" Lee asked, his gaze like a needle. "Can you explain why you felt such a method was necessary?"

Looked like he had no way of getting out of this. "I'm sorry, sir."

Lee held up a hand. "Stop with the apologies. Just tell me the truth."

Okay, then. "Ray has often boasted about his long association with you, going back to college days. I," he swallowed, "I did not trust that you could be unbiased in this situation."

"Didn't you just hear me say I've had my own reservations?"

"Yes, sir. But I didn't know that at the time. I find Ray to be very persuasive."

"Which can be a benefit, but also a hindrance when one needs to be sure one will hear the truth." Lee's eyes narrowed. "You at least are honest."

"I try to be."

"Hmm." Lee frowned again. "I don't like the implication that you think I would be persuaded by association with another."

"I'm," he bit back *sorry*, and replaced it with, "I underestimated you, sir." He closed his mouth to stop another apology from spilling out.

"That you did." Lee glanced at Helen, then returned his attention to Matt. "Ray will be back on Thursday, and I'll be speaking to him about these allegations, and to both of you about what is next."

Matt nodded. He expected nothing less.

"Now, I imagine you have some work to do," Lee said.

"Some," he allowed. From his read through of work emails it seemed many of his tasks had been assigned to others in the past week. None to Ray, he'd noticed.

"We will have another meeting on Friday once Ray has returned, and I want you to consider your future here. We do have some restructuring we'd envisaged in the future that may need to be expedited."

In other words, he'd be made redundant soon anyway. "I understand. And again, I apologize for all the hurt my actions caused."

"Hmm. Well, you know what to do. Go do it."

A glance at Helen revealed her nod, which shoved him to his feet. "Thank you, sir."

"Oh, before you go," Helen said, "I've emailed you some links to the forms you'll need to fill in online regarding your leave."

"Of course."

Matt nodded, thanked them both again, and stumbled to the hall and walked shakily to his desk, conscious eyes and whispers followed his progress. He slumped into his seat and exhaled. God had proved most merciful. Now if his fellow employees could only be the same.

CHAPTER 13

❧

"The article comes out tomorrow," Serena said.

Article? Oh, the feature in *Toronto Living* magazine. Excitement thrummed, pushing aside the concern for Matt's meeting with his bosses today. "That's exciting."

"I just got off the phone with Leanne. She said to expect a delivery of the magazines sometime this afternoon, ready for the weekend."

"I can't wait to see it."

"I imagine the publicity will do the resort a lot of good. And it all helps to get your name out there. Did you notice an uptick after the radio interview?"

Toni nodded. "We're starting to see an increase in people making inquiries about lessons."

"That's wonderful!" Serena beamed.

"It's amazing. And it's all due to you," Toni said.

"I think it's all due to your own skill and hard work, actually. If you hadn't painted those beautiful pictures in the first place, and kept at it even when you weren't selling many, then you wouldn't have had the stock to sell to people. So, when you look at it like that, it's actually your own fault, Toni."

"Yeah, but plenty of people work hard without ever receiving anything like the recognition I have. And I know that's down to what you've done. And what God has."

"Well, that's worth remembering, isn't it? Be faithful in what God places on your heart, and if you're dedicated when nobody's looking, God can trust you to keep doing it when people are finally paying attention. I think that's what faithfulness is about."

Faithfulness. It was a word Toni had rarely heard used to describe her. Someone like Serena had probably been described as diligent all her life. Until his recent blow up, Matt had been the epitome of conscientiousness. But Toni had always been considered a little more flaky than some. Unorthodox. The rebel. Faithful wasn't her middle name. But then, rebel wasn't true of her either, anymore. God really was doing new things.

"Now, do you have some art classes booked for next week?" Serena asked.

"A few."

"Well, brace yourself for more. I'm sure that phone will be getting a workout tomorrow." Serena flashed a smile. "I know Adrian is really pleased."

"I'm so glad."

Serena's diamond ring—Mom's old engagement ring—flashed in the morning light as Serena pushed her hair behind her ear, reminding Toni of her desire to help her friend.

"How are you doing? Is there anything I can help with for the wedding?"

"Oh, you're sweet, but really everything is under control. My parents arrive tomorrow, as you know, and I can't wait for them to meet you and Joel in person."

"Do you, um, think they'll be okay with Ethan?"

"Do you mean will they judge you for being a single mom? I hope not. I know they're still working on that grace thing. I think I've mentioned before that they're pretty straight-laced and conservative. But hey, at least it's not my sister Miranda. I don't think she understands grace at all."

"Ouch."

Serena winced. "Sorry, that sounded catty, didn't it? Even if it is true. I can't help but be glad she and her boys can't make it until just before the wedding. Let's just say encouragement is not her area of gifting. But don't let them bother you. It doesn't matter what they think, does it?"

"No." Not when a girl was working to get her self-worth from what God thought about her. The reminder—she was chosen, forgiven, beloved—brought a smidge of ease to her heart.

"Well, I'd better scoot," Serena said. "You'll be coming with Joel tomorrow night, won't you?"

Joel had arranged to go with Serena to pick up Serena's parents from the airport. While Serena had visited them in India a few months ago, this was obviously a very important occasion. "I'll be there."

"With Joel's best man?"

Heat flushed her cheeks. "Matt hasn't said anything to me about coming this weekend." Well, not definitively, anyway. He'd said he wanted to, but so much depended on how his meeting went today.

"Joel said Matt seems to be doing okay."

Okay might be overstating things. "He was pretty nervous earlier in the week, but from the last few phone calls we've had I think he's reconciled to the fact that he may eventually be 'restructured,'" she said this with air quotes, "out of the company."

Serena winced. "What will he do?"

"I don't know. I don't like to ask, because if I ask it seems like I don't believe he'll stay there. To be honest, when he describes his work, it's a world where I really struggle to understand a lot of what he does."

"It's a good thing you don't need to understand it to be supportive of him."

"I guess."

Serena studied her for a moment then smiled. "You know, he might not say this often, but your brother is so proud of you."

"Oh, he says it often. But don't let that stop you from saying anything more."

"Ha ha. Well, I'm glad you know that, because I see it too. It's wonderful to see that God is maturing you, and even though there have been some challenges, you've stretched and you're accomplishing things. It seems hard to believe at times that the bratty teenager-like girl I first met is the Toni of today."

Ouch. "Was I really that bratty?"

"No comment."

Toni winced. "Okay, then."

"Well, it's more okay now. Let's just say that."

But as Serena left, and Toni spent the rest of her Friday dealing with gallery visitors, praying for Matt, and working on her own painting, it did seem like life was more okay now.

She felt more settled, more positive, like her life had purpose and direction. Once upon a time everything seemed to be spiraling out of control. Now she could see a path forward. One of creative challenge and endeavor. One with friends and support. She felt a part of this local community, that people liked her, and wanted her in their lives. Sure, she might not get everything about being a new and solo mom right, but the last visit with Dr. James had revealed Ethan was tracking to meet his baby health goals exactly as he ought. Life was more okay now.

And that continued when she spoke to Matt that night, and he explained how the interview had gone.

"I was getting kind of worried about what Ray was going to say but he basically shot himself in the foot from the word go."

"What do you mean?"

"He blamed me for not fully preparing him, which to be fair, I didn't. He'd asked for information and I'd uploaded the basics to our shared group file in the cloud, but I didn't send him the specifics, because they were my own notes that I've used based on previous meetings, and I figured they wouldn't necessarily be of any use to him." Matt chuckled. "Or maybe I'm just not the team player I once thought I was. Regardless, Ray was supposed to have checked those documents, but he didn't, and it appears that far from taking initiative, Ray has proven himself to be overly reliant on other people's work. That's what Lee, our chief executive officer, said, anyway. He's given Ray a probationary period, with a review of his work when he returns."

"So what does this mean for you?" she asked.

"Ah, that. I'm already on a similar probationary period, though it's much shorter, only for a couple of weeks. I basically have to prove myself by mid-February, as that's when the conversations about 'restructuring' will begin."

"You mentioned that before. Do you think that will mean you still have a job?" she asked.

"I don't know. It's really hard to tell. And honestly, sometimes I wonder what it would be like to have a different job, to not work here with everyone's suspicion that I might go off the rails again. I get that impression from some of my colleagues, anyway. Whatever happens, I know I can trust God with my future. And I also know that I have to get better at managing my time. I can be a bit of a workaholic, so I'm looking for ways to cut down on the stuff that gets in the way of what I want to do."

"And what do you want to do?" she asked softly.

"I want to spend time with you. You and Ethan. And if that means leaving work so I can actually have a whole weekend and see you, then that's what I want to do."

"I could come and see you," she offered.

"For sure. That'd be great. But I have to admit I really love the idea of escaping the city and spending time in Muskoka Shores. I just feel like I can breathe easier there."

"Even when we're in the depths of a snow storm?"

"There's another headed your way on Sunday, isn't there?"

"If the roads are bad I might get a long weekend. Hey, you should definitely come and then you can have a long weekend too," she teased.

"That'd be awesome, right?"

Huh. That response didn't make it sound like that was something he'd actually do. Still, since returning to the city all the drama with his work meant it was like the man had lived the equivalent of five weeks in the past five days. She couldn't blame him for wanting to stay home. But a twinge of disappointment stole through her heart, nonetheless.

"So, how about you? What are you doing this weekend?" he asked.

"The magazine article comes out tomorrow, so prepare to be famous."

"Man, I forgot about that. Not that I need to worry, when all the attention will be on you. Your work is so good you'll be inundated with calls."

"That's what Serena said might happen, so I'm bracing for the fact that it may get a little crazy at work tomorrow."

"You'll be great."

His words seeded hope for the future. How could she have ever overlooked this loyal, encouraging man? Oh, she appreciated him. His words were like that proverb, 'apples of gold in settings of silver.' How she wanted to be a similar encouragement for him. "I hope tomorrow goes well. I've almost finished my latest painting, so it'll be good to finally check that off the list. Whatever happens, I'm supposed to meet Serena's parents tomorrow night for dinner at her house," she said. "I'm trying not to worry about what they will think of me being a single mom."

"Hey, don't worry about what others think. Their opinion doesn't need to affect how you see yourself. You only need to worry about what God says."

Emotion curled her heart, roaring into her throat.

"Toni?" he said, after several moments.

"You're so good to remind me. That's what I'm trying to do. God is good and He loves me. I know that. But I'm trying to *know* that if you know what I mean."

"I know exactly what you mean."

SATURDAY PROVED to be very like what Serena had predicted. Visitors and phone calls from people wanting everything from painting classes to purchasing a painting. Pity Chrissy and the other poor resort receptionists who had been kept busy sending calls to the gallery's phone extension, but Toni couldn't regret anything else.

Leanne had done an excellent job, her article and photos showcasing several of Toni's paintings, and including two pictures of Toni's lesson: one of her assisting Matt—his name was misspelled as Mark—and one of Toni standing out the front so the backs of the heads of Matt, Maude and Alistair were visible. She didn't think Maude would be pleased. But with such words and descriptions of the "warm and inviting studio space" and "stunning, evocative artworks" it was no wonder the response to the article was so positive. Toni even had a couple of former art college friends call her whom she hadn't spoken to in years. She'd been kept so busy, scheduling lessons, greeting visitors, preparing, and packaging artwork to be delivered, and answering congratulatory messages from her friends, that it wasn't until the afternoon that she finally got a chance to work on her art.

She set out her paints, wrapped an apron around her, and studied her painting. Another tree displaying the full glory of

Autumn color, with branches holding gold, burnished copper, and red. She applied a pigment that added a subtle shimmer, that really made the colors pop and appear almost luminescent, then slowly began filling in the details. She'd already done the base coats. Now it was all about adding those elements that made her painting come alive.

Her phone buzzed a message from Matt. She placed down her brush and read it. *Awesome article!*

Sorry they typed your name wrong, she typed back.

His reply came a moment later. *What's important is that they got yours right. You're famous!*

You're sweet.

You're right.

She laughed. *You're crazy.*

His reply took a little longer. *Crazy enough to know you're going to succeed, and that tonight will go well too. Nobody can argue with success. I'm proud of you.*

Her heart sang with happiness. Could her day get any better? Thanks to the article, she'd likely made over two thousand dollars in one day, with bookings and orders placed for more works. Matt was right. She really shouldn't worry about what other people might think of her, because it was obvious that things were going well. If only Mom and Dad could see her now, they might be proud of her too.

The door opened. The resort general manager, Adrian, smiled. "Here you are. I hear the phone hasn't stopped ringing for you."

"It was a nice article, wasn't it?"

"It was excellent. You should feel encouraged. I certainly do. This is one of the best ideas we've had for a long while. And all in winter, usually our slowest season."

"Serena is the one who made this happen."

"Yes, it was her idea, but I think you can take some credit for the work that people obviously want."

Maybe she could. Maybe this was some of God's blessing. "Thank you for the opportunity, sir."

"I think it's time you called me, Adrian." He smiled. "Okay, now I don't want to interrupt you, but just wished to pass on my congratulations."

"Thank you, sir—Adrian."

He laughed, lifted a hand, paused at the artwork near the door, and nodded before exiting.

Now that was encouraging. *Thank You, Lord.*

She sipped her water bottle then bent to her canvas again, concentrating on the tiny leaves, dabbing the carmine-tinted paint in precise strokes. Judging from the number of enquiries about her maple trees, it looked like her autumn series was going to be her brand for quite a while. God bless patriotic Canadians.

The next couple of hours continued with more visitors which meant more pausing from her efforts to complete the painting as she spent time explaining her works and process to guests and art-lovers who'd made the trip especially. It seemed crazy to think people would drive so far just to see her, but maybe that's what Adrian appreciated, the increased revenue additional guests were bringing in by staying at the resort.

The afternoon light was fading as she returned to her canvas, her heart resuming its ease as she sank into the bubble of creativity. While she appreciated all this interest, she couldn't help but wonder if this was how Staci felt when she was writing a book and had constant interruptions that disrupted the flow of creativity. It would be nice to have the time and space to just focus on her painting.

The door to the gallery flung open. She finished the last feathery strokes on her tree and glanced up. Then dropped the paintbrush. No.

"Hello, Toni."

"Bryant! What are you doing here?"

"What do you think?" He glanced at the pictures hanging on the wall, his expression unreadable. "Your work?"

"Y-yes."

"Hmm."

She tensed as he passed each painting, inching his way closer to her. After not seeing him for eighteen months it felt surreal to be seeing him for the second time in a week. She'd certainly never imagined him here in her space. *Her* space. Not his. What was he doing here? Her heart thumped. She hoped he hadn't learned about Ethan!

He wandered closer, wrinkled his nose. "Derivative as ever."

Wow. She pushed from her stool and braced herself. "You didn't answer my question before." She heard the wobble in her voice and pushed iron into her tone. "What are you doing here?"

"I'm here to see you." He twisted to face her.

His swarthy complexion seemed even darker than what she remembered last Saturday in the city. Maybe that was the effect of his graying beard, maybe it was the lines around his eyes that made him appear haggard. His hair was tied back, although a few strands had come loose, giving him a pirate-like look. A shudder crept through her. He was as slimy as when she'd seen him at the restaurant a week ago. But added to that, there was something desperate about him. Oh, why was today of all days the day Joel and Serena were out of town? Still, she didn't need her big brother as protector. She was tough. And the resort had security if absolutely necessary. "Well, you've seen me. Now you can go."

"I wanted to see you because you barely spoke a word last week, and I think I deserve an explanation for what you've done."

"For what I've done?" Her voice pitched up. "I don't owe you anything."

"I think you do." He flung a hand at the surroundings. "How

did you manage to scheme your way into something like this? What audacity to think of yourself so highly."

"Excuse me?"

"We both know your talent isn't worthy of such an honor. So, tell me. How did you manage this?" He gestured to the gallery space.

"I…" She swallowed, hoping the tremor in her voice would smooth away. "How did you even know about this?"

He picked up one of the *Toronto Living* magazines stacked on the service desk then flung it at her feet.

Her pulse increased with fear, but she clasped her hands together so he wouldn't see them shaking. "They like my work here." She lifted her chin. "They're using my design as their new logo."

"They don't know who you really are, though, do they?"

"I don't know what you mean."

She was thankful for the lack of visitors as he began to spew a stream of words that spoke of her lack of morals, her lack of humility, her lack of ethics.

Each hissed word fell like darts, puncturing her soul, piercing the words of faith she'd tried so hard to establish within. Her lack of creativity, her lack of sense—"You don't really think this will work, do you?"—and weirdly, her lack of honesty.

"That's rich, coming from you," she said. "Or did you forget the fact that you were married when you slept with me?"

His eyes pinched. "You broke up my marriage."

"The marriage you told me was over when you slept with me," she retorted. "Has your wife left you now? Was I the final affair that broke your poor wife's heart?"

He swore, and took a step closer, his hands forming fists.

She glanced at her phone. It was too far away. But she could always scream.

He called her another foul name, something that tried to

claw inside her soul. But met resistance in the way of righteous anger.

"Don't you dare blame me." Fury pushed her words out, clipped and fast. "You always told me that you and your wife were finished. You were the liar, not me. As soon as I found out you were screwing around on her, I ended things, or have you forgotten that?"

"I can't believe you had the nerve to report me to the college. Because of you I lost my job."

"Me? I'm pretty sure you managed that on your own. Or did you forget that you aren't supposed to mess with your students? I know I wasn't the only one. Exactly how many of your students did you sleep with?"

He stepped closer and she put up her chin, clenching her hands. *Lord, keep me safe!*

"I'll make you pay for what you've done."

"For what I've done? I think you're just reaping the consequences for what you've done, Bryant."

He lifted a hand as if to strike her, and she stepped back quickly. "I wouldn't if I were you. See that?" She pointed to a camera in the upper corner of the room. "There's security watching. The receptionist can hear me if I scream." She knew that because Ethan's tears one day had brought a concerned visit from Chrissy from reception.

"It isn't right that you're getting away with this," he hissed. "I'm going to tell them what you've done."

"I think you're forgetting that nobody here knows you, Bryant, and nobody here cares that you might have once been my lecturer. But everybody here knows me, and what's more they like me and they want me to stay. So you better not try anything, because they're not going to believe you."

Another expletive dropped from his mouth as he stepped even closer. "You're nothing but a scheming—" He called her another foul word.

She flinched, meeting his terrible dark-filled gaze but saying nothing.

"I bet that baby you tried to convince me of was another man's child anyway," he sneered. "Good thing you got rid of it."

Her heart quavered. *Lord, please let him not discover I kept his child. Please let Ethan not have inherited any of his natural father's evil traits.* What could she say to make him go away?

His eyes widened, before he strode into the other corner of the room. The corner where she kept Ethan's toys. His incredulous face swung back to her. "You did keep it?"

Lord, forgive me. "Those things are for when mothers of young infants want to take lessons but not have their child too far away." Well, they would be. If the baby of the teacher wasn't using it.

His gaze narrowed, as if not sure whether to believe her.

"You can leave now," she asserted, her voice wobbly.

"Did you keep it?"

No, she wasn't going to play this game. She had zero desire to lie, but if it meant he went away, she'd do all she could to keep this evil man out of her life. She drew up her last dregs of courage and clutched the edge of her desk to help her stand.

"What do you think? Do you really think I'd want to have any reminder of you?" Thank God Ethan never reminded her of the man standing in front of her. "And how do you think I would've managed all this," she waved a hand at her surroundings, "if I had a baby in tow? That'd be next to impossible, right? You've always been crazy, and saying stuff like this is more proof. Maybe it's time you took a good long hard look at yourself and started making amends for all the damage you've done over the years. You should probably start with your wife."

"Don't you lecture me—"

"Don't you try and bully me. Your word carries no weight here. You're a washed-up has-been and—"

Slap!

Waves of pain flashed colors across her eyes. "Get out!" she screamed.

When he didn't move, she screamed it again.

But it was only when the doors were flung open and Chrissy hurried in that he backed away. "What's happened?"

"Call the police," Toni said, putting a hand to her throbbing cheek. "He hit me."

"I'm not getting involved with any police," he said.

"You better leave, then." Oh, her jaw ached. Had he knocked loose some teeth?

"Get out," Chrissy said, lifting her phone as if she was about to talk into it, and he scuttled from the room. "Here, Toni, we need to get you some ice. Oh my gosh! You can see his hand print on your cheek. That's it. I'm getting a photo."

"What? Why?"

"If I get a photo of it the police can use it for proof."

Her day which had begun so well had made a screaming U-turn.

Chrissy snapped a picture. "I'm so sorry this has happened to you, Toni. I'm happy to be a witness for you. And don't worry, they'll have that on security footage too." She shook her head. "My sister was stalked by her ex for years, even when she took out a restraining order. Violence against women is not okay."

TONI KNEW she wouldn't make dinner with Serena's parents. After being forced by Chrissy to tell Adrian about what had happened, he insisted she close up and Chrissy travel with her to attend the community police station in the next town over. Here, she and Chrissy spoke to a helpful officer called Tom Woodmore who interviewed them both, then advised she had enough grounds to seek a restraining order, "Seeing there is a child involved."

But she hadn't admitted to Bryant about Ethan's existence. "Would he know then that Ethan is his child?"

Tom's face barely moved. "You're saying he's currently unaware?"

"I don't know how much he knows, but I don't want to alert him to the fact if I can avoid it."

He nodded. "Then a peace bond can have the same effect. The person is still legally bound to stay away, and if we prepare it, then it means you can avoid court."

"Anything to avoid court sounds great."

"It's only fair to tell you this will still require further investigation, and even when that is completed it can take at least six weeks before the order can be made."

"I don't mind. I just want him stopped." She rubbed her eyes. "I never thought today would end this way."

"I'm sorry." Officer Tom had kind brown eyes. "But it's good to be proactive and prevent things from escalating. We see plenty of cases where people's days have ended in far worse ways."

By the time she reached home, she was emotionally drained, but even sending a message to Joel seemed too hard. After double checking the locks, she collapsed onto the lounge with Ethan, holding him close to her heart. Her phone rang again. She checked the number. Joel. "Hey."

"Where are you?"

She closed her eyes. The dinner. "I'm sorry."

"Everyone is here, waiting for you."

"I got held up at work."

"Uh huh. Too busy celebrating all your success?"

Her lip quivered. Not quite. Should she tell him? But not telling him would be hard for him once he found out. But then, neither did she want to spoil his important night.

"I've only just got in," she said instead, glad her voice sounded steady enough. She'd tell him tomorrow. "And now

Ethan is really tired and I don't want to disturb him anymore. Please tell Serena I'm really sorry."

"You're missing out on a great meal."

"I'm sure I am. I'd be there if things had gone differently."

A beat. "Are you sure you're okay?"

"I'll be fine. I just need some down time. Today was insane."

"Okay. I'll be home after ten."

"Now her parents are here, you're not going to stay too late, huh?"

"Yeah, no."

She forced a chuckle. "Have fun, and please pass on my regrets."

They ended the call, and she clutched Ethan a little closer, as her thoughts spiraled down well-worn grooves. Fear wrestled faith, hope struggled against hurts as a list of past pains sought attention. The death of her parents. Toni's forays into drinking, then drugs, then sex. Meeting Bryant. Becoming enamored with the man of quick wits and a quicker smile whose interest in her art work soon led to interest in other things. Why hadn't she realized just what he was after? That he was only interested in power, in controlling her, that she was nothing more than a notch in his belt. Or on his bedpost. How could she have been so naïve?

Tears leaked from her eyes and she wiped them away, snuggling into the warm mass of Ethan. She was such a failure. And even now, way over a year since their affair started, she was still filled with fear. Officer Tom might have started legal proceedings against Bryant, but it would take time for the wheels of justice to be set in motion, and in the meantime what would this mean for her and Ethan? How long would it take for Bryant to discover Ethan was her child—was his child too? What could she do? But she had no one to blame for this except herself and her selfish decisions. It wasn't right to ask anyone else to be involved.

A knock came at the door. She froze. Who could it be? She checked her phone. No messages. So it was unlikely to be any of the girls, or the pastors, who were supposed to be at Serena's dinner too. It wouldn't be Joel, as he had his own key. Could Bryant be out there?

The knock came again. She carefully eased up, carefully placed Ethan down. She inched her way down the hall to peek through the peephole. Who—?

Oh. She unlatched the door and flung it open to the man holding a bunch of roses. "Matt! I'm so glad to see you."

Then she burst into tears.

CHAPTER 14

In his impromptu trip to Muskoka he'd imagined the way his unexpected arrival could go. Yeah, he'd known about the dinner with Serena's parents, and had counted on Serena's hospitality to find an extra space, as per Joel's earlier instructions. But when Joel had messaged to ask if he knew why Toni was still at home he'd changed course, glad that the lights were still on at Annette's Florist and she'd agreed to whip up a bouquet from the last of her flowers today. He'd expected surprise from Toni, sure. A hug too, he hoped. Excitement about her day's success, yes. But not tears. Not this distress.

He drew her closer, cradling her in his arms, drawing her head against his chest, which met with a wince. "I get the feeling congratulations aren't quite in order."

She shook her head, pulling away, then tugging him through the door before closing it firmly. Her hair swung to cover her face.

"Hey, what's wrong? I thought I was going to see you at dinner tonight."

She drew her hair back, then he saw her bruised face. "Toni!" His heart cramped. "Oh, sweetheart. What happened?"

She drew him to the lounge area and sat next to him on the sofa, holding his hand firmly. Then proceeded to tell him all that had occurred at the resort today.

Bryant. His fists clenched. Men who beat up women deserved to be beaten up themselves. But the fact that man had hurt this precious woman made him want to tear him from limb to limb. He forced himself to be still, to not scare her with the depths of his rage. "Is this the guy I saw you talking with last weekend?"

She shook her head again.

He wasn't? Then who—?

"He was talking to me. I wasn't talking to him." She shivered, then touched her injured cheek.

His stomach clenched. Her poor cheek. He wished he could kiss it all better. "I'm so sorry, Toni. This shouldn't have happened. The police will see him brought to justice."

"I hope so," she whispered. Another shiver meant he had to wrap his arm around her.

"Hey, you don't need to be afraid," he said softly. "I'm here, and you know that Joel and I and all your friends will do all we can to protect you, and keep you and Ethan safe."

"I don't know what I'd do if he tried to take Ethan from me. Bryant can't find out that Ethan is his son."

But wanting something to be so didn't mean it would be so. Witness his many years of unrequited affection for the woman he now held in his arms. He stroked her hair. "You're not alone. You have many friends and people who will vouch for you and will do all that they can to protect you. And remember, God is with you too. He loves you, and wants the best for you and Ethan."

For some reason this produced a greater volume of tears as she curled into him and sobbed against his chest. "It's okay," he soothed, as his prayers lifted and he gently rubbed her back. Eventually the tears lessened into the occasional hiccup, and her body relaxed. And somewhere in that moment he noticed how they were sitting, her leg pressed against his, her curves against his chest, and he grew very aware that she was very appealing, that they were very alone, and that he should move. "Hey, how about you have a rest here and I'll make you a cup of tea."

"But you're the one who drove all this way," she protested.

"Yeah, my day wasn't as huge as yours has been. Have a rest, close your eyes if you want, and I'll make us both some tea."

He put the kettle on to boil, found two cups, two teabags, and took a moment to exhale, gripping the edge of the counter top, before moving to fill a vase with water and then with his flowers. His call of, "Almost ready!" met with no response, but he figured maybe she hadn't heard him.

When he returned it was to find she was asleep, one hand flung to the side hanging off the sofa as she lay on her back. She looked so peaceful, even with the smudges of mascara underneath her eyes, that he didn't have the heart to disturb her. He placed his cup down, found a light blanket he draped over her, and sat opposite to watch her sleep.

He gripped his mug of tea as a million emotions battled for supremacy. He couldn't imagine what it must've been like for her today. To go from the heights of magazine fame to the depths of fear and police interviews and personal shame. But this vulnerability only increased his admiration. She might've been beaten, but she didn't quit. Once upon a time she would barely look at him. Now the fact she was sharing this with him when he suspected she hadn't even shared it with her brother made him feel special, like their relationship held a sense of trust that allowed them both to share the broken pieces of their lives. If Joel had known, he'd be here for sure. And Matt meant it before. Neither he nor Joel would leave her side so she'd have no chance to feel a moment's fear. And if that meant Matt moving back into the spare room then so be it.

The clock's hour hand completed a full circuit, then another. And in that time he had plenty of time to tend to the fire, flick on a muted TV, deal with a suddenly awake Ethan and his over-full diaper, and pray. His own troubles seemed far away, less important, not compared to those facing the woman he loved. The woman he *loved*.

He loved her. He'd long held her in affection, but now knew a depth of protectiveness and devotion he felt deep to his core. This feeling wasn't swayed by her revelations, wasn't dismayed by her past, but was still stubbornly devoted to wanting her best. Which was why the knowledge that some man had tried to hurt her—after blatantly using her—killed him.

His fingers clenched, and he slowly straightened them. Heat rippled through his chest and he breathed to release. He couldn't imagine how anyone could be so selfish that they'd hurt a woman, let alone hurt someone who had once held that man's heart. This Bryant wife-cheater must've loved Toni, to some degree at least, in order for him to risk his marriage.

Poor Toni. Matt's mind tracked through what he could do. At least she'd gone to the police, and a police investigation might keep Bryant from any likelihood of hurting her. But still, the fear would still be there, her concern that maybe he'd break his bond and try to see her. That is, if the bond was even able to happen. So, a bond was good, but still imperfect. There had to be another way. *Lord?*

The stillness of the house broke as a thought struck, but it seemed so extreme, so all-encompassing, that at first he barely dared explore it as an option. Then he gave himself a minute to trail down that path and imagine what could be. Could it work? Maybe.

Lights flashed across the shadowed room, signaling a car had turned into the driveway. Joel must be home. Matt glanced at the sleeping Toni and contemplated waking her up, but decided against it. She was obviously exhausted.

He pushed to his feet, careful to not make any noise as he tiptoed down the hall, opening the door as Joel searched for his key. "Hey."

"You made it then."

Matt nodded. "Your sister is in there, she's asleep."

"Okay." Joel hung up his coat. "How is she?"

"She's been asleep a while, so we didn't talk much."

Joel arched an eyebrow at him.

Matt held up his hands. "She was pretty tired. How about you tell me how things went? What are Serena's parents like? You collected them from the airport, right?"

It might be good to give the man a few minutes to transition from the bubble of contentment with Serena to the pain Toni had undergone.

Sure enough, Joel's eyes lit. "They were really cool. I might've got the impression they liked me on those Zoom calls, but now in person, I get the idea that they *really* like me. Serena said her mom is not much of a hugger, but it seemed like she couldn't stop hugging me."

Matt smiled. "You'll enjoy having that whenever you go to visit the in-laws, huh?"

"If it's the price I have to pay for being married to Serena then I'm okay with it."

"And her dad?"

"Yeah, he's cool, too. Or at least I think he will be, given enough time. I think it's sinking in that his baby girl is getting married in two weeks and I'm not sure if he's really reconciled to that yet. But that's okay." They walked to the living room. "It was good to have John and Angela there. They helped break the ice."

"I'm glad," Matt said.

"So, um, are you staying?" Joel asked, glancing at his sleeping sister then up at Matt.

"Thanks. I thought you'd never ask."

Joel grinned. "Okay, so the flowers tell me you didn't get them for me. This is for Toni, huh?"

"I like her," he said simply. "You've known that for ages. But you might not have known that she now likes me."

"Huh. Well, good for her for finally recognizing my excellent taste in friends."

Matt chuckled, glancing over at her sleeping form. His heart hitched.

"So, she had a good day? I gotta admit she didn't sound completely okay earlier on the phone."

"Yeah. There was a reason for that."

In a low voice, Matt filled Joel in on what Toni had told him, watching his friend's face go through similar expressions he'd bet he'd worn on his own. Disbelief, outrage, concern, anger, fear, sadness. Yep. Every one.

"I can't believe—why didn't she say anything?"

"Because she didn't want to spoil your night."

"But this is way more important than meeting Serena's parents. She should've told me. I would've come here."

"You didn't see her earlier. She really was wiped. But on the bright side, I think she'll feel better now that she's faced the threat, and by taking the situation to the police she's done all she can legally to protect herself and Ethan."

"Ethan." Joel shoved a hand through his hair. "Man, I forgot about the little fella for a moment. What does all of this mean for him?"

"Nothing, if Bryant doesn't discover that Ethan is his son."

"Yeah, and what are the chances of that?" Joel asked cynically.

Matt didn't like the chances of a small town keeping its mouth shut, either. "Who here knows that Bryant is the father?"

"Nobody, except you and me. And Ange and John McPherson, the pastors. I felt I had to tell them when I took the job, and Toni told me I could. But as far as I know she hasn't told anyone else, except maybe Serena."

Matt nodded. "So, there's no real way that Bryant could know for sure that Ethan is his child. Not if she doesn't disclose who the father is."

Joel winced. "I hate for it to appear that she is promiscuous, and that Bryant will think so."

"Who cares what Bryant thinks?" Emotion roared again. Matt tamped it down. "Hopefully, the police will be able to stop him getting near her again."

"I can't believe he dared hit her," Joel's jaw clenched. "What's going to stop him doing so again?"

Matt swallowed. Then squared his shoulders. And finally admitted the plan that had struck him earlier, the plan that, as he talked about it, seemed the embodiment of his dreams.

Joel's eyes rounded, his head against the sofa's headrest like Matt's words had sent bullets through his chest. "You would really do that?"

"In a heartbeat."

"Wow." Joel rubbed his hair. "I don't know what to say."

"As long as you're not dismissing the idea outright."

"Are you sure it's not extreme?"

Matt smiled. "I don't think it's extreme. Not when I have cared about her for years." *Cared about* was so lame. "Loved her for years," he corrected himself.

"You really are a dark horse, aren't you? Wow."

"Just an option to think about." Matt shrugged.

Joel's eyes narrowed. "How long have you two been a thing?"

Matt lifted his hands. "I don't know if I really know. But if it makes you feel any better, we haven't kissed."

"Whoa. This is a conversation I never thought I'd have." He grimaced. "My best friend and my sister kissing."

"It would probably be helpful to explore that side of things before seeing if she'd agree to the other."

"Probably would." Joel nodded.

"Anyway, I just thought I would mention that, in the interests of full disclosure."

"Appreciate it."

He could tell Joel was spinning out. Probably best to leave this here. The man had enough to get his head around. He got to his feet. "Now, I'm assuming your spare bed is still where I left it?"

"Yeah, go." Joel waved a hand. "You know what to do. Make yourself at home." His eyes narrowed again. "How long do you think you'll be making yourself at home in my home?"

"I'm supposed to be back at work on Monday, but I'm kind of hoping the snow storm that's predicted will mean I'll have to work from home. Even if that home is here."

"I see."

Matt lifted his brows, but Joel waved him away, moving to Toni's side and gently waking her and murmuring to her before clasping her in his arms in a long hug.

Matt was tempted to linger, but knew that was fraught with its own challenges so instead he went to the spare room and pulled out the sofa bed. He made up the bed quickly, visited the bathroom, and upon exiting found Toni in the hall again. "Hey."

"Thank you for before." Her eyes seemed huge in the night shadows. "I'm so sorry for falling asleep on you."

"Any time."

"And thank you for listening, for being such a good encourager, for being my friend."

"You know I really care about you."

"I do."

His heart thudded at the words, words he longed for her to say in a different context.

"Thanks for telling Joel about it too," she said softly. "I don't think that I would've had the strength to retell everything yet again."

"I'm glad that was okay."

She studied him, her eyelids heavy, remnants of makeup streaked across her face. But her courage in allowing herself to be seen, to be known, made her beautiful to him.

"What is it?"

She lifted her hand and traced it along his jaw, leaving a trail of fire in its wake. "I don't think I've ever really realized just how handsome you are until now."

"Handsome, huh?" His heart gloried in her praise.

"Very handsome," she whispered, as her body swayed toward him, until her lips hovered tantalizingly close to his.

He gripped her upper arms. He yearned to kiss her, to feel the sweet promise of her lips on his, but not like this. Not when she was so tired she would likely struggle to remember this tomorrow. And definitely not anywhere where his best friend and her brother was likely to interrupt. "You're really tired," he murmured.

"I am." She seemed to droop as she said that.

"You need to go to bed."

"Probably."

"Have a good sleep, Toni." He pressed a kiss to her forehead.

"You have a good sleep yourself," she whispered.

Yeah, he'd struggle to get any sleep tonight.

~

It was funny how fear could be chased away by the arms of a big strong man. Yes, she thought herself more of a twenty-first-century woman than this, but there was something so comfortably reassuring when Matt held her in his arms and whispered assurance in her ears.

The comfort of his presence lasted all of Sunday and Monday, when the big snow storm that had threatened actually did appear. Matt had worked from home—Joel's and her home—on Monday, and she'd reveled in his presence even as she'd pottered around the house, making cookies, making coffee, trying to prove she was domestically able like she knew she wasn't, as she thanked God for Adrian's earlier message saying all non-essential resort staff could stay at home to avoid the treacherous conditions.

Joel's presence must be the main reason Matt hadn't kissed her before he'd returned to the city early this morning. She'd put it down to that at least. She'd seen the heat in his eyes, noticed how often his gaze fell to her lips, and how his hugs lasted longer than before. And while she suspected he was giving her time to really know her own mind, and she appreciated that, she also was growing hungrier to know what exploring his kiss would be like.

She could kick herself for taking so long to notice him, because he was, as Rachel insisted on saying, "A divine specimen of manhood."

She bit back a smile, trying to concentrate on her artwork.

The heavy snow had now been cleared enough to return to work, but the day dragged, Saturday's flurry of interviews and dozens of phone calls seeming a lifetime ago. She felt self-conscious, and hoped the double application of makeup hid the greening bruise on her cheek, and that Chrissy and Adrian hadn't advertised the incident too much. She felt anxious, edgy, wondering if Adrian's promise to have security monitor this space would be enough to protect her in case Bryant returned. She also wondered if Ethan's increased fractiousness was because he'd picked up on her tension caused by Bryant's actions. Had she been right to put him in the daycare? She'd figured it had to be safer than having him here, and Bryant discovering him. Her heart hiccupped with fear. *Lord, keep that man away from us.* The prayer was one she'd prayed a hundred times since Saturday.

The door opened, and Serena walked in. "Toni, sweetheart." Serena wrapped her in a long hug that drew moisture to Toni's eyes again.

"Stop it," she said, pulling away, wiping under her eyes. "You'll make me cry."

"How are you doing?" Serena drew a hand down Toni's arm.

"Better than Saturday night," she admitted.

"I'm so sorry that happened. But so glad Chrissy was there and able to help. I still feel bad that I was elsewhere."

"Why? You wouldn't have known what Bryant was planning to do. And it's in the hands of the police now."

"Still, it's not something that would be easy to get over."

No. But Matt's arms around her had helped. God bless him.

"I think you need a distraction."

"Love one."

"Okay then. How do you feel about helping me plan the Galentine's Day meal for next week?"

"I thought you and Joel would be doing something together."

"Well, I still plan to, but I thought I'd see if we could swing it so we can cover all events. Do something with everyone who wants to, then maybe those who are coupled up could go on to do whatever else they think appropriate for Valentine's Day."

"Leaving those non-coupled to do something super fun like a movie marathon?" Toni wrinkled her nose.

"Hey, I thought you liked movies."

"As long as they're not too predictable or filled with clichés. Honestly, how many movies have you watched where the high-flying executive woman goes back to her hometown and meets the guy of her dreams and then gives her career away? Lame." She dusted her hands. "There. I called it. I don't find that inspirational or romantic at all."

"You'd rather the highflying executive man give up his high-powered career and move to the small town for the girl?"

Well, yes. Maybe. But she didn't trust that smirk of Serena's, so she wouldn't say that aloud.

"Don't answer that question," Serena said, her expression melding into something that definitely qualified as a smirk. "Anyway, Galentine's really is about friendship and celebrating our awesomeness, and I don't see why we can't celebrate that, single or not."

"You know Galentine's Day is actually supposed to be held on February 13, don't you?" Yeah, she'd researched it. It wasn't something she'd ever done with her city friends. Mostly because she hadn't had many.

"Well, we've always celebrated on the big one four, although Anna has long said we should hold ours on the fifteenth, so we can take advantage of the discounted chocolates at the stores."

"That's smart, too."

"Anyway, the big day is next week—well, *that* big day, anyway, so I was hoping you could help me plan some fun for the ladies." Serena grinned. "Even if you might be distracted by a tall and handsome highflying executive from the city."

"I don't even know if he'll be in town."

"You don't think he'll be here to see you on the most romantic day of the year?"

"It's not like he lives next door."

"It's not like he's overseas. And I think, judging from how I've seen him look at you, that he wouldn't want to miss this opportunity for anything."

Toni drew in a deep breath. Okay, so maybe she could afford to get a little excited. Maybe on Valentine's Day she might finally know his kiss.

.   .   .

THE NEXT WEEK passed in a blur of art, art lessons, wedding preparations—including the weekend's bachelorette spa day at Muskoka Shores, where some of the stress of past weeks was massaged away by the expert fingers of Yvonne—and by lessons with her heart. Each day Matt and she would share messages or phone calls, sometimes they would FaceTime. His work was slowly getting back to a degree of normal, although the Thursday before Joel's wedding was the day scheduled for another important meeting with the chief executive officer where the threat of a 'restructure' loomed. She prayed for him, like she prayed for Joel and Serena, her prayers a good reminder to not focus on herself. But she prayed for her own situation too, thanking God that she was seeing an increase in both gallery visitors and enquiries about art lessons too. Things seemed to slowly be steadying back onto course, even if she'd love to know how Tom's police investigation of Bryant was progressing.

Tom had called her four days ago, his 'update' holding little real news. Not that she had expected much, but it was nice to know her complaint hadn't been completely forgotten.

"I'm afraid these things take time," Tom had said, which she knew was true.

History had shown her that, when her complaint to the art college about Bryant's behavior had taken weeks before anyone had taken it seriously. But at least she had done something, rather than let him get away with it and prey on other girls. Her actions—and those of others—had eventually resulted in his dismissal. Now if only he could be kept away from her.

But now wasn't the time to focus on that. Not at today's Galentine's occasion. Serena was once again hosting, having off-loaded her parents to John and Angela for the night before Joel was expected to collect her for a romantic evening at Alphonse's. Matt had messaged earlier to say he hoped to visit, but it was dependent on work. So she was here, enjoying the company of her friends, as she tried not to think about what a romantic dinner with Matt might look like.

"What are you thinking about?" Jackie asked.

Toni exhaled. "Just thinking." Owning her private thoughts about Matt to her friends still felt a little funny, like she was exposing a piece of her heart she wasn't sure of yet. At least Jackie wasn't so inclined to get all single gal-bothered like Anna was.

"Wondering about later tonight, huh?"

"I didn't want to say anything," she admitted.

"It's okay. I'm safe." Jackie's head tilted to where Anna sat. "I don't know if the same could be said there."

"She's not exactly feeling her inner awesomeness, huh?"

"Not this year, no." Jackie sipped her mocktail. "I don't like to say this, but I feel like the more she compares herself to others the more discontented she's going to feel."

Toni nodded. She knew all about comparison. "It's hard."

"It's something that never stops if you choose to live that way. There will always be someone prettier, someone smarter, someone richer, or who seems to get more opportunities. It's not easy to find contentment, especially in this world that's so focused on achievements or acclaim that can so quickly crumble, but it's necessary if you ever want to find peace." She smiled wryly. "But I get the feeling that Anna doesn't really want to hear a sermon from me."

"So are you content?"

"Yep." Peace on Jackie's features said it was so. "I've long been reconciled to the fact that I'll never be the pretty one, or rich, or anything like that. But that's okay. I know that God loves me, that He thinks I'm special, and that's enough. I'm me, and some people can like that, some people will not, and that's okay. Although just quietly, on a day when we're celebrating inner awesomeness, I can't help but think that that is their loss."

Toni chuckled. "Here's to awesomeness, then." She raised her glass.

Jackie tapped the rim with her own. "And to finding our security in God, and not needing to find it in another."

"Amen." The glass rims gave another ting, while Toni's heart did the same.

Is that what she'd done? Sought comfort and assurance in Matt's arms instead of God's? Maybe she hadn't learned too much from that girl who'd once sought to escape the pain of her parents' death by seeking comfort and validation in a man's bed. *Lord, I'm sorry. Help me rely on You instead.*

It might've only been a micro prayer, but in that moment her heart seemed to tip back into peace, to settle, to know that God's love for her was deeper than any human's could be. It was like in a mere fraction of time the truth she'd known for years finally clicked into place. She didn't need to worry, didn't need to compare, didn't need to carry worthlessness, not when she now *knew* that God loved her.

"Amen," she whispered again. Amen and amen and amen.

"Hey, what are you two Amen-ing about over there?" Rachel asked.

"Recognizing our inner awesomeness is because of God," Jackie explained.

Toni nodded, her heart too full to speak. But that was true. She could be secure, she could know that God had created her uniquely, which meant that her focus could be heavenward, instead of comparing herself to others.

"Ooh, that reminds me of something in Psalms," Serena said, squinting as if she tried to remember. "For you created my inmost being; you knit me together in my mother's womb. I praise you because I am fearfully and wonderfully made; your works are wonderful, I know that full well."

"You've memorized that?" Staci asked.

"She has to," Rachel said. "It's part of the deal with marrying a church minister. You need to be able to recite at least fifty verses by heart. Am I right?" She winked.

Serena laughed. "No. But I've memorized that one because there were plenty of times last year when I did not feel fearfully and wonderfully made. Saying it to myself and reminding myself that that's how God sees me really has helped a lot in my self-esteem."

"And that's part of why it's good to have memory verses," Jackie said.

That was a verse Toni needed to speak more often over herself, too.

"Well, come Saturday night, Joel is going to know just how wonderfully made you are," Rachel said, downing her glass as the room exploded with laughter.

"Rachel!" Serena's cheeks were pink.

"What? Come on. Don't tell me you're not excited about *that.*"

Serena cut Toni a look that held apology. "Forgive her." She rolled her eyes before glancing back at Rachel. "I don't really feel too comfortable talking about this in front of Joel's sister."

"Hey, if it makes you feel any better I'm pretty sure Joel is excited about that part of marriage, too," Toni said.

Speaking of... Maybe she should take up Serena's invitation and move into her house soon. She'd discuss it with Joel tomorrow.

"Ew. I'll never be able to look at him during a sermon the same way," Anna complained.

Staci joined the new chorus of laughter and clapped her hands. "This is the best."

"Don't go putting this in a book, okay? This here is the circle of trust," Serena said. "What happens in Muskoka stays—"

"—in Muskoka," they all cried, and tapped glasses again.

"So how goes all the preparation for Saturday?" Jackie asked, once the laughter and teasing had died down.

"It's all tracking well," Serena said. "No hiccups yet."

"No hiccups, period," Jackie said. "I kind of hate how people say things like that, like they expect things to go badly."

"What do you mean?" Anna asked.

"Oh, I know," Staci jumped in. "Like when I read a book review and the person says, "I'm enjoying the book so far," like they're implying they might not later on. Just say you're enjoying the book, people. Don't suggest you might soon not enjoy it."

"I never thought about it like that," Serena said.

"Well, now you can." Staci's phone buzzed, and a smile lit her face. "Looks like my carriage has arrived. I'm going to have to love you and leave you."

"Good to see an author never using clichés," Rachel teased, as Staci moved to the door.

"Have fun," Serena called.

"Yeah," Anna said, her expression holding a degree of misery.

When the door had closed Jackie turned to Anna. "Are you still not over James?"

Anna shrugged, her earlier girl-power declaration of awesomeness looking far away.

"Come on, girl," Rachel said. "It's getting embarrassing."

Anna stiffened. "I can't help how I feel."

"You actually can, you know. If you keep focusing on what you don't have, you'll never notice all the good things you do have," Jackie said.

"Thank you, Pastor Jackie," Anna said. "Maybe you should be the one marrying Joel."

"I think he's perfectly suited to Serena here, and I wouldn't have it any other way."

"What kind of man would you like to marry?" Toni asked. Jackie might say she was content, but every girl had some idea of the kind of guy she found attractive.

"I don't know."

"Come on," Rachel prodded. "You must have some idea."

Jackie shrugged. "I don't think about it, to be honest. I figure that if God has someone for me to marry then God will draw my heart to his and his to mine, so I don't really need to worry."

"Oh, that's hardly an answer," Anna complained.

"Maybe it's easier to say what you don't want in a guy," Serena suggested.

"Okay, that's easier, yeah. I hate being in the spotlight, so I don't want him to be famous," she ticked off her fingers, "I don't care how rich he is, and honestly, I really don't care if he's handsome. I want him to be a Christian, and have a good sense of humor and a nice smile and to love me. That's all."

"Nice." Rachel settled back in her chair, and lifted her glass again. "Here's to your mystery man, wherever he may be."

"My mythical man, you mean," Jackie said with a grin.

"Hey, don't knock it," Serena protested. "You never know what good things may be coming your way. I certainly didn't, and now it's only a few days until I'll be married."

"Rub it in, why don't you?" Anna complained.

"Come on, let her be happy," Toni said. "Here's to the bride and groom. May all your dreams come true."

"Amen!" the others declared.

"Especially on Saturday night," Rachel added slyly.

Toni's phone vibrated with a new message, pulling her from new laughter. She glanced at the screen. Matt. Her heart double-thumped.

"Is that lover boy?" Rachel asked.

Someone should talk to Rachel about her cocktail addiction and how it left her filter free. "Um, yes."

"He's coming?" Serena sat up straighter.

"He's out the front," she confessed.

"Ooh, well go and have fun then." Rachel winked. "But not too much fun, if you know what I mean."

Mmm. Toni knew exactly what she meant. "I've already got

the baby. I'm not repeating that experience again until I'm married."

"Good to know." Rachel lifted her glass.

"Have fun," Jackie called.

That was the plan. She blew them a kiss. And went outside to see her Valentine.

CHAPTER 15

⬥

*I*n all Matt's dreams he'd never dared imagine going on a Valentine's date with Toni. And then for a Valentine's Day date to be their first official date? Mind blown. And even though life at work was still crazy, he knew he'd never live it down if he didn't make the most of this time tonight. So although he probably should be at home preparing for the interview with Lee and the company's other bigwigs in two days' time, he was instead sitting here, feeling all the warm and fuzzies as Toni smiled at him across a candle-lit table. Well, a candle-lit booth, actually. He might pride himself on being organized and planning several steps ahead, but the busyness of the past few days had completely stolen any clue that he was supposed to have booked a restaurant for Valentine's Day, which is why Alphonse's at the resort was full, and his next best bet was to visit The Coffee Blend. It wasn't the most romantic place, but with the candles and red-and-white checked tablecloth, it had a certain rustic Italian vibe. It might not be his first choice, but the twinkly lights draped across the ceiling gave a mellow romantic feel, and the pasta-based meals he'd seen others downing looked appealing, so he didn't think Toni would mind. Too much.

Besides, this place was probably better suited for Ethan, seated in the high chair that the owner, Suzy Morris, had dragged in from the back. "You three are so sweet," Suzy said, gently patting Ethan's cheek. "It's not every year I open up for dinner on Valentine's Day and have such a handsome young man come to visit. And to think this year I've got two." She shot Matt a wink. "She's a lucky gal, this one."

"Very lucky," he said, as seriously as he could.

Toni laughed, and his heart lightened. He loved to make her laugh. Loved to think he might add some sunshine to her day. Especially considering the last time he'd seen her had been under more challenging circumstances. But she didn't look so stressed when he'd collected her before, her face holding a peace that he longed to know the reason behind. Even if it held something that looked more like tease now.

"You know, you really should think about working on your humility," she said, after Suzy had walked away.

"You keep me humble."

"How so?"

"How do you think it felt to be ignored for so many years?"

Wait. Judging from the wince she gave that probably wasn't the best way to make a woman feel special on Valentine's Day. Man, he was rusty at romance.

"You know I regret that," she said softly, looking down at the table. "I can't believe how blind I was for so many years."

"It's okay."

She shook her head. "See? You're still being so generous with me. You know, it might sound weird, but I think you reflect a lot of who God is."

He blinked. Okay. An unexpected direction on Valentine's Day. But hey, he'd go with it. "What do you mean?"

"You've been so patient. You're so caring, even when," her

eyes grew shiny, "it must've felt like I'd gone astray. And I guess I never really realized until tonight when I was chatting with Jackie that knowing we are loved by God, means we can truly extend that love to others."

His skin prickled, his palms grew clammy. "What are you saying?"

"I'm going to be okay, and so are you, no matter what happens in the future, because I know, I *really* know now, that God loves me and has good plans for me." Her smile held peace and light. "I don't know how many times I've heard Joel talk like this, but sometimes it takes a few times before it truly sinks in. And I feel like it's here now," she placed a hand on her heart. "Like it's truly sunk in. That I'm God's creation, that He loves me, and He loves you, and Ethan," she brushed a knuckle down her son's cheek, "and it means no matter what others try to do to us, we can always trust Him."

Part of his heart that he had never known was clenched suddenly released. He knew she was a Christian, and they'd touched on matters of faith before, but this felt more real and poignant and important than any of the conversations they'd had before.

"You know when I said before that you keep me humble," he said in a low voice, "what I should've said is that I see God's hand on you, in the way He has made you to reflect His creation through the amazing creative ability He's given you. I think you're amazing, Toni."

Her face went soft.

"I mean, I shouldn't really be surprised," his mouth added, going rogue without a clear thought to direct words. He felt a moment's panic that calmed as he concentrated on the woman sitting opposite him. "When I see you, I see someone who is so wonderful, and strong, and so talented." He shrugged. "That's all."

"That's all?"

"Oh, you want more?" He grasped her hands. "How about I'm so impressed with your courage, your beauty, and how you mother this little boy."

"That's because you don't see me every day."

"I'd like to, though."

The words slipped out before he thought too hard, and seemed to surprise her as much as him, judging from the way her eyes rounded. "What do you mean?"

He swallowed. Okay, it was way too soon to be talking forevers, even if he'd known her for what felt like half his life. Besides, he didn't want her freaking out about the idea. But he'd talked about the possibility of this with Joel and got his blessing, even if he hadn't exactly planned to say this on Valentine's Day. But hey, he was learning that sometimes going off script wasn't always a bad thing. "You asked me before about what a relationship with you might mean for the future. I'm telling you that whatever your future holds, I want to be a part of it."

Her breath caught, and he suddenly wished there wasn't this fake wooden table between them and they were someplace way more romantic. That he and she were alone on a tropical beach under stars. Or maybe in New York's fanciest restaurant. Or at the top of the Eiffel Tower. Then he could hold her the way he really wanted, and maybe kiss her, like he'd imagined in his dreams. Right now he'd have to settle for gently squeezing her hands instead. "You know today is Valentine's Day."

She nodded.

"And that you got a chocolate heart from me before." All he could find at the nearest store when he'd decided to leave his city office at five.

"I didn't get you anything," she murmured, her face holding regret.

He lifted a shoulder. "That doesn't matter. What matters is this." He wet his bottom lip. "You have my heart, Toni. You always have, and you always will."

Her eyes shimmered, and she blinked rapidly. "You're so incredibly sweet."

"I," he swallowed, and finally dared to say the words brimming in his heart for years. "I love you."

"Oh, Matt." She placed a hand on her lips, glanced at Ethan, then down at the table.

Sweet he may be, but right now he felt like he'd gotten caught up in the romance mojo of Valentine's Day and had just run off a cliff, and now he was falling and there was no way to find firm ground. What had he done? Had he really gone crazy and placed his heart in her hands only for her to abandon it and leave him to bleed dry?

"Matt, I… I don't know what to say."

Right now, anything along the line of "I love you too" would be great. But he'd settle for nothing, if he could figure out a way to save himself from complete and utter embarrassment and get out of here.

She let go of his hand and slid from her seat. Okay, so his declaration had made her run away. Good to know. Was it possible his heart could shrink any further?

But before he could hurry too far down this path, she slipped around Ethan's high chair and into Matt's side of the booth, twisting on the seat to face him. "You were too far away," she breathed.

"Too far away for what?" he asked.

"Too far away for this." And she inched closer and closer and tilted her head until her lips finally met his.

Oh.

In all his dreams he'd never imagined kissing Toni quite like this, a little too tightly ensconced in a booth, a little too public as half the town looked on. But he barely noticed as her lips seemed to impart divine fire that burned through every fiber and melted his body like wax.

She drew back, her eyes holding a smile he'd never seen

before, one that matched the one dancing across her lips. Her beautiful, glorious lips. "I think—no, you don't like me saying that kind of thing, do you?"

Right now he didn't care, he was desperate to know what she thought. That had been an awesome kiss, hadn't it? He thought so, anyway. Although awesome didn't cut it. That kiss was only the best kiss of his life. "What do you think?" he asked.

"I *know*," her eyes danced, "that you're going to have to kiss me again."

"More than happy to," he murmured, before capturing her mouth once more.

She sighed, her lips caressing and moving against his, her hands on his cheeks, sliding up to cup the back of his head and drawing him closer, deeper into desire. Now he really wished they were at a tropical beach, and not squished beside a plastic-wood table.

"Well, it certainly looks like it's a happy Valentine's Day here."

He drew back, his mind, his senses whirling, as a wide grin threatened to split his face.

Suzy wore her own grin—he bet it wasn't as goofy as his—as she placed their meals on the table. "Are we celebrating something in particular, or just celebrating new love?"

Ah, the fun of a small town where everyone had an opinion and could comment on your life. "We're taking things slow," Toni said.

"Mmm. Didn't look too slow to me." She winked at Matt again and waggled her left hand. "You might want to put a ring on it so you can get on with making another one of these." She caressed Ethan's downy head.

"Oh, but—" Toni's words faltered as Suzy winked again and walked away.

Okay, he was officially never coming here again. He didn't

care if this was the best coffee spot in town, or if this food tasted like it was made for angels. No way did he ever—

"Wow." Toni turned, and he caught how her expression melded from embarrassment to amusement to something else. "I promise I did not put her up to saying that."

His mind slowly waded through the awkwardness of a minute ago to grasp her meaning. "Do you mean you want a diamond ring?" His voice was husky.

"One day." Her eyes were intent on him. "I have zero desire to have another baby without one. Actually, I'd really prefer to have two rings, because I'd rather be married than do it alone."

In all his dreams he'd never imagined having this conversation with her on their very first official date. But somehow, the fact they'd known each other for so long, that they'd been friends before anything else, made it seem like a conversation he could pursue. Although, she hadn't yet said—

"I love you, Matt."

He blinked. Could she read his mind?

"I'm sorry it took me so long to realize just what an amazing man you are, but hey, I know it now. And I am glad, *so* glad, you never gave up on the idea of us."

Us. His dreams were now officially pushing into new territory. There was no checklist to consult any more. "So, you're happy to be considered a couple by others?"

She chuckled. "I think coming here and then kissing me like that pretty much announced it to all of Muskoka."

"I kissed you? I thought you kissed me."

"I don't think you can kiss alone," she said, her lips quirked with tease.

"I didn't mean to put you under any pressure."

"Do I look like I mind?" She picked up his hand and kissed the back of it. "Come on. Let's eat. Then you can take me home and we can do more of what we were doing before."

~

IT WAS QUITE possible she was going to explode from happiness. Why had she never realized just what a great kisser Matt would be? She'd almost thought he'd had lessons he was so good. These past two nights she'd gone to sleep and dreamed of kissing him until she'd woken up, then read his good morning text message that he always signed off with a *Love, Matt.*

Her heart shuddered, threatening to leak joy. Matt was a good man. Such a *good* man. And she still didn't know what she had done to deserve his affection. But whatever it was, she gloried in it, thanked God for it, and was determined to do whatever she could to show him his regard was not misplaced. And today, on his day of reckoning at work, he was at the topmost of her prayers.

The door to the art gallery opened. Toni grinned. "Good morning. How's the bride to be?"

"Feeling very bridal." Serena grinned. "I wanted to see how my maid of honor was getting on."

"Anna? I haven't seen her since Tuesday at your house. Ooh, which reminds me: if it's all the same with you, I think I will take you up on your offer to move into your place. Rachel's conversation made me realize that there are things no sister should ever see."

"Stop it. You'll make me blush again. But yes, if you can wait a week or so, until Mom and Dad are gone, that'll work well. Unless," she eyed Serena, "you'd be happier where you are, and Joel can just move in with me. That way you wouldn't have to move all of Ethan's things, and can still paint that incredible view of the lake."

"How about we talk it over with Joel tonight?"

"Sure. Oh, and back to what we were discussing before. Anna wanted me to pass on her wish that you take her place.

Apparently, it's all over town that you and a certain best man were seen kissing at The Coffee Blend—"

"It's all over town?"

"All over town." Serena grinned. "Hey, what did you expect? Anyway, Anna thought that it might be a better look if you and Matt were seen to be together on Saturday."

"What? I didn't need to be partnered with him. Believe it or not I'm actually secure enough for him to be partnered with somebody else."

Serena studied her. "You are, aren't you? I can see it in your eyes. Like there's a new confidence."

"And I know this might seem hard to believe, but it's not based on Matt, but on finally understanding what God thinks about me."

"That's what you and Jackie were discussing on Tuesday, wasn't it?"

Toni nodded. "She's pretty awesome. I just wish Anna could find some of Jackie's contentment. Why didn't she say anything about changing bridesmaid roles to me?"

"Anna is a little sensitive about these things, so don't worry about that. And when we go to have our nails done tomorrow, try not to say anything."

"Okay."

Serena gestured to the phone. "Have you heard anything from Matt yet?"

"Not yet."

"We're praying for him. That God will make a way, not just for his job but for you two as well."

"Thank you."

"Okay, I better leave you to it. Got any students today?"

"Two at eleven. Sisters from the city. Apparently Maude sent them, would you believe."

"Ha. Well, wonders never cease. That gives me an idea.

Maybe we could see about a discount on referrals, that way you could get repeat customers perhaps."

They discussed a couple more marketing strategies before Serena continued on her way. For someone getting married in two days she seemed awfully calm, but then her giant checklist had most things crossed off so it was little surprise she was looking so tranquil.

The morning continued, and Toni took calls, worked on her painting, and prepared for her class, hoping against hope that Matt wouldn't call with news about his work when she was beginning the class. It might look pretty unprofessional to have to pause the introductory spiel in order to take his phone call, but that's what she was prepared to do.

Her phone buzzed a message. Matt? No. Her heart tensed. Officer Tom.

Call me?

She sank onto a seat and pressed the button to return his call.

"Hey, Toni. Thanks for getting back to me. I wanted to give you an update on where things are at with Bryant."

She braced.

"I'm sorry this isn't better news. It seems our investigation has met some opposition with the art college, and they're not being especially forthcoming with some of the details about the allegations you made last year. And it also seems that Bryant is proving hard to track down. His wife no longer has anything to do with him, and his parents have recently died so it appears that Bryant is a little desperate, and may be in an unstable frame of mind."

Her pulse increased. "Are you saying that he might attack me again?"

"I'm saying it's wise to remember that he's out there. I don't know if he would try to come after you again, because he seems to have made his point already, but it won't hurt to be aware and on your guard."

She slowly exhaled, her blithe words to Serena about confidence earlier seeming to have run shrieking away. *Oh Lord, help!*

Except…

Jackie's comment to Anna had been correct. Just as Anna didn't have to dwell in her regrets and envy neither did Toni have to buckle under dread. She didn't have to be at the mercy of fear, blown this way or that according to her feelings. And just because she might feel afraid didn't mean she had to *live* afraid. She could still trust God, and trust Him with this news now, just as she had before.

"Toni?" Tom asked.

She sucked in a deep breath. Released. "Thank you for telling me."

"Hey, I know it's not the news anyone wants to hear, but know we are doing what we can. And in the meantime, until you hear otherwise, make sure you stay with people around, okay?"

"Okay. Thanks."

The call ended, and she propped her head in her hands as she stared at her desk, as a million thoughts crammed for attention. It was all well and good to say, 'stay with people,' but in two days' time Joel would be leaving on a honeymoon with Serena, so what would happen then? And while she had other friends she could stay with, or even John and Ange MacPherson, the thought of having to leave and uproot Ethan from their usual routine and quiet existence seemed so unfair. Why was it that the perpetrator was allowed to roam free and she, the perhaps not-so-innocent victim, was left feeling caged?

But focusing on the unfairness probably wasn't going to help. Neither was allowing any more air time to the thought that she deserved his harassment because of what she had done.

She closed her eyes. Remembered what Joel had said. Remembered a counsellor's words. Ange and John. Bryant had taken advantage of her, just as he had taken advantage of other female students, and nothing made his actions right, or gave him the right to treat her with disrespect. And the reminder of two days ago, that she was created by God, drew new purpose. She was loved, not because of herself but because God Himself loved her. She was valuable, not because of what she had done but because of what God had done. She was forgiven, not because she deserved it but because Jesus's death on a cross had wiped the slate clean. And it didn't matter what names Bryant might call her, or even what names she might secretly call herself, as far as God was concerned Jesus had washed her sins away, and she was now as white as snow. That was what she had to remember. She was loved, valuable, forgiven. *Lord, help me to remember this.*

"Okay." She could do this. She would do this. She opened her eyes, only to see two ladies standing at the gallery's doors who must've thought her pose rather strange. She found a gritted-teeth smile and lifted a hand. "Good morning. Are you here for the art classes?"

Two nods. Bless them for not being scared away. Just like she refused to be, either.

She lifted her chin. "Excellent. If you'd like to come this way then." She gestured to the art studio space. "My name is Toni Wakefield." *And I'm loved, valuable and forgiven.* "Let's get started."

CHAPTER 16

⁂

The conference room held Lee, Helen from HR, two other executives, and Matt and Ray. He tried not to take it as a sign that things were not going to go too well by his positioning next to Ray on one side of the boardroom table from the others. He unscrewed a bottle of water, and took a swig, before setting it back down.

"Thank you for coming, gentlemen," Lee began.

He then proceeded to give a long spiel about professionalism, compliance policies, and Sage Investment's company policies concerning workplace practices. He glanced at Ray, then at Helen, before inviting her to speak.

She spoke at length about anti-bullying and outlined various ways workplace issues could be resolved, all of which only underlined Matt's obvious failures to do so. He kept his gaze on her, his expression neutral, even as his jaw clenched. Sure, there were times, many times when he should've said something. But he hadn't, and neither had anyone else he'd mentioned in his now-infamous email. They had all been complicit in allowing Ray's bullying behavior to continue.

Ray, he noticed, was fidgeting, his gaze lowered so he didn't meet anyone's eyes.

Lee cleared his throat. "So, given these circumstances, it should come as no surprise that the partners and myself have come to the conclusion that the promotion we had originally spoken of last year will be no more."

Matt swallowed. No, he wasn't surprised at all.

"This situation, as unfortunate as it is, has at least allowed for a degree of soul-searching," Lee continued. "And it has also permitted us to take a review of the company and our management and it's with this in mind that we have decided that a corporate restructure of certain elements is past overdue."

A corporate restructure. Yep. The language of redundancies the world over. His stomach tensed. Here it came.

"Ray, I am dismayed that our investigations seem to corroborate a lot of what has been said as being true. It has proved extremely disappointing on both a personal and professional level to learn about your conduct, and I will be talking with you about this in more detail soon."

Lee looked Matt's way. "Matthew, I feel it's only right to say that we have looked at all of these things and taken your years of service into account. The way you handled these matters was not according to company policy, nor did it display the professionalism that we all expect from you. You may leave us for a moment while we speak privately with Ray."

Matt dipped his chin, glanced at Ray whose gaze remained fixed on the table, then left the room to find his office.

Okay. It was only a matter of time before he'd be saying goodbye to these four walls and that view. Which probably meant it was only a matter of time before he needed to leave his apartment and find someplace his non-existent salary could afford. Did he have to stay working in investments? What else might God have for him? He leaned against the windowsill and gazed out to glimpse that sliver of Lake Ontario. Maybe this enforced restructure would restructure God's plans for him and propel Matt into what God actually wanted for him. And to be fair, he'd always had more of a heart to invest in sustainable projects that Sage had never been too enthusiastic about. Maybe this was his chance to apply for a job with a company who actually believed what their website said.

He spent the next quarter hour praying, for his work, for his future, for Toni, his prayers interspersed with checking his phone for any messages from her. She'd sent one earlier, telling him she was praying for him, and he'd responded with a heart. But he now felt too edgy to do anything more than touch his phone then lift his finger immediately. Whoever had said he was addicted to this piece of technology was right. Looked like he could really do with a second round of cold turkey and have his phone out of reach for another week or two.

The murmurs of the other workers in the office suggested they all knew the significance of today's meeting in the boardroom. He wondered who they would prefer to see fired, Ray or him. He always thought he had a reasonable relationship with his colleagues, but over the last month, ever since his brain snap, he wasn't so sure. Like Lee had said: his colleagues needed to know that they could trust him, and that what they said and did wouldn't be exposed to the wider company community. How he wished he hadn't sent that email.

He was absently fiddling with his watch strap when a tap came at the door. "Matt? They want you now."

Awesome. He nodded, then cast his office a final glance, before heading out to the main office area. His walk of shame, perhaps, as people's eyes lowered, although a few colleagues offered wince-like smiles he guessed they thought were encouraging. There was no sign of Ray in his office, so he knew what that meant, and he wasn't about to ask anyone.

He returned to the boardroom and resumed his seat, drawing back his shoulders as he gazed at the expressionless faces of the executives. No matter what happened he would remember that God was with him, that God was making his path straight, and that his future ultimately wasn't to be found in what was said next, but in what God ordained for his life. His heart eased and he found a more genuine smile.

"Is there anything you would like to say to us?" Lee asked.

Pressure ramped inside, as everything screamed that this was his final chance to save his job. Except, it wasn't. Not really. Not if God was in control. He exhaled and clasped his fingers on the table. "Thank you, but I have said all—and way more—than I needed to. And you know my deep regret for all that's occurred. I'm truly very sorry."

There was a beat. Two. Then Lee frowned. "Yes, yes, we know that. Is there anything else you wish to add?"

"No, sir."

The executives glanced at each other. "Truly?"

They wanted more from him? Very well. "I wish to say thank you. I have enjoyed—for the most part—my time working with Sage, and found this experience invaluable. I'm especially grateful for the chance to encourage investments in those kinds of programs and schemes that have helped to strengthen communities and have demonstrated social responsibility, and most proud to know that where we have invested has truly made a difference in the lives of others."

Lee stared at him hard. "That's it? Nothing more to add?"

"I don't know what else you wish for me to say. You know that I'm profoundly sorry for having embarrassed members of this company by speaking honestly about things that I should've dealt with in a different way. I do feel like I have served you well, and yet I am fully cognizant of why you have made the choices you have regarding my role here. So, once again I thank you. I am deeply appreciative of the chance to work here."

Lee glanced at Helen who hitched her eyebrows and gave a

little nod. His gaze swung back to Matt. "You don't wish to plead for your job, like some others have recently?"

So that's what had been happening while Matt had been out of the room. "I fully understand the decision you have made."

A bark of laughter escaped Lee.

Matt's eyebrows lifted. "I'm sorry, sir?"

"You." Lee sighed, then shook his head. "This isn't easy for me to say, but I feel it is only fair that it is said. Your email exposed many of the frailties within our company and really cast a spotlight on practices that we long chose to disregard. It was not easy reading, and it still isn't easy to accept that this company is not tracking in the way that we originally planned. Our goal was never just to make money for our clients, but to incorporate best practice in our dealings with our colleagues, our clients, and the wider community. Which is why your email showed us that that has not been the case. And now, your comments about sustainability and social responsibility have just reminded me why you've been such a valued member of our organization all these years."

Matt's fingers straightened. While it was nice to be praised, he was still a little confused about exactly what was being said. But a, "Thank you, sir," never went astray.

Helen wore a little smile, one that hoisted a little bit of hope into his heart.

"We are restructuring," Lee said, "and I'm afraid your job will no longer be required."

There. He should've known it. The emotions of the past few hours must've made him misread that smile. He covered his fast-plunging hopes with a flattened lip and nod.

"Instead, we'd like to offer you a new role, as head of corporate responsibility."

What? His mouth fell open. He snapped it shut.

"This is a new role that we have been thinking about for some time," Lee continued. "It would involve the oversight of our environmental and climate issues and policies, in addition to further developing the company's social responsibility efforts in impact investing, strategic philanthropy, and corporate community involvement. We believe that you'd be the perfect person to engage our employees more deeply with these causes that really stem from our original purpose in establishing Sage Investments."

"Sir, I—"

"Let me finish. We've been hesitant to introduce this role, knowing that none of us have, well, let's be honest, the interest or have developed the connections that you have in this area. And we haven't wanted to rush into this, knowing that this is an area that can easily be mismanaged or can lead to fraud, so it needs to go to somebody who is honest and trustworthy. And we believe you are that man."

"I… I don't know what to say."

"You don't need to say anything yet. While we have been thinking about this for some time I'm afraid we need more time to fully flesh out just what this role would mean. But at this stage I think it's fair to say you would be able to develop this role in the way you see fit." Lee tilted his head to Helen who nodded.

"We will be fine-tuning some details in the next week, but we would like you to consider whether this is something that you might feel is a good fit for you."

A good fit? It felt more like a God gift. "Is this a role that you think will require as much travel?"

"Why? You're not a family man, are you?"

"Not yet. But I have plans to marry soon."

"Really?"

Helen beamed. "I'm so glad. When can we meet her?"

As soon as he convinced her that she needed two rings on one finger. "Soon, I hope. She lives in Muskoka Shores."

Lee smiled. He actually smiled. Matt was tempted to glance

out the window in case a unicorn flew past. "This may come as a surprise, but I had dinner with someone the other day who met you in Muskoka."

"Really?"

"Mm. My aunt and uncle stay every year in a resort, and this year their trip was delayed until last month. Apparently during their time there they took some art classes, and Maude happened to mention the delightful Matt man who she mistook for a waiter, due to his kindness in overlooking her overbearing nature." He held up a hand. "She's my aunt, I'm allowed to say it."

Matt bit back a smile.

"Alistair was most complimentary about the artist, I forget her name—"

"Toni." Matt glanced at Helen, and smiled.

Her grin widened, and she nodded.

"Maude insisted on showing off her work, which likely doesn't surprise you, not if you've spent more than ten minutes with her. But I digress. My point is that the kind of person you proved that you are when you're on vacation, or when you're coming to grips with a world-shaking situation, is the kind of person we have benefited from these past ten years, and it would be a crime to let someone leave our organization who is honest, ethical, and has a compassionate nature, yet who is also extremely shrewd and capable. We want you, Matt. What I said before wasn't me blowing wind. You are valued by us. You're valued by me. And I hope you will consider this opportunity."

His lungs might burst from trying to hold in a yell of victory. He settled for a fist pump under the table and the widest grin his cheek muscles had ever felt.

There was brief discussion about what this might mean for his pay, for his working conditions, and his tentative suggestion that he cut his overtime to standard hours was received well.

"I'm extremely grateful for the opportunity, and will give

you my all for the days I'm at work," he promised. "But at this stage in my life I am very keen to spend as much time as I can in Muskoka as Toni and I work to see what our future could be like."

"Toni?" Lee's gaze sharpened. "The artist girl my aunt was raving about?"

Helen beamed. "And she had a profile piece in *Toronto Living* magazine recently."

"Huh. Well, in that case we'll definitely have to meet her. We want you, Matt, so we'll make it work so it works for you," Lee promised, before glancing at Helen. "Once we've ironed out more details, you'll get a contract drafted and sent to Matt in the next week or so, right?"

"Absolutely."

Lee stood, which seemed the signal for the others to follow suit.

"Thank you, sir," Matt said. "I'm a little overwhelmed right now."

"Think it through, talk with your lady friend, and then say yes. Okay?"

Matt smiled. "I'll certainly be thinking about this over this weekend."

"That's right. I noticed on your records that you've got a day off tomorrow."

"I'm the best man for a friend's wedding."

"Well, you could save us all some time by getting married yourself." Another smile from Lee. Would wonders never cease? "Just joking. Enjoy yourself. And that young lady. And come back on Monday and let's discuss how we can best get this new role happening."

"Thank you, sir. I will give it much thought."

"Thank you, Matt."

"Sir?"

"For not wasting our time like Ray did with all his excuses."

Lee shook his head. "I thought I knew the man, but it seems I was gravely mistaken. As if his actions weren't shameful enough, he embarrassed himself with his exit." Lee's smile held no joy. "It may come as a relief to learn that his position has been made redundant, and we will not be engaging his services anymore. Our investigations have uncovered further breaches of company policy and we believe it's in our company's best interest to part ways with him effective immediately. And I believe it's only fair to offer our apologies for not recognizing this earlier, or investigating this to the extent we should have before."

"I think losing him is a good call."

Lee chuckled. "For all that compassion there's still a man who likes to play hard ball, I see."

"I like to play fair, yet firm. And be sure that those whose actions negatively affect the company are curbed, while standing up for the rights of the downtrodden."

"Then you'll be perfect for the role. But that's enough. Take an early mark, enjoy your weekend, and we'll discuss more details next week."

He shook hands with each of them, then made his exit from the room. Only to stumble to his office and close the door. Then with great heaving breaths, he gripped the window sill as moisture slipped from his eyes. Who would have thought? God obviously had. And God's great mercy made him want to curl up in a ball and howl.

∼

"OH, LOOK AT THESE BOUQUETS, GIRLS," Anna cried.

"They're gorgeous, Annette," Serena said, a hand on her heart. "Thank you so much."

"Only the best for you, my dear," Annette said gruffly.

And the best is what they'd seen, with everything from

247

Annette's beautiful flowers to Alphonse's sculptural masterpiece of a wedding cake being expressions of loveliness and skill. Proof that today's bride had earned the love and support of so many in Muskoka and beyond.

Toni swore she could see a tear sparkling at the corner of Annette's eye. The woman had a flair with flowers, and a soft spot for Serena. Likely, as a long-time church member she knew something of Serena's history, with the broken relationship with a loser named Dwight which had opened her heart and eyes to see the excellence to be found in Toni's brother. And to think these two were getting married in under two hours!

The dressmaker was fluffing out Serena's dress as Alexa, the photographer, called for Serena to resume her place in front of the grand mirror that stood against one wall of the resort's bridal suite. Originally the plan had been to host the wedding party at Serena's house, which would've been closer to the church, but with various members of Serena's family moving in, it had been deemed easier for Serena to stay in the bridal suite, which she admitted enjoying, as it helped to know exactly how bridal guests must feel. It probably helped that Adrian had gifted this to her, and that Cherry was close by for any last-minute details. With yesterday's arrival of Serena's sister, Miranda, and her family from the west coast, Serena's house was full, necessitating her removal here.

Toni shifted to the dining table that held Serena's wedding day checklist, and marked off the flowers. Thanks to Serena's exceptional organizational abilities—and that of her assistant, Cherry—Toni's maid of honor duties had been few, limited to driving her here to the resort last night, where Serena, Anna, Jackie, and herself had spent the night—with Ethan, of course.

Serena's mom and sister had arrived at the resort this morning, and now most of Toni and Anna's time was spent keeping either of these Williamson ladies from saying or doing anything that might impair Serena's joy. Mrs. Williamson was pretty encouraging—it helped that she truly did seem to regard Joel as a son already—but the same could not be said of Serena's sister. Miranda was the kind of gal to see a glass half empty, and her reproaches disguised as praise sure sounded like criticisms to Toni. And to Anna and Jackie, judging from their rolled eyes and hasty interferences.

"How about we go check on how your boys are doing?" Jackie asked. "I know that you'll want to make sure that they are dressed and ready so they're on time."

Miranda sighed. "You're right. I should probably check on them. I'm sure that husband of mine hasn't even thought about getting them dressed yet." She shot a look at Serena. "You might think that getting married means all your troubles are over, but there are days, like today, when it feels like just the opposite."

"How about we go now?" Jackie said, steering her away, mouthing a 'Sorry' over her shoulder.

"I suppose I should go as well, and check my husband is ready," Mrs. Williamson said. "How long until we need to be here to take you to the church?"

Serena glanced at the clock, but Toni knew the answer. "If you're back in forty-five minutes, then that will work."

"But that barely leaves enough time—"

"Mom, I'm determined to be the first bride ever who was on time, so please make Dad hurry. I do not want to be late."

"I know, I know. But you know what he's like in the mornings."

Serena shot a look at Cherry, who nodded, and did her own escort-from-the-premises of Mrs. Williamson. Serena sighed.

"Hey, it's going to go okay," Toni said. "You look beautiful."

"You're honestly the prettiest I've ever seen you look," Anna said.

Aw, was that now a tear in Anna's eye? They group-hugged, laughed, and then endured the photographer's good-natured, "Now you'll need to fix your hair," when Serena paused. "Oh, before I forget, Toni, can you look after this for me?" She slipped off her engagement ring and handed it to her. "I know this was your mom's, and it would mean a lot if you can wear it until after the ceremony."

Toni fingered the delicate gold band with its humble solitaire. Her parents had never been very wealthy, so this diamond was not as large as some, but her parents had loved well, until a car accident cut their lives short four years ago. Emotion threatened. Shoot. Was she now about to cry? She blinked, blinked again. Waved her hand at her eyes.

"Toni, honey? Is everything okay?"

She nodded. "I'd be honored." Her voice sounded strangled, so she cleared her throat, and slipped the ring onto her right hand. It would help her feel like Mom and Dad were close today.

The next hour and a half passed with more moments of photos, smiles, and laughter, then finally they were released to head to the church, Serena traveling with her parents in one car, while Anna, Jackie, Toni, and Ethan traveled in the other.

At the church—they were on time—Angela met them at the front steps holding a big smile. "Oh, you girls look so beautiful! I'll go in and tell them you're ready. Oh, and I hope you don't mind, but I've arranged a special surprise."

The day was fine, but crisply cold, although adrenaline was making Toni warm. Or maybe that was anticipation at seeing Matt again. She knew the man would look as handsome as anything. She'd seen photos of him online wearing a tuxedo for charity events, and it was obvious the man knew how to wear a suit very well. And after his arrival Thursday afternoon, following his awesome work news, and their reunion kiss which had set the bar high for new passion, she'd found spending yesterday apart while he spent time with Joel and Wade and she was with the girls was just too long. But soon, in a minute or so, she'd see him again. Her heart fluttered.

The cold weather meant they were glad to enter the vestibule as the music—Pachelbel's Canon—played across the loudspeakers, and Anna started her slow glide down the aisle.

From her position here, Toni could see the pews were heaving with congregation and community members, dotted with a few faces she didn't recognize. One of the advantages of a small town was the fact that nearly everyone knew each other, and times like this, when one of their own was marrying their church's assistant minister, made it very special indeed.

Toni received the nod from Cherry, then began her journey down the aisle. For a moment she dared wonder what it would be like to be the bride, to have all these people here for her, to be marrying the man of her dreams. She glanced up, and sure enough the man of her dreams was waiting at the end of the aisle, with a big smile on his face. Matt.

Her heart glowed. She was so proud of him, so glad for him, so amazed that this super smart, conscientious man loved her. *Loved* her. She still got goosebumps thinking of what he'd said only a few days ago. And yes, it might be early days, but she knew him, had known him for years. And would like him to be part of her future. Forever.

She drew her head up and smiled, smiled at Matt, then at her brother, whose face softened as she drew close. "Love you, kiddo," he mouthed.

"Love you, Doofus," she whispered back, sparking his laughter.

Laughter that quickly faded as a stir at the back revealed the bride's entry. Oh. Was her big brother now crying? Well, at least tearing up?

Matt handed Joel a handkerchief—see? That's what conscientious guys did. They came prepared—and Joel blinked hard and shoved it in his pocket.

But it wasn't any wonder he was emotional. Anna was right. With her dark blonde hair pulled up in an intricate twist, and the gown that showcased her hourglass figure, Serena was the most beautiful Toni had seen, and a world away from the girl she had met in Brandi's bookstore last year, back when Serena had looked so defeated.

Toni's gaze drifted across the congregation, nodding to her aunt and cousins, before settling on the redheaded woman beside Angela McPherson against the far wall. Wait, was that Sarah Walton?

Sarah's own gaze, up until now focused like everyone else's on the approaching bride, pivoted to meet Toni's, and her smile hitched higher, then she placed a finger on her lips like they shared a secret. Sarah was Angela's surprise? She must be doing something with the music. How awesome was that?

Serena reached the end, handed her flowers to Toni, and the service began. Toni drank in all the details—the church floral arrangements, the prayers, the vows, and just how well Matt filled out a suit—as she waited for Angela's surprise. For someone who reveled in planning things down to the nth degree she couldn't wait to see Serena's reaction when her favorite singer took to the stage.

But when the rendition of *Amazing Grace* was sung by the regular church musicians Toni didn't know what to expect. And as John preached his sermon she wasn't sure what to think. Why was Sarah here? Maybe her husband was on a road trip. Still, it didn't matter. If Toni got the chance she would say, 'Thank you,' for their support and that she hoped Sarah liked Toni's painting that her husband Dan had bought. This couple probably would otherwise never know the difference their act of generosity had brought to her life.

John's message about love—what else?—concluded, then it was time for the vows, and the exchange of rings. Then came the moment everyone always waited for at a wedding. The proclamation that they were husband and wife, and, "You may now kiss your bride."

Joel took his time to kiss Serena thoroughly, in a way that probably bode well for tonight. Her gaze slipped past to encounter Matt's, who looked similarly amused, before his eyebrows hitched, like he couldn't wait to kiss Toni like that too.

Her heart fluttered, then Joel and Serena broke apart to the cheers and applause of the congregation. The signing of the register was next, and Toni handed Serena back her flowers then joined them at the table. Then she noticed a certain redhead go up to the piano.

Alexa snapped a photo of Serena's stunned expression as she realized the first bars of one of Heartsong Collective's famous songs were being played by Sarah live, and not on the recording as she'd planned.

"Surprise," John whispered. "Sarah was in town, as Dan's on a trip, and when she heard what was happening today and that you'd planned to use her song, she wanted to come as a thank you for all you did in pulling together her wedding last year."

"I don't know what to say," the stunned bride said.

"Thank you will work."

Certificates were signed, more photos were taken, then John prayed a final time before announcing, "Please be upstanding for Mr. and Mrs. Joel and Serena Wakefield."

The room filled with cheers, and Toni stepped close to Matt, placing her hand on his arm as she shifted the bouquet to the other. Their progression back down the aisle was slow with the bride and groom receiving so many hugs and kisses. Toni even received a few of her own. Outside there was a flurry of more photos, then a chance to join the little crowd around Sarah.

"After all she did for me in making my dreams come true so quickly last year, it was the least I could do." Sarah's Aussie accent stood out. "Hey, Matt? Wow! You sure scrub up well." She hugged him. "We're neighbors in the city," she added kindly, as if conscious of Toni's confusion.

"You know this is Toni Wakefield, Joel's sister, the famous artist," Matt said, wrapping an arm around her.

Famous? Oh, let the man have his fantasy. "It's a pleasure to meet you."

"Oh! You did that amazing picture of the maple tree? That's my favorite painting ever. I *love* it. I have it hanging in our apartment in the city and it always reminds me of how beautiful Muskoka is. Ooh, I need a selfie with you." She drew out her phone and took a picture of the two of them, then swapped details so they could be Facebook friends. "Hey, if you've got more like that, let me know."

"Actually, she has an exhibition happening at the resort," Matt said.

"Muskoka Shores?"

Toni nodded. "It's on until April."

Sarah's eyes lit. "In that case I'll be there, with bells on. I'll check it out after Pilates with Ange on Monday."

This was surreal. And also the time to say what needed to be said. "I just wanted to say thank you for your support," Toni said shyly. "My life has changed because of people like Serena and you."

"Well, what does it say in the Bible? The world of the generous gets larger and larger. I've seen it be true for me, and I think it definitely can be true for others."

Sarah was soon whisked away by others who wished to speak to her, like Trudy, the church secretary, Enid, one of the more ancient members of the music team, and Jenny Wells, which left Toni with Matt.

"Finally," Matt murmured.

"Finally?"

"Finally," Matt said, wrapping his arms around her back and swooping in for a kiss.

Pleasure rippled from her lips to the very ends of her fingers and toes. Oh, this man could kiss…

Click!

She drew back, as Alexa laughed and moved to capture other candid shots. They joined the others in the church hall for a special tea for the church members before the afternoon reception would be held for family and close friends.

The next hour passed in photos, kisses, and finger food, then they were finally driven back to the resort. Matt held her hand as he drove her car, Ethan in the back. God bless Jackie for looking after him for much of today.

"Do you know how beautiful you look today?" he asked, pressing a kiss to her knuckles.

"I think you'd better tell me."

He pulled into the resort parking lot and killed the engine. "Maybe I should just show you."

He took his time kissing her, enough that the windows started to fog, and she was pretty sure all her lipstick was kissed off. But she didn't mind. This pocket of affection in the busyness and noise of today was just what her heart needed.

"I love you," he said, his eyes deep on hers.

"I love you, too." Oh, to think she was responsible for making his face light like that.

A tap came at the window, then Wade called, "Come on, you two. They want more photos inside."

Of course they did. Still, the maid of honor and best man had duties to fill. So they'd better follow inside.

CHAPTER 17

The reception venue was much like many others Matt had visited in his life, except this one was on the edge of the beautiful frozen lake. There were more photos, then after the first course was served and Joel and Serena were making the rounds of the tables and talking to various guests, he finally got another chance to talk to Toni. She looked beautiful today with her hair caught up and her peach-colored shiny gown begging him to touch her. He refrained, but was thankful there were people staying in Joel's house again tonight. He needed others around to help him deal with the temptation that was Toni.

Toni exhaled and fanned her face. "Is it me or is it hot in here?"

"How do you really want me to answer that question?" he asked.

She laughed, which sparked her child's attention and cry, Ethan's little arms reaching for her from the high chair. Toni unclipped him and drew him out to sit on her lap, where he instantly nuzzled to her chest.

"Poor baby," she said, stroking his head. "Mommy's been too busy, hasn't she?"

His heart knew a savage pang for this. This. Toni and Ethan as part of his world. Part of his family. His right to love and protect them.

Ethan's whimpers soon escalated into a full-blown crying. Jackie hurried over. "Want me to take him?"

"Thank you, but it's okay. We probably need to do some mom and baby time." She glanced at him. "I might take him for a walk."

"Do you want me to come?"

"I'll be fine."

"Are you sure?"

"Didn't Tom tell you to be careful?" Jackie asked her with a worried frown.

"Tom?" He glanced between them.

"The police officer who is investigating Bryant."

"He told you not to go anywhere by yourself, didn't he? Not until they found him."

Matt scraped back his chair. "I'm coming with you." Last night Joel had mentioned a car kept going up and back past their house but that he hadn't seen the plate or color. Neither of them had wanted to worry Toni or Serena, and the busyness of then and now had chased it from his mind. But what if it was the missing Bryant?

"Not to the ladies' room you're not. Hey, I'll be right back as soon as this little man is settled. Besides, the next course is going to be served soon, and I don't want to miss that."

"I'll go with her," Jackie said to him before smiling. "Hey, congratulations on your promotion. Toni told us last night. That's awesome, eh?"

"God is good."

"All the time," Jackie responded, before turning to Toni and Ethan. "Okay, let's get you two sorted."

They disappeared through the doors, and Wade slumped

back in his seat. "Looks like you and Toni will be heading down the aisle soon."

Matt tugged at his collar as he loosened his bowtie. "One day. That's the plan."

Wade's eyes rounded. "You've asked her?"

"Not yet. But I think she knows that's where I want to go. But I'm not pushing things, not when it's still early days yet."

"You'll have a bit to figure out with your new job too, so that's probably wise."

"I keep forgetting about that," Matt admitted. "It's hard to believe, but there's been a lot going on."

"So you'll take it?"

"I think God opened the door, there's no other way that everything fell into place like that, so yeah, I feel a sense of peace that this is what I should do."

"But what about you and Toni?"

"I've already discussed with the bosses how we can reduce the overtime. I think they're eager to see how this can work, not look for ways in which it won't. And if it means I work from home, whether that's in T.O. or here, then we'll get it done."

"So what will your new job involve?" Wade asked curiously.

He'd explained this a few times recently but was happy to say it again. "It's about building partnerships with companies that are working with environmental and socially ethical causes. You've heard of Liam Darcy?"

Wade nodded.

"His Pemberley Green Foundation does a lot of good, including work that supports wells in Africa."

"Huh. That's good."

"It's about building partnerships with companies that are working with environmental and socially ethical causes. It's such a blessing to get this job. We're sorting out details on Monday."

"Awesome."

"Yep. God is good." He glanced at his watch. How long did a bathroom break need to be? There was still no sign of Toni.

He pushed back his chair. "I'll be back in a moment. "I just need to check on Toni."

"Sure."

Matt passed Joel who was being hugged by Serena's mom again. He bit back a smile and held up a hand. "I'll be five."

Joel nodded and returned his attention to the table, and Matt exited. Okay, so where were—? Oh, there. He followed the bathroom signs, including one for those disabled / parenting which had noise coming from inside. Maybe Ethan was having a diaper change. He waited outside for what felt like forever, then finally tapped on the door. "Hello?"

A flush came then he heard sounds as the lock unlatched. Then an elderly woman poked her head out. "Oh, I'm sorry, dear. Do you have bowel issues too?"

"Uh, no." Too? TMI. "Sorry. I thought you might be someone else."

"Well, sometimes I wish I was. Like some of those young things who look so good. I had a lovely figure once upon a time. I bet you didn't think that, did you?"

What was the polite answer to that? "I'm sure you did." But he would make a point of not thinking about elderly women and their figures. "Excuse me."

He moved to the women's bathrooms, but knew he couldn't push in. What should he do? Relief filled him as Rachel drew near, holding her little girl's hand.

"Did you want to know you're giving off stalker vibes standing there?"

Not especially, no. "Sorry, would you mind seeing if Toni is in there? She's been gone from the reception for a while, and I wanted to make sure she's okay. Jackie went with her, but I haven't seen either of them for ten minutes."

"I'm sure it's nothing to worry about but I'll check."

He clenched and unclenched his hands as he waited.

She reappeared. "She's not in here."

His skin prickled. Okay, so maybe they were just somewhere else. "Thanks."

"I'll just finish with Jemima then I'll help you look."

"She's probably back there, so don't stress. Thanks, anyway."

But when he returned to the reception room she wasn't there, and the next course was being served. Jackie had returned though, so he went to her. "Where's Toni?"

"Oh. She didn't come in?" Jackie's expression grew worried. "She was right behind me. I'll go look for her."

"Everything okay, Matt?" Cherry, Serena's assistant asked. "Your food has been served."

He returned to his seat, but ate only a mouthful of steak before he got up again.

"Where's Toni?" Joel asked, as Serena's brow pleated.

"She's coming," Matt said, a statement more of faith than anything else. "I'll be back in a moment with her. Don't let them take away our food," he joked, with a smile for Serena. No way did she need to be worrying on her special day.

He hurried outside, this time not bothering to knock as he entered the bathroom. Fortunately—or unfortunately—it was empty. Panic ramped up. So where was she?

He hurried down the long hall to where a door marked 'Employees Only' led to the kitchen. He opened it, startling a waiter, who asked "Can I help you?"

"I'm looking for a woman, with a baby." Then he realized this employee might know a fellow staff member. "You haven't seen Toni Wakefield have you?"

"Nobody apart from us has come in here."

"Thanks." He turned, and ran back down the hall to the glass doors that led to the patio outside. He pushed open the door, meeting the frigid air, the sky holding an eerie glow as sunset blanketed the lake and trees in buttery light. His good shoes skidded on the icy boards, and he heard voices. Then heard Ethan's wail. Toni!

He rushed around the corner and saw her, Ethan held to her chest, as a man with greasy black hair and a knife stepped closer.

∿

"I SAW YOU at the church earlier. There were too many people around before." Bryant's evil grin reminded her of the Joker. "But there's nobody here but us now."

"Hey!"

Toni's terrified gaze slipped from Bryant to Matt as he hurried closer. Whatever he said or did next would be critical in either escalating or calming this situation.

"Hi." Her breath ballooned into a white puff of air. She was so cold.

"Here you are. Hey, aren't you freezing out here? It's time you came inside." He wrapped an arm around her then glanced at the man. "I don't believe we've met."

"Who are you?" Bryant snarled. "Are you two together?"

"Yes," Matt replied. He gently encouraged Toni to come with him, but she could barely move. Her feet were frozen in her shoes. "Come on, it's too cold out here. And everyone is wondering where you are."

"Sure. I, uh, didn't mean to take so long." She followed his lead, and took a step when Bryant blocked their way.

"No. You don't get to just leave," he slurred.

She could smell his alcohol-soaked breath which made her shudder.

"Is the kid yours?" he asked Matt.

Toni glanced up at Matt, begging him to say yes. The monster there might have contributed to Ethan's genetic makeup, but in no way was he Ethan's father, and Ethan did not belong with him any more than she did. They both belonged with Matt, whose protective arm was securely around them.

Matt glanced down at her, and in the midst of his tension his face softened as he smiled. "I sure hope so."

Bryant swore. From the corner of her eye she saw another figure in the distance. Jackie. She finished speaking on her phone, then held it up like she was recording. Toni returned her gaze to Bryant, so he wouldn't be distracted by or attack her.

"So, one minute you're telling me you're pregnant with my child, then the next you get knocked up by him?" Bryant jeered, then called Toni a word that Serena's parents would definitely not approve.

"Whoa. Not in front of a lady," Matt said. "Here, let me take my boy."

His boy. Oh, how she longed for the day when it was true. She passed Ethan over.

Without Ethan's bulk her arms felt empty, and she shivered, her teeth beginning to chatter as she rubbed her hands together. Matt seemed to notice as his grip around her waist tightened.

"Dude, we don't want any trouble, we just want to get back inside. It's cold out here or haven't you noticed? I don't know how many times you need us to say this, but Toni is with me, so you need to leave."

"I don't believe you," Bryant snarled.

Toni angled away from him, subtly swapping Serena's engagement ring to her left hand, and spun it so only the gold band shone. "Do you believe this?" she said, holding up her finger.

She caught the way Matt's breath hitched, his quick glance at her. "That's right," he said, not missing a beat. "Now leave. Or do you want us to call the police?"

Bryant bared his teeth, and for a second his expression exactly resembled a painting she'd once seen of a demon. "You won't be calling the police," he said, stepping toward them.

"No, because they've already been called," Toni said. That's what Jackie's phone call had been, right?

"Hey, is that a security guard?" Matt asked, pointing behind Bryant, away from where Jackie stood, then hustled Toni away, before giving Ethan back to her and telling her to scram.

Toni hurried, her feet sliding on the ice, her peripheral vision catching sight of Rachel holding a phone, a security guard, and then Bryant as he shouted and changed direction to follow Toni. Matt blocked his way, and there came the swish of a knife, a gasp, then a scream.

Then the sound of splintering wood as Bryant fell to the ground, as Jackie lowered a Muskoka chair.

∼

THE NEXT HOUR was filled with all kinds of commotion, as security and police and wedding guests meant noise and chaos and interviews. So much for Serena's stress-free wedding. Even if Cherry and the others had somehow shielded Serena and Joel from it all.

By the time Toni and Matt returned for the rest of the reception, dessert was underway, and Toni was immediately surrounded by her friends.

"Here, girl, you need one of these," Rachel said, shoving a cocktail in her hand.

Yes, she did. She drained it, not caring about the alcohol content. "You'd better get one for Jackie as well. She's the real heroine."

"I don't drink," Jackie protested when one was shoved into her hand.

"It's medicinal. You've had a shock," Rachel said. "And been a heroine. I'm so glad I got out there when I did. And recorded it on my phone. I couldn't believe my eyes. Who'd have thought our little skinny mini Pastor Jackie could be such a superhero?"

Jackie's cheeks pinked. "I don't really know what came over me. I felt a bit like Samson though."

"You looked it," Rachel said. "Guns of steel, like you're Wonder Woman or something."

"Definitely Wonder Woman," Toni said, clasping Jackie's hand. "I'm so grateful."

Anna snatched up Toni's hand. "What's this?" she cried, eyeing the ring. "Don't tell me Matt proposed too?"

"Please." Toni found enough energy to slide off the ring and place it on the table. "It's Serena's. I need to give it back to her, but I haven't had a chance."

"Hey, you've had a lot to deal with. At least Bryant won't hurt anyone for a while."

Tom Woodmore had said as much. Bryant's actions had been recorded by the witnesses—Rachel, and Jackie, who after her phone call had recorded his threats on video—meant he'd likely be locked up for a long time.

"Ooh, and here's the other hero," Staci said, as Matt hovered back into view. "He looks like he has something to say, so we'll give you two some privacy, hey?"

Jackie motioned for Ethan who happily went to her, leaving Toni and Matt alone.

"Wow. What an afternoon."

"Right?" He slumped into the seat next to hers and exhaled, wrapping an arm around her shoulders. "Are you okay?"

"I'm better now."

"Warmer?"

"Yes." She had someone's jacket on her legs, and Anna's coat around her shoulders. "I can't believe Jackie was able to lift that chair. Talk about a miracle."

"I know. It's like those times when people get a supernatural shot of adrenaline and can lift cars."

"I'm so thankful she was there."

"Me too. And that she and Rachel had the presence of mind

to record it on their phones. It certainly made those interviews easier."

She shivered and drew closer. The police had assured her they now had enough evidence to put Bryant away for a long time. "How is your arm?"

"Okay. James bandaged it, but it was only a graze. I'm going to need a new watch though." Matt showed her where the knife had grazed his skin before glancing off the watch.

"Good thing you've got a pay raise coming your way, eh?"

"Mm." He pivoted in his seat, eyes on her. "But it's not a pay raise or even a new watch I want."

"What do you want?" she asked, although she suspected she knew.

His smile was crooked. "It's what I've always wanted, and what I said before. I want you and I want Ethan, and I want to be part of a family with you. I want us all to share the same last name, to have the right to protect you. I don't care if it seems too soon. What we just went through makes me not want to waste a second longer."

"I don't want to waste a second longer, either," she whispered.

He drew her into his arms, into his kiss, and she spent a few long, blissful moments finding peace there before a cleared throat drew attention up to Joel and Serena's faces.

"What's this about a fuss outside?" Joel asked.

"It's all taken care of," Matt assured.

"Nothing to see here," Toni reiterated.

"Uh huh." Joel picked up the ring. "Wait, isn't this mom's?"

"I meant to give it back to you," Toni said to Serena. "Sorry."

"Dude, are you serious? Have you proposed to my sister and didn't tell me?"

"Well, I was trying to."

He was?

"I don't care how long it takes until we actually get married, but I want her to know she has a home with me." Matt shifted to face her, as other guests drew Joel and Serena's attention. "Regardless of what happens, you have my heart, and I hope that I have yours."

"You know you do," she murmured.

"So, is that a yes?" Matt asked.

Her heartbeat thumped erratically. "A yes to what?"

"Toni Wakefield, I love you, and want to spend the rest of my life with you. Will you marry me?"

Her heart glowed with certainty, with love, with devotion. "Yes."

She glimpsed Matt's look of delight before he drew near for another kiss, taking his time to savor her lips as she relished his.

Quiet laughter drew their attention back to the bride and groom. "Did I hear a yes?" Joel asked, grinning.

"You may have," Toni said, feeling suddenly shy.

"Well, you two are perfect for each other." Joel bent to give her a hug, before hugging Matt, too. "Really, I couldn't have chosen better for you both."

"Wow." Serena's beaming smile could light up a city. "Well, I guess we're ready for the toasts. Which means an extra special one for the maid of honor and the best man."

"The best man? The only man," Toni said, before turning to capture Matt's face in her hands, and murmuring against his lips, "And my hero. The most perfect man for me."

THE END
If you enjoyed this book, then make sure you read the next in
the Muskoka Romance series,
Muskoka Spotlight

A NOTE FROM THE AUTHOR

Thank you for reading *Muskoka Hearts,* the third book in the Muskoka Romance Christian contemporary romance series. This book is based on my visit to the beautiful Muskoka region of Ontario, Canada, and springs from *Muskoka Blue,* the sixth book in the Original Six contemporary romance series, that enters on Sarah and Dan's romance story (grab your copy of *Muskoka Blue).* If you've enjoyed this book, please check out the pictures from my visit to Muskoka on my website at www.carolynmillerauthor.com

∼

Reviews help other readers find new-to-them authors, so if you can spare a moment to write a quick review at Goodreads / your place of purchase, I'd be very grateful.

Enjoyed this taste of Muskoka? Then make sure you read the next book in the Muskoka series, *Muskoka Spotlight.*

If you enjoy Christian contemporary romance you may want to check out the books in the Original Six hockey romance series, a sweet & swoony, slightly sporty Christian contemporary romance series.

The Breakup Project
Love on Ice
Checked Impressions
Hearts and Goals
Big Apple Atonement
Muskoka Blue

Romance and hockey fans may also want to read *Fire and Ice*, the first book in the new Northwest Ice series, releasing in 2023.

I'd love for you to check out my other books and to sign up for my newsletter at www.carolynmillerauthor.com where you can be the first to learn all my book and contest news, and discover more behind-the-book details and photos. Newsletter subscribers can also get an exclusive bonus book free, so grab your copy of *Originally Yours* here.

A huge thank you to the following people for their encouragement and eagle eyes: Kaye, Rebekah, Brittany, & Becky - I appreciate you all so much! Big hugs to my brother, Michael Weaver, for his insights into the world of financial investments. Big thanks to the ladies in my Facebook group, Carolyn's Books & Friends, for all your support in helping promote my books.

ABOUT THE AUTHOR

Carolyn Miller lives in the beautiful Southern Highlands of New South Wales, Australia, with her husband and four children. A long-time lover of romance, especially that of Jane Austen, Georgette Heyer and LM Montgomery, Carolyn loves to write contemporary and historical romance that draws readers into fictional worlds that show the truth of God's grace in our lives.

To find out more about Carolyn's books, and to subscribe to her newsletter, please visit www.carolynmillerauthor.com

You can also connect with her at

Historical:

<u>Regency Wallflowers</u>

Dusk's Darkest Shores

Midnight's Budding Morrow

Dawn's Untrodden Green

<u>Regency Brides: Legacy of Grace</u>

The Elusive Miss Ellison

The Captivating Lady Charlotte

The Dishonorable Miss DeLancey

<u>Regency Brides: Promise of Hope</u>

Winning Miss Winthrop

Miss Serena's Secret

The Making of Mrs Hale

<u>Regency Brides: Daughters of Aynsley</u>

A Hero for Miss Hatherleigh

Underestimating Miss Cecilia

Misleading Miss Verity

'Heaven and Nature Sing' from the Joy to the World Christmas novella collection

Printed in Australia
Ingram Content Group Australia Pty Ltd
AUHW021900061023
384664AU00001B/3